## *She really was very leggy, he thought. And very blond.*

And she appeared to be moving in next door.

The woman set a large box down on the front porch of the house. Then she froze. And slowly turned her head and looked right at him.

Ian jerked back from the window, startled.

*You can't be sure she was looking at you, not with those dark glasses,* he told himself, as he tried to puzzle out his scientific problem.

And then she smiled at him.

His heart did a crazy flip-flop. He told himself it wasn't the smile that rattled him, although even from here it was a killer smile. It was that she sensed him watching. Such instincts made his scientific mind wary, he thought as he turned his mind back to his old problem.

And hoped he hadn't just acquired a new one.

Dear Reader,

This month we have something really special on tap for you. *The Cinderella Mission*, by Catherine Mann, is the first of three FAMILY SECRETS titles, all of them prequels to our upcoming anthology *Broken Silence* and then a twelve book stand-alone FAMILY SECRETS continuity. These books are cutting edge, combining dark doings, mysterious experiments and overwhelming passion into a mix you won't be able to resist. Next month, the story continues with Linda Castillo's *The Phoenix Encounter*.

Of course, this being Intimate Moments, the excitement doesn't stop there. Award winner Justine Davis offers up another of her REDSTONE, INCORPORATED tales, *One of These Nights*. A scientist who's as handsome as he is brilliant finds himself glad to welcome his sexy bodyguard—and looking forward to exploring just what her job description means. *Wilder Days* (leading to wilder nights?) is the newest from reader favorite Linda Winstead Jones. It will have you turning the pages so fast, you'll lose track of time. Ingrid Weaver begins a new military miniseries, EAGLE SQUADRON, with *Eye of the Beholder*. There will be at least two follow-ups, so keep *your* eyes open so you don't miss them. Evelyn Vaughn, whose miniseries THE CIRCLE was a standout in our former Shadows line, makes her Intimate Moments debut with *Buried Secrets*, a paranormal tale that's as passionate as it is spooky. And Aussie writer Melissa James is back with *Who Do You Trust?* This is a deeply emotional "friends become lovers" reunion romance, one that will captivate you from start to finish.

Enjoy! And come back next month for more of the best and most exciting romance around—right here in Silhouette Intimate Moments.

Leslie J. Wainger
Executive Senior Editor

Please address questions and book requests to:
Silhouette Reader Service
U.S.: 3010 Walden Ave., P.O. Box 1325, Buffalo, NY 14269
Canadian: P.O. Box 609, Fort Erie, Ont. L2A 5X3

# One of These Nights
## JUSTINE DAVIS

Silhouette®

INTIMATE MOMENTS™
Published by Silhouette Books
America's Publisher of Contemporary Romance

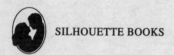 **SILHOUETTE BOOKS**

ISBN 0-373-27271-5

ONE OF THESE NIGHTS

Copyright © 2003 by Janice Davis Smith

This edition published by arrangement with Harlequin Books S.A.

Visit Silhouette at www.eHarlequin.com

**Printed in U.S.A.**

**Books by Justine Davis**

## JUSTINE DAVIS

A former policewoman, Justine says that years ago, a young man she worked with encouraged her to try for a promotion to a position that was, at that time, occupied only by men. "I succeeded, became wrapped up in my new job and that man moved away, never, I thought, to be heard from again. Ten years later he appeared out of the woods of Washington State, saying he'd never forgetten me and would I please marry him. With that history, how could I write anything but romance?"

Once upon a time, there was a genre of books that was sadly misunderstood by anyone who didn't read them. Those who did read them loved them, cherished them, were changed by them. But still, these books got no respect on the outside. In fact, these books were belittled, denigrated, held up as bad examples, while their readers and authors were sneered at and insulted by people who, although they never read the books, had somehow arrived at the idea that it was all right to slap others down for their choices. But those readers and authors kept on in the face of this horrible prejudice. Why? Because they found something in these books that they found nowhere else. Something precious, which spoke to them in a very deep and basic way.

Then one day, this beleaguered genre was given a gift. A fairy godmother, if you will, a person with an incredible knowledge of these books and why they worked, and an even more incredible generosity of spirit. A one-person support system who gave so much to the writers of these stories, and was ever unselfish with her time and that amazing knowledge. And her endorsement counted for something; readers took her word and knew they would rarely be disappointed. She was a rock, a pillar on which the genre depended. Her loss has left a gaping hole that can never be filled, and will always be felt by those who love these books—and loved her.

For those reasons and so many more, the Redstone, Incorporated series is dedicated to

### MELINDA HELFER

Lost to us August 24, 2000, but if heaven is what it should be, she's in an endless library, with an eternity to revel in the books she loved. Happy reading, my friend....

# Chapter 1

"Hey, Professor, you've been ordered to the boss's office right away."

Ian Gamble swore that if one more person called him Professor, he was going to ruin his image and punch whoever said it.

*At least they aren't saying the absentminded part,* he told himself.

But it didn't help much when he knew they were thinking it. He was *not* absentminded, nor was he a professor. What he was was an inventor, and that, as he'd told them all more than once, should be enough of a job title. It had been enough for Joshua Redstone, after all. He'd hired Ian when nobody else would. Josh hadn't cared about a piece of paper with the name of some college on it.

"Did you hear me?"

Ian gave his high-energy, and occasionally wearing, assistant a sideways look. The young college student was bright and had a lot of potential, but she was also in a very big hurry to receive the kind of acknowledgment she thought she already deserved. Even Stan Chilton, the easy-going head of this safety-oriented section of Redstone's research and development division, admitted he sometimes found her tiring.

"Were you speaking to me?"

Rebecca Hollings let out an audible, put-upon sigh as she pushed a lock of rather dull brown hair out of her eyes. "Yes, sir."

"Mr. Redstone *ordered* me to his office? That's unusual." He watched her steadily until she gave in sheepishly.

"Well, I guess what he really said was he needed to talk to you."

That was more like it. Most of the time if Josh needed a face-to-face with someone in his own headquarters building, he went to them. Summoning the peons to the tower wasn't his style. Besides, as he'd told Ian once, he wasn't one to pass up any chance to get out of his office.

"But he did say soon," she added. "And he was headed for his office."

"Then he didn't stay long," Ian said as a movement at the doors to the research and development lab caught his eye. A split second later Joshua Redstone poked his head in the door.

Rebecca blushed and turned away. Ian supposed he should go easier on her. She worked hard, often late into the night. And she went out of her way to help him, even brought him sandwiches when he forgot to eat. It was just his own nature that made him feel she was hovering too much.

"Ian? Take a walk with me?" Josh said in that easy drawl that made it painless to follow what from another man in his position would have been an order.

Ian nodded at Josh, hit the keys to blank the screen he'd been working with, signed out and locked the system, then got up and headed for the doors. Without a backward glance at his assistant.

They walked in silence until they reached the end of the hall and the huge bay window that looked out on the courtyard. The building that was the main headquarters of Redstone, Incorporated, was built around a cool green garden with a big pond and waterfall. In the heat of a California summer, it was a favorite spot for all the employees, and this window alcove lined with comfortable chairs was Ian's favorite retreat when he needed to get out of the bustle of the lab. He wasn't surprised that Josh remembered that. Redstone people got used to that kind of thing after a while.

"How's it going?" Josh asked as he folded his lanky frame into a chair. The laziness of his drawl, an odd combination of all the places he'd drifted through during formative years, didn't fool Ian one bit.

"Backing up a bit after the last results," Ian said as he took the next chair, "but we're still on the right track."

He knew Josh already knew this, because after the last round of experiments he'd filed a report that had shown they had further to go before the explosive-sensitive material he was working on would be effective in a configuration to be of use. Something else must be on his mind, Ian thought.

"If you can do this, it's going to be a wonder, Ian. Maybe we can't prevent everything, but I'd give a lot to never read about another Lockerbie or lose another of the family to a bomb on a plane."

Ian knew he was referring to the death of Phil Cooper a few years ago. As it turned out Cooper hadn't been the stellar citizen they'd thought, having died in the process of abandoning his wife and child, but that had all worked out for the best in a typical Redstone way, with new, happy beginnings for all.

"You're already giving a lot," Ian pointed out. "You're

supporting this research.'' And if he could just figure out what was wrong and fix it, so the material could line the cabins and holds of any aircraft as he intended, it would be worth everything Redstone was putting into it.

"And I'm not the only one."

Ah-ha, Ian thought. Josh was on that horse again. "Josh, the only one even close on this is Trektech, and Baron's stumped."

"He is?"

"I was talking to a old prof of mine at Cal Tech. He said Baron's called him three times in the last month, with wilder questions each time. He's lost. I know there are others working on it, too, but I'll get there first," Ian promised.

"I believe you. As long as you're left alone to do it. And that isn't what worries me."

"Oh?" Ian said, fairly sure now of where his boss was going with this. And the fact that Joshua Redstone, founder of the entire Redstone empire and veteran of innumerable corporate and personal battles, looked uncomfortable told Ian he was exactly right.

"I got a call from a friend today," Josh said. "He heard something interesting."

Ian knew Josh had an incredible network of people who, thanks to his penchant for lending a helping hand, were more than happy to repay him with bits of information.

"Interesting?"

"TriChem has had some inquiries about two of the chemical components you're using."

"Two?"

Josh smiled as Ian zeroed in on the crucial word. One might be coincidence, two was suspicious but not conclusive.

As if he'd read his mind, Josh added, "One of them is the compound, Ian."

Well, that changed things, Ian thought. It wasn't likely

anyone else would need that particular combination at this exact moment in time.

Josh's voice was dangerously quiet. "I think we have to assume we have a leak."

Ian hated to agree with that summation, but he knew it was true. "You're right," he said reluctantly. "It's such an odd combination."

"And unlikely someone else would have come up with it within a month of your breakthrough."

Ian grimaced. Why couldn't he just get on with his work? He hated to think about things like this. About someone he knew, someone he worked with and trusted, betraying him.

He glanced at his boss and saw something in his eyes that reminded him that this was a betrayal of Josh, as well. Josh, who'd earned the loyalty of everyone who worked for him. A generous, staunch ally who also made a dangerous, lethal enemy.

"There's more," Josh added. "Personnel caught another one."

"Trying to get hired?"

Josh nodded. "He had the perfect credentials. Would have been just what we were looking for."

"But?"

"A little digging turned up a JetCal connection. Not a close one—a roommate's brother or something—but it was there. Again."

This was the second time someone tied to JetCal had tried to get a job in Redstone Technologies' research and development division. Ian knew Josh hadn't thought much of Joe Santerelli's business methods already, and this only confirmed he was right in his judgment.

"I'm not sure we can make the lab any more secure than it already is, without limiting access entirely," Ian said thoughtfully. Josh had already spared no expense in setting up safeguards for the R&D section, Ian's work in particular, but if the leak was already on the inside, that might not be enough.

"We may have to do that. But I'll deal with the inside. Outside is where the real vulnerability is."

Ian frowned. "What do you mean?"

"You, Ian."

Ian blinked. "Me?"

"It's not a secret that you do a lot of work at home. If they want this badly enough to try espionage from the inside at Redstone, they might try something there, too."

"I've made some security arrangements there," Ian said. "The work will be safe."

Josh smiled, that gentle smile that warned Ian he'd somehow missed the point. "They might want it badly enough to come after you."

"That would be crazy," Ian protested.

Josh Redstone's gaze never wavered. "Yes. But it's a crazy world, my friend."

Nobody knew that better than Josh, Ian realized. But the idea that someone might come after him seemed too absurd to Ian to contemplate.

"What good would I do them?" he protested. "It's not as if I'd ever work for them."

"Voluntarily." Josh's voice was grim. "I want you to have protection, Ian, until this project is concluded one way or another."

Ian couldn't help it, he burst out laughing. "Protection? You mean like a bodyguard? You're not serious!"

"I am, Ian. I don't compromise when it comes to the safety of my people."

Ian had never seen quite that glint before in the steady gray eyes of the man who was Redstone. But he couldn't give in to this. He liked his life as it was. He knew his own mental processes well enough to know that the kind of disruption Josh was talking about would rattle his thinking, and he'd likely never achieve a breakthrough on this project. He didn't like change, anyway, he needed things in his personal life stable so he could free his mind to think about his work.

"I appreciate your concern, but it's out of the question."

"Ian—"

"No," he repeated.

It was not, he supposed, wise to interrupt and argue with your boss, but if Josh had been the kind of man who took offense at such things, Ian knew he would have been fired long ago.

"I mean it, Josh. Somebody around all the time, at my home and wherever I go? I can't work or think that way."

Josh studied him for a moment. "And if I made it an order?"

Ian let out a compressed breath. "Then, with great difficulty because of my tremendous respect and liking for you, I would disobey."

Josh's mouth quirked upward. "I was afraid of that."

"Josh, I'm sorry, but—"

Josh waved a hand at him. "Never mind. I had to ask."

"And I had to refuse."

"I understand."

Relieved, Ian stood up. Then he asked, "Was there anything else?"

Josh shook his head. "Just tell your assistant to lighten up."

Ian chuckled. "I have. She's a little hyper, so it hasn't gotten through yet."

Josh looked concerned. "Is she turning out to be a problem?"

Josh himself had talked Ian into taking the girl on, saying she was bright enough to learn from the best. Ian had a sneaking suspicion Josh also thought having the young woman around might loosen him up a bit. In any case, he didn't want Josh to think he'd made a bad decision when in fact it was mostly Ian's own problem.

"No, not at all. I'm just not used to her yet, and she's anxious to do it all now."

"Keep trying with her," Josh said.

Keep Trying. One of the Redstone mantras, Ian thought as he headed back to the lab. Along with Hire the Best and Let Them Do Their Best, and Redstone Likes Happy People. To the outside world, he was sure they all sounded like idealistic dreamers, but everybody on the inside knew it was for real. Because of one man, Ian thought as he keyed in his pass code for entry to the lab. One man with a vision, and the determination to make it happen. Josh had—

Ian stopped dead in the doorway to his office. Rebecca was in his chair, at his computer.

"Looking for something?" he asked.

"Oh!" She jumped, spun in the chair, her hand pressed dramatically over her heart. "You scared me."

Normally it would have been time for an apology, a statement saying he hadn't meant to scare her. But Josh's warnings were still echoing in his mind, and he stayed silent, simply watching her. He'd learned it was a rare person who could allow such silence, and Rebecca definitely wasn't one of them.

"I was just leaving you a note."

Her voice still sounded tight. Again he waited, and something odd flickered in her eyes.

"I need to leave early," she said hastily. "I have a doc—er, a dentist's appointment."

If she'd only been leaving him a note about that, why was she so flustered? Had she been doing something else? Trying to access his files on the computer? The screen was as he'd left it, blacked out, but if she'd been here long enough…

As Rebecca scuttled out of the room, Ian told himself he was being paranoid. Yet he had enough respect for Josh to take his worries seriously. The man was no fool, and those who had mistaken him for such, perhaps judging him by that lazy drawl or the way he had of strolling along with his hands in his pockets, were the sadder for it.

He turned to his computer and did a quick check. He could find no trace that anyone had accessed any of his files in the past half hour. That decided him. In this case Josh was being overly protective. Wasn't that part of the Redstone legend, taking care of his people? Wasn't that why they were consistently at the top of the national list of the best places to work?

*I want you to have protection, Ian....*

No. No way. He couldn't tolerate it. He hadn't even been able to tolerate his wife around all the time. His need for space, while Colleen had needed people and socializing, had driven her away after a mere ten months of trying to put up with him.

No, he was a loner, a borderline recluse, as Josh's personal pilot, Tess Machado, had called him more than once. And he would stay that way, happily. He didn't need a wife, or any woman to complete him. He had his work. That was enough.

"Thanks for getting here so quickly, Sam."

"No problem," Samantha Beckett told her boss.

Actually it had been a problem—when he'd called she had just stepped out of the shower, her hair dripping wet. But she'd have dealt with a lot more than wet hair to come running at his call, and she hoped he knew it. Joshua Redstone had done more for her and Billy than anyone ever had, and she owed him more than she could ever repay.

"How's Billy?" Josh asked, as if he'd read her thought.

"He's doing great. That new residential skills center is working well for him. He likes the people and he's really happy."

"That's good to hear."

Sam knew he wouldn't take it in words, so she tried her

best to put her thanks into her smile. If not for Josh, Billy would probably be locked in an institution somewhere, taken away by some bureaucrat who thought they knew better than she did how to take care of her little brother. Instead they'd stayed together, and she was able to afford to have him well looked after when she had to leave on assignment.

Speaking of assignments, she thought, why was the usually direct Josh taking so long to get around to the point?

She studied him, thinking as she often had that you'd never guess by looking at him that this former pilot had built a small airplane design company into an international corporation the scope of which she could hardly comprehend. But she also knew that was one of his strengths. Josh didn't come across as a shark, not with that tall, lanky frame, sometimes tousled hair and that lazy smile. He was very unassuming and laid-back, but people who assumed he was as slow as his drawl didn't discover the sharpness of his teeth until it was too late.

"This is an unusual one," Josh finally said, sounding a bit uncomfortable. That in itself was odd enough for Sam to sit up and pay close attention.

"In-house, I gather, since you wanted to meet here?" she asked, gesturing at the restaurant they were sitting in.

He nodded, confirming her guess that the "unusual" case involved something or someone inside Redstone, and that he didn't want to risk anyone seeing them meet. This despite the fact that the Redstone security team was low profile by intention. They reported directly to Josh, had their own office off-site, and other than those in the upper echelon, like Noah Rider last month, the majority of Redstone employees wouldn't know any of them by sight.

"Undercover, then?" Sam asked, already running through logistics in her mind.

"Sort of," Josh said.

Sam looked at the man across the table from her. It

wasn't like him to equivocate. For the most part, Joshua Redstone preferred plain speaking. Which made this hesitancy even more interesting to her.

"Would you like to just cut to the chase, sir?"

"I need you to bodyguard somebody who doesn't want one."

Well, that was blunt enough, Sam thought. "All right," she said. "How far under?"

"What?"

"You want me to sleep with him?"

Surprise flared in Josh's eyes, as she had intended. "You know better than that!"

"Yes, I do." She grinned at him. "You just seemed a little vague about the specifics here."

Josh let out a wry chuckle. "Now I know how the guys who go up against you and lose feel."

"Is there any other kind?" Samantha said, her grin widening.

"Not many, I'd guess," Josh conceded, returning her grin finally. "I have to say I knew what I was doing when I hired you for this job."

"And the people at the Sitka Resort are eternally grateful you pulled me out of there, I'm sure."

*And no more so than I,* she added silently, knowing she would have gone slowly insane working in such a routine-laden world, even if it was for Redstone.

"You weren't happy," he said candidly, and for a moment Sam marveled at the simplicity of it; one of his lowliest, most distant employees wasn't happy, so he took steps to fix that. Amazing. "I'll have Rand relieve you periodically, because I don't know how long this assignment will be."

Samantha nodded. She and Rand Singleton had worked together frequently, often taking advantage of the striking resemblance between them. With matching nearly platinum-blond hair and blue eyes, they were easily able to pass as brother and sister. She thought of him that way, too, as a sometimes bossy big brother.

"So who's this guy who doesn't want to be guarded?"

"Ian Gamble. He's in R and D."

Sam frowned. The name sounded vaguely familiar. "What's he need guarding from?"

"He's working on a very important, very secret project for Redstone Technologies. He's close to success, and there are a lot of other people who would like to get there first. JetCal has already tried twice to get a mole in. Plus, there's a possibility we have a leak."

There was an undertone in his voice that was razor sharp, and if there was a leak, Sam didn't envy her or him when Josh found out who it was. Which he would, she knew. She thought about asking what the project was, then decided if it made any difference in her task, Josh would have told her. Besides, her mind had already leaped ahead.

"People who might want to interfere with him or his work in one way or another?"

Josh nodded. "Or stop him from working at all. On the financial front, the Safe Transit Project could be worth billions to whoever gets there first."

"That's a lot of motive," Sam said. "Why the resistance?"

"In part because he doesn't believe he's really in danger."

"Naive?"

"Not exactly. Ian is…different. Brilliant, but a bit eccentric."

Eccentric, in her experience, was a kinder euphemism for crazy. A vision formed in her head, a sort of Einstein-needing-Prozac image that had her smiling inwardly even as she calculated just how difficult this task might be.

"He has a very particular way of working," Josh explained, "and he refuses to let anything or anyone intrude on that."

"Even for his own safety?"

"Especially that. He agrees his work needs protecting but won't have anything to do with a bodyguard. And I can't say that I don't understand. He needs space and time to let that incredible mind of his run."

"He's that smart?"

"Not in the traditional sense. He thinks outside the box, as they say. That's why he's so good at what he does."

"Which is?"

"They call him 'the professor,' but he's an inventor."

Einstein suddenly shifted to Edison in her head. "We still have those?"

"A few," Josh said with a grin. "Most inventing is done by committee nowadays, but Ian is a throwback. Lucky for us."

"And where did you find this one?"

It had become legend, Josh Redstone's knack for finding gold in the most unlikely places. It seemed every employee had a story of how Josh found them in a place they didn't want to be and gave them the chance to find the place they belonged.

"He was trying to market a new deicing chemical for planes that he'd come up with, and after he got turned down by all the big and small airlines, he came to Redstone Aviation. He'd already invented a new computer cable that reduced signal noise, and a fireproofing treatment for already existing roofs, but hadn't been able to sell those, either."

And on the strength of what would likely be seen in the business world as three failures, Josh had hired him anyway, Sam thought. Typical.

"They didn't work?" she asked.

"They worked," Josh said. "But Ian is in no way a salesman."

Sam smiled inwardly. *Not necessarily a bad thing in my book.* "So Redstone took that off his hands?"

"And let him do what he does best."

"Invent."

Josh nodded. "And nobody else can quite follow the way his mind works, so he works alone. And lives alone."

That could make things either easier or harder, Sam thought. "Not married?"

"Not for several years."

Burned, or impossible to live with? Sam wondered. "How alone is he? A recluse?"

"No. He doesn't socialize much, outside of Redstone, but he does get along fine inside. He works out in the gym with a regular group, that kind of thing."

Something in Josh's expression told her she was wasting her time trying to think of an approach. "You've already got this set up, don't you?"

One corner of her boss's mouth quirked upward. "I always did say you were perceptive."

"So what's the plan?"

"I hate lying to him, but I'd hate even more having to negotiate for his safety. Or go to his funeral." Josh reached into his pocket and pulled out two keys on a ring, with a paper tag attached. He slid them across the table to her. "You just bought a house."

Sam blinked. She looked at the keys, then at her boss. "Lucky me," she said.

She picked up the ring, glanced at the tag, at the address scrawled on it.

"Let me guess," she said. "The professor's nearby?"

"Right next door."

Already planning her packing, she lifted an eyebrow at him. "Did they want to sell?"

Josh's mouth quirked. "They did in the end."

"At twice market value?" she guessed, knowing how Josh worked. "Enough to set them up in a brand-new house with cash to spare?"

Josh shrugged. "The important thing was to get you close. So Ian's got a new neighbor."

Sam pocketed the keys with a grin. "There goes the neighborhood."

# Chapter 2

Adhesion.

That, Ian thought as he paced his living room, was the problem. The formula itself was working perfectly, it was the practical logistics of use that were being evasive.

He paused at the side window, his mind intent on the puzzle. No matter what they applied the explosive-sensitive material to, it started to peel away. Steel, aluminum, even plastic—after a month to six weeks under normal usage in a cargo hold or passenger cabin it always happened.

He turned, crossing the room once more, his path clear because all of the furniture was pushed up against the walls, leaving him lots of free space to roam as he thought.

They'd tried embedding the material in a plastic that could then be shaped, but the process greatly affected the efficiency and sensitivity of the product. They'd tried every known kind of primer, with little success. The problem was finding something that didn't react with the active ingredient in the sensor medium. The only thing they'd found

so far was lead, but lining an airplane with that was a
problem for more reasons than just the weight factor.

He came back to the window.

He had to be overlooking something. There was some
simple answer, he could just feel it. It was probably so
simple he was looking right past it. He was looking—

He was looking at a rather incredible woman.

He blinked as his conscious mind finally registered what
his subconscious had already known. There was a tall,
leggy blonde next door, carrying a large box. Carrying it
more easily than he would have expected, given its bulk.
She was wearing faded jeans, a yellow tank top and a pair
of wraparound sunglasses. Her pale hair was pulled back
into some kind of knot at the back of her head and secured
with what looked for all the world to be chopsticks. How
did women learn such things? he wondered.

She really was very leggy, he thought. And very blond.

And she appeared to be moving in next door.

He frowned. Not his usual reaction to the sight of a
beautiful woman, but his quiet, older neighbors had sold
out and moved so quickly, barely pausing to say goodbye.
True, they'd been longing for a place with less upkeep,
but had been certain it would be years before they could
afford the luxury town house they wanted. Obviously,
something had happened to change that.

And the day after their moving van had pulled away a
furniture truck had appeared, unloading several items. And
now this woman.

She didn't seem to have brought much. Maybe the rest
of her personal items had been with the new furniture.
Then again, probably not. It had been a delivery truck, not
a moving truck. Yet what he'd seen her carry in amounted
to less than his mother took on a weekend trip. Of course,
his mother didn't know the meaning of traveling light.

He supposed he could go over there and simply ask.
Maybe introduce himself. Even offer to help, although it

looked like she didn't need it. It was what his mother would do.

But she, Ian thought rather glumly, would do it with ease and charm. He would fumble and stumble and feel thoroughly awkward about it.

The woman set another large box down on the front porch of the house, straightened, started to turn to go back to the blue pickup truck that was parked at the curb. Then she froze. And slowly turned her head and looked right at him.

Ian jerked back from the window, startled.

*You can't be sure she was looking at you, not with those dark glasses,* he told himself.

And then she smiled and waved at him.

His heart did a crazy flip-flop. He told himself it wasn't the smile that rattled him, although even from here it was a killer one. It had to be that she seemed to have sensed him watching. Such instincts, while he knew they existed, made his scientific mind wary.

He pulled back even farther, and with a discipline born of years spent learning to focus, he turned his mind back to the old problem.

And hoped he hadn't just acquired a new one.


Sam took the last box straight inside, set it down and plopped herself down on the cushy couch that had been delivered just yesterday.

"Well," she muttered to herself, "that'll teach you to make assumptions."

Obviously her Einstein image was now blown to bits. She hadn't been able to see all of him, but already it was clear that Ian Gamble was anything but the wild-haired old man she'd been picturing. In fact, his sandy brown hair had looked thick and shiny and had that endearingly floppy quality that always made her want to touch.

She jumped to her feet. She wasn't *that* rattled, she told

herself. All she needed was a little readjustment of her
perceptions. So he was younger than she'd thought. All
that meant was he might be a bit more active than she'd
figured. She could deal with that. In fact it would be easier.
Stakeouts and long surveillances always made her crazy
because she wasn't used to sitting still for so long.

That thought cheered her, and she got up and went about
the business of unpacking. Since she'd have access to laundry facilities here in the house, she'd been able to pack
even lighter than usual. She usually lived in jeans and cot-
ton shirts when she had the option, but she'd have to wear
office clothing to convince Gamble she had a job somewhere. At least the Armani gown and the dressy clothes
she'd acquired—at Josh's recommendation and expense—
in the course of other assignments could stay home this
trip.

It didn't take her long to empty the two boxes of clothing, and to set aside the dark jeans, sweater and knit cap
she had selected in case she had to do any late-night re-
cons. The bathroom was another, smaller box. The kitchen
was the smallest box of all; her cooking skills were limited
to coffee, scrambled eggs and packaged macaroni and
cheese, so she didn't require much in the way of gear. Into
the fridge went the items from the cooler she'd brought
from home, to save her from throwing the stuff out when
she went back to her apartment. Then she unpacked the
bag of items she'd picked up at the grocery store around
the corner on her way here; she couldn't order in *every*
night. Well, she could, but not without drawing more attention from the neighbors than she wanted.

Lastly she took her two-inch Smith & Wesson revolver
out of its case, along with a trim holster with a belt clip
and an ankle holster. She'd spent yesterday sharpening her
skills with the small weapon. Anything larger than the
small gun would be harder to hide from Gamble, and she
didn't want to have to worry about it.

When she was done unpacking, she went back into the living room. She'd already seen that the windows on the north side of the house were the best spot to watch Gamble's home. And smiled to see that Josh had already arranged to have the rather ornate floral draperies left by the previous owners replaced with pleated shades that allowed in sunlight from outside yet were semitransparent from inside, so she could see at least motion if not details without raising them.

Upstairs, the master bedroom had a window seat alcove that looked out on that same side. She suspected most of her in-house time would be spent there, since she could see the windows on the side and back of Gamble's house, plus both the front and back yards. The yards themselves were an almost scary sight; gardening, it was clear, was not on the man's list of priorities.

Which could be a good thing for her, she thought. A way to get closer. She'd have to watch for a chance.

She was glad the lower bank of windows around the window seat bay opened. She needed to be able to hear the slightest noises from next door. She preferred to sleep with windows open, anyway, especially in spring and summer, but in this case she'd have to even if it was cold out. Not that she'd be sleeping all that much at night, and when she did, it would be with one ear open. She'd have to catch up during the day when Gamble was safely tucked away at Redstone.

Speaking of her target, she thought, it was time to get moving on that front. She went to the kitchen, grabbed her favorite coffee mug, and headed for the door. It was old and corny, yes, but it also happened to be true. She was out of sugar.

She had to go down to the sidewalk then up the walkway to the house; there was no way she could cut through the overgrown honeysuckle that grew along the property lines between the houses. It had to be at least six feet tall and incredibly thick. That, she thought, could be a problem if she needed to get over there in a hurry. All the more reason to pursue that, she thought.

She paused for a moment before knocking on the front door. First impressions counted, and never more than in this kind of work. She debated between sheepish, shy or harried, decided on a combination of the first two, with a touch of flighty blonde just to see if it would work.

She knocked. Waited. Knocked again. Finally the door swung open.

Samantha Beckett took her first close-up look at Ian Gamble and immediately abandoned her plan. There was nothing naive or absentminded about those vivid green eyes, and the wire-rimmed glasses he wore did nothing to mask an intelligence that fairly crackled. His hair was lighter than she'd thought, almost a sandy blond on top, but it was as thick and shiny as it had seemed from a distance.

He was tall, she realized. At five foot nine herself, she noticed that. He didn't tower over her, but if she looked straight ahead she was looking at his nose, not his forehead as often was the case. And he was lean, not pudgy, as she'd half expected someone who spent their days in a lab to be.

*I've got to work on my preconceptions,* she told herself. *And,* she added silently as she realized he was looking at her rather quizzically, *I'd better say something here.*

''Hi,'' she said.

*Well, now that was clever. Get it together here, Beckett. You've done this before, what's your problem?*

She tried again. ''I'm Samantha. Samantha Harrison.'' She and Josh had agreed that while it was very unlikely, there was just enough chance Gamble might stumble across her name or someone else who'd seen it in connection with Redstone to make a cover name wise. So as she usually did, she used her mother's maiden name. "I just moved in next door."

After a moment of hesitation that made her wonder, he nodded. "I saw."

At least he didn't try to deny he'd been watching, she thought. After the way he'd jerked back when she'd sensed his gaze and looked over at his window, she'd half expected that.

"I know this sounds like an old joke, but I really am out of sugar, and if I don't have it for my morning coffee, it gets pretty ugly. I'd really like to avoid another run to the market if I can. I'm kind of beat."

His mouth quirked slightly. At first she thought it was in amusement, but then she got the oddest feeling it was in self-consciousness. Or embarrassment.

"You moved alone?"

In another man she might have thought this a not-too-subtle way to find out if she was married or otherwise attached. But there was nothing of subterfuge in his eyes, and she realized on a sudden flash of insight that he was uncomfortable because he hadn't offered to help her.

"Just me, but all I had to do was my clothes and personal stuff, so it wasn't bad." She gestured with the mug. "Except I was out of sugar and didn't realize it until I unpacked the coffeemaker."

"Oh," he said, as if suddenly remembering why she was here. "Uh, sure, I've got some sugar."

"Thanks," she said, handing him her mug.

He took it, then hesitated, and she wondered if he would just leave her standing on the porch while he went to the kitchen. That wouldn't do; she needed to see the inside of the house. She knew the layout, thanks to Redstone's research department, who had miraculously dug up the original plans from when the tract had been built twenty-five years ago, but she needed to see how he had it set up, to know where he worked, slept, watched TV, whatever he did.

At the last second he pulled the door open. "Come on in."

"Thanks."

She stepped in after him, but instead of following him toward the back of the house, where the kitchen was, she stayed near the door. At least, until he was out of sight. Then she swiftly went to the windows that faced her new residence; first thing she needed to know was what he could see. Her living room was on almost a direct line with his, so that was out for stealth. She noted that he'd have to lean out to look past his chimney to see her bedroom window; another point for it being the prime observation post. She turned back to the interior.

She'd noticed the chaos, but only peripherally in her focus on the windows. What was supposed to be the living room clearly was serving as his office. Judging from everything he had here, none of the bedrooms would have been big enough. Two computers, a door-size table piled with papers, a lower table covered with what looked like computer printouts, and two huge bookcases crammed with books, notebooks and pieces of equipment whose function she could only guess at.

On a normal surveillance, she'd be looking for places to plant bugs or cameras. But Josh had been quite clear on that; Ian was one of them, an innocent victim of his work at Redstone, and he was to be protected, not treated like some kind of suspect.

She walked to the other side of the room, where an arched opening led to what was supposed to be a den, according to the floor plan. This, at least, looked almost like what it was supposed to be, although there were piles of papers and books here, too. There was a television in one corner, and a leather couch that looked, from the pillow and blanket tossed to one side, as if it had been the scene of more than one night's sleep.

So, did he sleep on the couch for the traditional reasons, a tiff with a significant other that Redstone didn't know about? There was no sign of a feminine hand in this place, and rare would be the woman who could look at all this and not want to do…something.

More likely, she thought, as she heard footsteps and dodged out of the room and back into the entryway, he got so involved in his reading or work that he crashed here on the couch because it was closer. That fit with what Josh had said about him.

Of course, it could simply be that the bedroom was full, too, she thought, stifling a grin.

"It's a bit lumpy," he said apologetically as he handed her the mug, now nearly full with indeed lumpy sugar.

"No problem," she assured him. "It'll still dissolve just fine."

He seemed a bit more at ease now, and she wondered if she could stretch this a bit.

"I and my bleary, morning eyes thank you."

He managed an actual smile. A nice smile. In fact, a very nice smile. It changed his entire face, from that rather somber, serious mien to something that could pass for the proverbial boy next door. Which he was, in a way, she thought, smiling back at him.

"Have you lived here long? I don't know the neighborhood at all," she said, hoping to draw him out.

"Almost all my life. My parents bought this place when I was seven." He frowned slightly. "I didn't even realize the Howards had put their place on the market."

"They didn't, actually. A friend who knew I was looking for a place out here put us together." She didn't want to over explain and draw his curiosity, so she asked, "Your parents don't live here now?"

This time the quirk of his mouth was almost a grimace.

"They don't live anywhere. They're never in one place long enough. They visit here now and then, but live? No."

"They travel?" She knew that already, but schooled her features to friendly interest.

"In the extreme," he said. "The old phrase *the jet set* was invented for my parents. When I was a kid, every summer we were off to some exotic place. Now that they're retired, it's constant."

"Sounds like fun," she said, as if she hadn't had her own experiences of round-the-world travel since she'd joined the Redstone security team. Of course, her travel was hardly for pleasure, and often she barely got to glimpse whatever exotic part of the world she was in.

He lifted one shoulder. "It's okay, if you don't mind not having a home base."

She thought about that for a minute, then shook her head. "No, I'd have to have someplace to claim as home." She grinned at him. "Or that would claim me, at least."

He grinned back then. A quick, flashing grin as lethal as any she'd ever seen. And she'd seen a few. Again she had to reassess Ian Gamble.

Who hadn't, she realized, told her his name.

"So tell me, where's the best pizza, Chinese takeout and ice cream?" she asked, knowing full well those were his weaknesses.

He blinked. And the grin widened. "Luigi's, Wong Fu's and The Ice Cream Factory. All within walking distance, if you like to walk."

"Hallelujah."

"Luigi's and Wong Fu's even deliver," he added helpfully.

"I may survive," she said. "Thanks—" She lifted a brow at the place where normally she would have said his name. He didn't miss the hint.

"Ian. Ian Gamble."

She held out a hand. "Nice to meet you, Ian." No macho posturing here. His handshake was firm but not crushing. "I'll replace the sugar."

"Don't worry about it," he said.

"Okay, then I'll buy the ice cream one night."

"I...uh..."

He looked so startled it disconcerted her. He was a reasonably attractive man—well, okay, more than reasonably—surely he'd had a woman ask him for a casual date before. Hadn't he?

He was, she knew, only thirty-two, hardly old enough to be of the mind-set that women simply didn't ask men out.

"How about tomorrow afternoon?" she asked, thinking perhaps a Sunday afternoon might seem less threatening. "Besides," she added, "that way you can show me where it is."

That practicality seemed to convince him, and he nodded. "Okay. If it can be late afternoon, I've got some work to finish up."

"Work? On Sunday?" He shrugged. She looked at the two computers. "Are you some kind of dot com guy or something?"

He laughed. It was as nice as his smile. "Not hardly. I'm just a...researcher."

Had he hesitated over using the word inventor? And if so, why? she wondered. Because it was too hard to explain to strangers?

"You work at home?" she asked.

"No. I work downtown."

"So do I."

As if the need to be careful had just come back to him full force, he asked, "Where did you move from?"

"An apartment so small I could barely breathe," she said, with total honesty. She never spent much time in the place she'd moved into after Billy had settled into his own new home, because she was on the road so much for Josh.

But when she was there for more than a few days, it seemed cramped. She had the feeling that by the time this was over, she'd miss the extra room. This house wasn't huge, but it was three times the size of her apartment.

"This will be worth the extra drive," she added, and he seemed to accept the implication that her apartment was closer to her work.

"It's a nice neighborhood. Quiet."

"Good. I've already picked out my favorite reading spot, up in the window seat," she said, figuring she'd supply the reason now, in case he noticed and started to wonder why she was up there so much.

"You read a lot?"

"Not as much as I'd like. That's why I'm planning on more."

He smiled at that, the understanding smile of a fellow reader. She gestured around at the living room office. "Do you read anything but work?"

"I try, but like you, not as much as I'd like. I read history, mostly. But now and then a good mystery will keep me up nights."

"Me, too," she agreed, knowing she meant it in a totally different way than he did.

She'd about pushed the limits of the cup of sugar, she decided. "I'd better get back to my unpacking. And I've got to get my friend's truck back to him yet today. Thanks again for the sugar."

She felt his gaze on her all the way down the walkway, and then heard the door softly close.

Ian felt exhausted. He'd only spent five minutes with the woman and he was worn-out. He sank down on the couch, fighting the urge to pull the pillow into place and lie down. What the hell was wrong with him? Had he become so reclusive, so withdrawn that a short conversation with someone was such an effort for him?

After a moment he discarded that notion. It wasn't just someone, it was someone like Samantha Harrison. Life and energy simply radiated from her, and that kind of person always had this effect on him. Because he was so much the opposite, he supposed. He was always one step back from life, an observer rather than a participant. People like her lived life to the fullest, with passion and élan. People like him just stood back and watched, admiring but not partaking.

And sometimes wishing they could be different.

# Chapter 3

It wasn't just a Monday morning, it was a rotten Monday morning. Rebecca was really starting to get on Ian's nerves. When they'd first assigned the intern to him, he'd thought she might be a help with all the paperwork and reports tracking the progress of the project. And he couldn't deny she was efficient at that. Too efficient, perhaps. She had too much time left to hang over his shoulder, too much time to poke her nose into new work that wasn't ready to be added to the logs yet.

He'd tried telling her he worked alone; he couldn't tolerate somebody hanging around so closely. But she'd told him she was just so excited she couldn't help herself. One time he'd snapped at her, and the sight of tears welling up in her eyes made him feel like such a jerk. She was barely more than a girl, after all. So now he found himself making up things for her to do, just to get her out of his way for a while. Like now, when he asked her to track down a new cartridge for the printer, when he knew a simple shaking of the current one would keep him going for a couple of weeks. He didn't care, he just needed her out of here so he could concentrate.

It didn't work.

He swore under his breath as his mind insisted on returning to yesterday, a Sunday afternoon unlike any he'd had in years. Samantha was filled with such energy, such a passion for life it put him in mind of his mother, which did little to explain his wary fascination. He and his mother—and his father, for that matter—did not see eye to eye on much of anything, except that they loved each other and shared the wonder at how on earth they had wound up as parents and child.

A simple walk down the street for an ice cream, something he'd done countless times before, had somehow been turned into an adventure. Being new to the neighborhood, she'd seen and asked about things he took for granted. But he was glad. It let him relax and answer questions instead of trying to think of things to say. At one time he'd been perfectly able to carry on a conversation without strain. Once again he wondered how he'd come to this.

The Martins' multicolored Victorian-style house had earned a grin, the Bergs' cheerful border collie, a croon and a pat, and Mrs. Gerardi's lavish formal garden had rated a stop and look.

"Gorgeous, but a bit too tidy for my taste."

"You ought to love mine, then," Ian had said wryly.

She'd laughed, that lively and musical sound. "I noticed."

"I don't have the time," he'd said, then added frankly, "or the knowledge."

"I do. I love gardening, and there's not much to do around my place. Too much concrete," she'd said with a grimace. She'd turned a smile on him then that made his breath catch. "So why don't I tackle your yard? You'd be doing me a favor, letting me putter."

"You want to work on my yard?" He'd gaped at her but hadn't been able to help it.

"If you wouldn't mind," Samantha had said, sounding utterly enthused.

"If you wouldn't mind," Rebecca's voice said in his ear now, sounding utterly meek.

Ian snapped back to the present. For a moment he just stared at his assistant, who was looking at him as if she'd been talking for a while. He hadn't heard a word.

"Mind?" he asked, hoping the ploy would work. It did, sort of. She repeated enough that he was able to get the gist of her request but with an expression on her face that clearly indicated she was wondering about his sanity.

"I know you said last week's data wasn't ready yet, but I thought since I have some time I'd enter it, anyway, and then I can make any changes you want later."

Sometimes her eagerness wore on him, Ian thought. Maybe it was simply her youth. She made him feel much more than just thirteen years older than she was. He wondered how old Samantha was. Younger than he, he guessed. But not as young as Rebecca. And her enthusiasm didn't wear on him in the same way. For all her light-heartedness, he sensed in Samantha depths that weren't shown to the world. She'd had shadows in her life, he thought. She—

"Well, Professor?"

Yanked again back to the present, he resisted the urge to again snap at her for calling him that. He shouldn't be angry at her. She was always so nice to him, bringing him lunch when he forgot to eat, tidying his office, making sure he remembered a jacket when it was cool.

"Go ahead," he said, rather sharply.

*And just leave me alone.*

Even as he thought the words, he realized they had become a mantra. He'd even stopped adding *to do my work* to the phrase. And for the most part, people were doing just that. Leaving him alone.

For the first time he wondered if maybe he'd gone too far into isolation.

"Hey, Professor, how goes it?" Stan Chilton's voice cut into his thoughts. "Data ready yet?"

*He's your boss,* Ian reminded himself, albeit with jaw clenched. *You can't punch out the head of research and development, even if he is the one who started that damned "Professor" thing.*

And the man was nearly as bad as Rebecca, hovering, flitting around the edges until Ian thought he was going to lose it. Odd, Stan hadn't always been that way. But it seemed everybody was strung tight over this particular project—even Stan, who, while bright enough, was more of an administrator than anything. His talent lay in the research, not in the development. Along with his computer skills, which were legend around the division, paperwork and organization, things that were an anathema to Ian, were Stan's pride and joy.

*And without him, you'd be stuck doing that,* Ian told himself. So with a sigh he reined in his temper and set about updating Chilton, which in essence meant telling him that in hard data they were exactly where they'd been the last time he'd asked.

"So far, so good," Sam reported.

"He doesn't suspect?" Josh asked.

"No." She lifted a shoulder to hold the phone receiver against her ear as she finished pouring icy soda water into her glass. "I've got a good watching post for when he's in the house at night, and a way to stick close to him on weekends. The only problem is transit between here and Redstone. Right now I'm following him in and then back home, but I don't think that's going to work forever."

"You think he knows you're following him?" Josh asked.

"I told him I work in the same direction. But he works unpredictable hours, and that makes it tricky for me to match his schedule without him getting wise."

"Shall I have somebody else do the tail, so you can be less obvious?"

"That would be a good idea, for the interim."

"The interim?"

"I still don't like him driving alone. Too much could happen. If somebody was really prepared, they could grab him before we could get to him."

"Unacceptable," Josh said. And she knew he meant it.

"I've got a way around it, but I think I need to wait a bit. He needs to know me better, get used to me being around."

"It's your call."

She understood what trust and faith were implicit in those words. Josh didn't need details, he trusted his people to do their jobs. Never once had he even hinted that she was any less capable than any of the men on the team, or that she needed backup. Josh had hired her, Draven had trained her, and she carried her share.

"I'll arrange for someone to track him in the meantime," Josh said.

"Thanks. Have you heard from Draven?" she asked, now that the head of her section had come to mind.

"This morning. He's wrapping up in Managua and will be headed back the end of the week, with the package."

*Way to go,* she thought. They'd all wondered if they would be called in on that kidnap situation. *Should have known better, with Draven on it.*

"How's Billy?" Josh asked.

"Fine. I just got back from the school. I'm able to see him every day now, as long as our boy is in the lab. It's working out well."

She knew Josh had somebody on the inside watching— his longtime and rather spookily omniscient assistant, St. John, she suspected—ready to call or page her if Gamble left unexpectedly. That left her quite free during the frequently long work hours the professor put in, hours she put to good use visiting her brother and catching up on her sleep.

"I'd like to stop by and see him," Josh said.

"He'd love that. You know you're always Uncle Josh to him."

She could almost see him smiling, and there was no denying the genuine pleasure in his tone when he answered. "He's a special kid."

"Yes," Sam said quietly. Her little brother was a very, very special kid. And it took a man the caliber of Josh Redstone to realize that.

After she'd hung up she sat still for a moment, thinking once more how lucky she was. If Josh hadn't pulled her out of her old job, who knows where the restless streak she'd been born with would have led her. Her parents, had they lived, would have been aghast at her work now, at the danger of it, the very thing that kept her exhilarated and buoyant.

But they would have been pleased that she'd taken care of Billy. Not that there had ever been any question. Her sweet-natured, always happy brother was considered handicapped by some, but to her he was the base of her world, the center that kept her sane.

And sometimes the single thing that kept her restless streak from becoming a reckless one.

Ian nearly drove through his garage door.

He wasn't really accident-prone, just sometimes he got to thinking and lost track of what he was doing. Fortunately his reflexes were fast enough to keep him out of trouble most of the time, but there was a reason he always bought used cars.

Thinking had nothing to do with it this time, however. When he pulled into his driveway and saw Samantha in his garden, wearing only a bright-blue tank top and cutoff jeans that bared too much of those long legs for his equilibrium, he completely forgot what he was doing. That is, driving.

He stopped a fraction of an inch away from an expensive repair job on both garage door and already recently repaired car. Samantha looked up then and gave him a cheerful wave. She held a small pair of clippers, he saw then, and other gardening tools were in a small bucket on the ground beside her. She had on those dark, wraparound sunglasses, and a lime-green baseball-style cap, with her long, pale hair pulled through the back in a makeshift ponytail.

And the three-foot section of garden in front of her had been reclaimed. It wasn't anything drastic, just…tidier. The profusion of color his parents had loved was still there, it was just that you could see it all now.

Slowly he got out of his car and walked toward her. It was still warm out, even though it was after five, and he could see that she'd been at this a while, as she'd worked up a sweat. She seemed utterly unconcerned about it, which he thought was nice. He also saw a large bottle of water beside a tube of sunscreen in the tool bucket. She was careful, he thought. And wise. With her fair skin she could truly suffer from too much sun without protection.

"I hope you don't mind," she said as he stopped before her. "I wasn't going to start this until Saturday, but I got off a bit early today. I only did a little, until you could see and approve."

"I do. Approve, I mean," he amended hastily. "It looks just like it used to, when my mother was here."

"She planted the garden?"

He nodded. "Most of it. They're both big on bright colors and the exotic, so she added that to what was already here."

"She got both," Samantha said with a grin. "What a great place. I presume the bird of paradise was her pet?"

"And the lilies, I think."

"Then the passionflower vine must be hers, too."

"Is that that one, with the odd, round flowers?" he asked, pointing to the vine that was now so heavy it was nearly collapsing the trellis that was supporting it.

"That's it," Sam said.

"Yes, that was one of hers, too. I guess it was the only way she could let out what was inside. She was trying to be a homebody, for my sake."

"Trying?"

"It just wasn't in her. Oh, she did it, until I graduated high school. Then I went off to college, and they…just went."

"You don't sound particularly bitter about it," Samantha said.

"Bitter?" he asked, startled. "No. Not at all. It's so against her nature I'm amazed she lasted as long as she did. But she did it for me. I don't begrudge her now." He smiled. "Miss her, yes, and my dad, too, but not begrudge her."

She smiled at him. She pulled off her sunglasses, and he saw the smile was echoed in her eyes. "They're lucky you understand."

He shrugged. "I do, more than they do, I think. They're exotic, sophisticated. They did the best they could, but they never quite understood how two peacocks ended up with a raven."

She blinked. "A raven?"

"Clever, sometimes even deep, but hardly flashy."

She looked as if his blunt assessment startled her. But then an odd expression came over her face. "I saw a raven once. In a tree. While he was there, he was just another shadow. But when he took wing, and flew into the sunlight, those black feathers flashed green and blue in a way that was more amazing than any peacock's display, because it was subtle, hidden, and you had to pay attention or you'd miss it."

At the near poetry of her statement, Ian found himself staring at her. He told himself not to take it personally, she'd only been comparing birds, not people. But still...

"And besides," she added, "a raven is much more useful than most peacocks."

"Useful?" His voice sounded almost like that raven's squawk to his own ears.

"They find things," she said. "And they are very, very smart."

He wondered if there was a compliment for him in there, but decided that was reading far too much into a vague conversation. Besides, it didn't matter. Compliments weren't something he sought out or needed.

Although one from this woman might be rather pleasant, he admitted.

"You really don't have to do this whole garden, you know," he said before he could take that ridiculous train of thought any further. "I'm sure you have lots to do, unpacking and all."

"I enjoy it," she said. "And as I said, except for a few pots and planters, there's not much for me to do over there."

He suspected the view out her windows of his yard wasn't the nicest, and that might have something to do with her eagerness, but he chose not to say anything.

"I guess I should have hired a gardener, but I never seemed to have the time to do even that."

"You do put in some long hours, I noticed."

Something about what he himself had said suddenly registered. "I...can I pay you for your time, at least?"

The minute the words were out he was afraid they would offend her. Damn, he was no good at even this, a friendly chat between neighbors.

But if she took offense, she hid it behind another smile. "You could find me something cold to drink," she said.

"I...sure. I think I have some soda or even a beer if you want."

"Soda's fine. Whatever you have."

When he came back, she was working again, and for a moment he just stood there, watching the smooth, easy way she moved. Then she straightened and turned to him, swiping her brow with a gloved hand, leaving a trace of soil on her forehead.

"Thanks," she said, taking the cold can he held out to her.

He liked that she didn't apologize for her appearance, as he thought most women would. She was working hard in a garden; she was going to sweat and get dirty. And her casual attitude silently said that if you couldn't handle that, it was your problem, not hers.

Of course, most women probably wouldn't look as good as she did doing it, he thought when she took a healthy swig of the drink. And then she rested the cold can against her neck, and he felt a ripple of an odd sort of heat that had nothing to do with the sun.

It was lucky for her Ian Gamble was no party animal, Sam thought as she watched him pacing his office from her lookout window seat. She'd been here for nearly a week now, and he didn't seem to have any social life at all. She didn't understand. He was an attractive man. She supposed the frequent usage of historical rather than contemporary analogies she'd noticed might bother some, and some women would find his frequent slides into deep thought, sometimes midconversation, disconcerting. But there had to be someone out there who would find the traits rather endearing. And impressive, given what those slides into thought often produced.

Not, she told herself, that it mattered to her job why he was the way he was. She was curious, that was all.

*Just accept it and be grateful that you don't have to tail him all over town.*

She ran the brush through her damp hair once more. If he ran true to form, he was in for the night. Only once had he gone out after he'd arrived home, and since he'd walked she'd been able to follow easily enough. The ice-cream place had been his destination again, and once more she'd had to laugh at his idea of walking distance; it was at least two miles each way. But it was also why he was able to indulge without it showing, she supposed.

But tonight he seemed settled in, so she chanced ten minutes with her blow dryer to finish her hair. Then she returned to her seat and took up the vigil.

When he finally turned out the lights at close to midnight, she stayed put, watching. At one in the morning she added a dark knit cap to her black jeans and sweater and went downstairs. It was time. And she knew he had a meeting in the morning, so it was the right time.

He'd left his car in the driveway, as usual. She wondered why he didn't use the garage, then guessed with a grin that it probably looked something like his office did, so there wasn't enough room. Whatever the reason, it was making things easier for her.

It took her under three minutes. She was back inside in five, again watching the house until she was sure he hadn't heard. Finally she went to bed, with the window still open, knowing she would awaken at the slightest out-of-place noise.

The quiet of a California summer night settled in.

"Damn it," Ian muttered, slapping the steering wheel of his uncooperative car.

He turned the key again. Nothing. Not even a click to indicate it was thinking about turning over.

He guessed he shouldn't be surprised. Cars tended to break down on him. Something about forgetting maintenance. He just had better things to do with his time and his mind, that's all. How could he be expected to keep track of things like oil changes and tire rotations when he was trying to solve this damned adhesion problem?

Maybe he should have taken Josh up on the offer of a Redstone company car. He'd said no because he tended to ding them up, and no matter that Josh had said that didn't matter, he would be too embarrassed to turn the thing in at the end of the lease period. It would only add to the perception of him as the absentminded professor.

He'd have to call a tow truck. Then he'd—

"Problem?"

His head snapped up. Samantha was standing beside the driver's side window; he hadn't even heard her approach. And she was dressed in a sleek navy pantsuit with a long jacket and crisp white blouse that made her look sharp and businesslike, totally unlike the casually dressed woman he was used to seeing. He wondered if she had to have things custom-made for those long legs.

"Won't start," he muttered, feeling as if he was stating the obvious.

"Dead battery?"

"Could be," he said, not wanting to admit he had no clue at all. Guys were supposed to know all about these car things. How could he explain he'd never spent any time mulling over things that had already been invented? "And I've got a meeting this morning."

"Come on, then. I'll drop you off. You can worry about the car later."

He hesitated but only for a moment. This meeting was important. Stan would have a cow if he didn't show up; he was picky about things like that. The man was picky about anything he thought reflected badly on the efficiency with which he ran his department. And as much as Ian was focused on the Safe Transit project, there were others already in the pipeline, and he'd insisted on being kept in the loop by marketing and production. He could hardly be late for the meeting they'd set up to fulfill his own demand.

And she did go the same direction, he'd seen her, he told himself.

"Thanks," he said, reaching over to gather up his briefcase and the traveler's mug of coffee he usually downed by the time he got to Redstone.

As he climbed into the passenger side of her sleek—and dingless—blue coupe, he couldn't help thinking how nice it was that she'd been there at just the right moment.

# Chapter 4

"Something wrong?"

*At last,* Sam thought. "Wrong?"

"You're…quiet."

"Maybe I'm just tired of carrying the entire conversation," she said. "I don't mind talking, but I don't usually chatter."

"Oh."

He sounded abashed, and she hoped he was, but she couldn't look at him at the moment and still deal with the cross traffic. This was the third day she'd taken him to work, and it was the third day he'd barely said a word unless in answer to a direct question.

"Sorry," he said after a moment of awkward silence. "I'm just not used to…"

"Small talk?" she asked, finally completing the left turn.

"Something like that."

She glanced at him. "Not even with yourself?"

His glasses had automatically darkened in the sunlight,

so she couldn't see his eyes clearly, but she did see him blink. "Myself?"

"I'm not sure I trust people who don't talk to themselves," she said, quite seriously.

He chuckled then. "Then I guess you can trust me."

She gave an exaggerated sigh of relief. "Ditto," she assured him. "You can even talk to me."

"I don't mean to be…uncommunicative. I just never got used to talking about…inconsequential things."

"So everything has to be important?"

"No, I don't mean that," he said, sounding a bit defensive. "I mean I never acquired the knack." His mouth quirked. "My mother and father were both born with it, but neither of them passed it on to their only offspring, I'm afraid."

"Your parents sound fascinating."

"They are," he said. "And charming. They can hold court for hours, and people still hate for it to end."

There was nothing but admiration in his tone, but Sam couldn't help wondering if he'd always appreciated his parents like this. It would be hard to grow up with two larger-than-life parents if you didn't feel you were able to live up to their example.

But it was harder to grow up without parents at all.

"That made you sad," Ian remarked.

A little startled at his perception, she shrugged. "I was just thinking of my own parents. And how much I miss them."

"They're gone?"

She nodded. "Over seven years ago now. Car accident. It's not raw, but it still hurts."

He shook his head slowly. "I'm sorry. My folks may not be around much, but I can't imagine a world without them in it."

"Treasure them, Ian. While you have them."

She shocked herself with her own words. She rarely spoke of her loss, and wasn't sure why it had popped out now.

"You must have been young when they were killed. What happened to you?"

Somehow she hadn't thought about what she would tell him about herself. She'd always prepared cover stories before, but this was different, guarding one of Redstone's own, so she hadn't done it this time. After a moment she decided the truth would be okay.

"Since I was only nineteen it took some doing, but I won the battle to keep my little brother with me."

"Little brother? That must have been tough."

"It would have been tougher if he'd lost me, too. He's...pretty sensitive, and he was already devastated."

"I'll bet." It wasn't until after they'd made the turn into the Redstone driveway that he said, "Not every nineteen-year-old would take on a kid like that."

She slowed the car. He pointed to the side door that was closest to the lab. She nodded and pulled over to the curb there.

"You do," she answered finally, "when you love him and there's no other acceptable option. I'll pick you up six-fifteenish?"

"You don't have to—"

"I know, but I can, so why not?"

He gave in. "Thanks."

He pushed open the car door and gathered up his briefcase and cup, and put one foot out. Then he stopped and looked back at her.

"Next time I'll chatter," he said unexpectedly.

She grinned at him. "This I want to see."

He returned her grin rather sheepishly. She watched him walk toward the side door. He stepped into a patch of sunlight, and it gleamed on that thick mop of hair.

He really was, she thought as she watched him, quite charming in a studious sort of way.

* * *

"I brought you a sandwich, Professor."

Ian took a breath, held it for a single second, then answered congenially, "Thank you, Rebecca."

Her startled look told him he'd been as snarly to her as he'd feared. And her sudden smile made him feel even more guilty about it.

It also made him doubt the suspicions that had become chronic since Josh had planted the idea of a leak inside the lab. Rebecca was simply young and overeager, he thought, not devious. She just thought she wasn't getting the credit she deserved. But he also feared that she wanted glory without having earned it, and that was a mentality Ian simply couldn't understand. What was the point of being praised for something you hadn't really done? For him the joy was in the process and the final success, not in the accolades that came after.

He smothered a sigh as he took a bite of the turkey sandwich. It was from the Redstone Café, so it was much tastier than the vending-machine fare that was standard at most places.

"Did you look at the paper I gave you yet?" Rebecca asked.

For a moment Ian looked at her blankly, then remembered the project paper she'd so excitedly presented him the other day. She'd done that before, come up with some idea she thought they should pursue, and this time he'd made the mistake of telling her to write it up, simply to get her out of his hair for a while.

"I did glance at it, yes," he said.

"And?" Rebecca asked, hope brightening her angular face.

He tried for tact, feeling as if he needed to apologize in some way for being suspicious of her.

"It's clever," he began.

She beamed.

"And the process is very thorough. At first look, I'd have to say it appears solid."

"Great!"

She looked so thrilled he almost hated to go on. But teaching was part of having a student assistant. He sighed inwardly; he'd told Josh he was no teacher.

"What's your goal?" he asked.

A crease appeared between her brows. "Goal? Just as it says, to create a new polymer."

"To what end?"

The crease became a frown, and she gave him a look that hinted that she was thinking him deliberately obtuse. "To do it, of course."

Irritation spiked through him, but he fought it down. As gently as he could, he asked the crucial question.

"Why?"

Rebecca blinked. Twice. "Why?"

"For what purpose? How will this polymer be better for that purpose than anything that already exists? What about it will make it worth going through this lengthy and expensive process? Will it make something stronger, lighter, more durable?"

She took a step back, staring at him. "Is that all you care about, whether it will make money somehow?"

Idealism, Ian thought with a sigh. It was the most wearing thing about children.

"What I care about," he said, "are things that will make lives easier, better, safer, and even give hope where there is none. Spending months to design a polymer we have no use for is a waste of effort, intelligence and, yes, money. But most of all it's a waste of the most valuable, finite resource you have, and that's time."

Her expression turned troubled. "Haven't you ever wanted to invent something just to see if you could?"

He was glad now he'd been gentle about it. "Yes. And I have. But eventually you come to realize the truth of the old saying about the scientists who got so wrapped up in the fact that they *could*, they forgot to question whether they *should*.''

''Yeah. Right.''

She turned and walked away, and he wondered if he'd inadvertently accomplished his goal of keeping her out of his way. Even if she wasn't the leak, it was best to find out now. If the simple rejection of an idea could stop her, she wasn't cut out for this.

Still, he hadn't liked smashing her hopes. And it was still bothering him when he got into Samantha's car that evening.

''Rough day?'' she asked, discerning his mood so quickly it startled him.

''Sort of. I had to rein in my assistant today, and she wasn't happy.''

''Rein her in? Was she messing something up?''

He settled into the seat and fastened the seat belt— something he didn't always do when he drove by himself but that Samantha demanded before she would even turn the key—before he answered her.

''No, she just wanted to take off on a project that was a bit...misguided.''

''Misguided?''

''With no real purpose. And somewhat self-indulgent. But she's young, so I tried to cut her some slack.''

Samantha smiled at that. ''You say that like you're ancient.''

''Sometimes I feel that way,'' he admitted. ''Her methodology is good, she's got the 'how' down pat. I hated to see one simple question take all the wind out of her sails.''

She studied him for a moment. ''You asked her... why?''

He was startled anew, but realized a perceptive woman like Samantha could have figured it out from his own words.

"Yes." His mouth quirked. "I told her not to feel too badly. A very wise *real* professor once said, 'Science is wonderfully equipped to answer the question How?, but it gets terribly confused when you ask the question Why?'"

"And how many eons ago was that?"

"Recently. Erwin Chargaff of Columbia, 1969."

Samantha chuckled, but it somehow didn't sting. He knew he tended to older trivia, and she was too perceptive not to have noticed. Her next words proved it.

"Only you, Ian, could consider that recent. Do you have any quotes from this quarter century?" she asked as she started the car.

"Sure." He thought a moment as she negotiated the parking lot. She glanced at him as they waited for cross traffic, and he grinned and said "'It's hard to be religious when *certain* people haven't been struck by lightning.' Calvin and Hobbes."

She burst out laughing this time, and it pleased him more than he wanted to admit.

"If you'd told her that instead, it probably would have gotten through," she said. "How angry was she?"

"Not angry, really," he said, thinking back to Rebecca's reaction. "More...unhappy, I think."

She seemed to consider her next words carefully before saying, "How unhappy?"

It hit him in that moment—what hadn't before but should have. He must have been too preoccupied with how to let her down easy. But he should have thought of it. Should have wondered if Rebecca was—and perhaps had been for a while—unhappy enough to do something foolish.

If she felt unappreciated enough to sell out Redstone.

"How's it going?"

Sam finished her last bite of salad, then raised her gaze to the man who looked enough like her to be her brother.

The first time she and her partner, Rand, had come face-to-face, it had been an eerie sort of shock for them both. Later they laughed when they discovered they had both started checking the family history to make sure there were no unclaimed siblings floating about. Since her parents were dead, she couldn't be absolutely positive, but Rand's parents were alive and well and had been somewhat insulted by his questions. That is, until he'd brought Sam home to meet them. Two jaws had dropped, and all was forgiven.

"Fine," she answered his question. "He's not a tough job."

"I've heard he doesn't do much, outside of work."

"Doesn't seem to."

Rand had called this meeting to give her the final sale papers on the house, in case she should need them. It never ceased to amaze her how fast the Redstone name and horsepower got things done, even government paperwork.

They were at the restaurant where she'd met Josh when she'd started this assignment. She had grabbed the chance at a decent meal; this job was making her rethink the wisdom of never having learned to cook. Rand, as usual, was drinking a soda, while she sipped at a surprisingly good lemonade.

"Is he as odd a duck as they say?" Rand asked.

Sam felt strangely defensive. "I haven't seen him do anything particularly odd. Yes, he thinks differently, but that's good, not odd."

Rand raised a brow at her.

"Like this morning," she said, "we heard a story on the car radio about some firefighters who were killed in a forest fire. The report said they made it into their fire shelters, that it was breathing the superheated air as the fire burned over them that killed them. So Ian immediately began thinking about developing some device small enough to carry that would give them just enough breathable air to survive a burn over.''

"I see what you mean," Rand conceded. "And if Josh is right about him, he'll probably do it, eventually. Although St. John says the Safe Transit Project is his only focus right now."

She nodded.

He paused before saying, "It's Ian, now, is it?"

She grimaced at him. "Well I can hardly call him Gamble to his face, now can I?"

"Sorry," Rand said, with a grin that belied the words. "Didn't mean to hit a nerve."

"So what's up back home?" she asked, not caring if her subject change was obvious. "I feel like I'm totally out of the loop."

"You heard Draven got McClaren out?"

"Josh told me," she confirmed.

"So his record is still perfect."

"Was there any doubt?"

Rand shrugged. "You never know."

That was a truth anyone on the Redstone security team soon learned, Sam thought later as she drove out of the restaurant parking lot. In an empire as varied as the one Josh had built, anything could happen. It was their job, impressed upon them from the moment they were accepted on the team, to see that no matter what happened, no Redstone people were hurt. Property, both physical and intellectual, came second.

She was waiting at what had to be the longest traffic light in the city when her cell phone rang.

"Beckett," she answered.

"He's leaving." There was no word of identification, but she recognized St. John's deep voice.

She glanced at her watch. "This early?"

"I believe there was some tension in the lab today."

"Tension? Ian?"

"Ian is rarely tense."

And that was all the answer she was going to get, it seemed. She had no doubt Josh's omnipresent assistant knew exactly what had happened, but she didn't press for details. No one pressed St. John except Josh, and she'd bet even he picked his battles carefully.

"All right."

She disconnected and pondered a moment, still waiting for that blessed light to change. She and Ian had come to the agreement that she would come by when she got off, wait no longer than fifteen minutes, and if he wasn't out by then she was to leave and he'd find his own way home. So far there had been only one day when she'd waited longer, nearly an hour, but he'd seemed to accept her story of heavy traffic. She knew from St. John that this regularity in itself was unusual; Ian had a tendency, St. John told her, to lose track of time.

She could go to Redstone now, but Ian might wonder why she conveniently happened to get off this early on this particular day. He had her cell number. She'd given it to him and told him to call if his schedule changed, but she doubted he would, not when as far as he knew she was working a regular job and got off at six.

Instead, she decided to swing by the Chinese takeout, grab some food, and then go get him. With luck the food would be distraction enough that her apparently flexible hours wouldn't become a topic.

It worked. The moment he got into the car and smelled the luscious aromas, talk of mere time was forgotten.

"I was starved," she explained. "I hope you don't mind, I got enough for two, as long as I was there, anyway."

"Mind? I could kiss you."

*Well, now that was a visual,* Sam thought, shocked at the tiny jolt the idea gave her. He was digging around in the bags, seemingly unaware of what he'd said.

Of course, there was no reason to think he meant it as anything more than a joking remark. Something people just said. In fact, if the growl his stomach had just sent up was any indication, he was hungry enough to have meant it no matter who had provided the food.

*It's you who's out of whack here,* she told herself. *Get your mind in the game, Beckett.*

"How long have you worked for Redstone?" she asked.

"Four years." He opened a bag and peered in.

"You like it?"

His head came up. "Yes. Yes, I do. Josh Redstone is one of a kind. He gave me a chance when no one else would, and I owe him everything."

"It's nice to have a boss like that," she said, meaning it in the exact way he did, although he didn't know it.

"Yes. He's the best. It's why everybody who works there stays, and he's got hundreds of applicants to chose from for any job that opens up." He dived back into the bag before he said casually, "How did you know I'd be leaving this early on a Friday?"

She made a note to herself never again to assume she could distract this particular mind. At least not for long.

"Actually, I've been off since four-thirty. My boss went out of town," she improvised. "So I figured I had time to grab food."

He looked up from the bag of small white boxes. "You really don't have to be my taxi service every day."

"I know, it's a sacrifice," she said with mock melodrama. "I have to drive an entire one hundred yards out of my way to cruise the Redstone driveway."

"Yeah. Well." He sounded rather embarrassed. "I got a call today that they have to order a part for my car. And they don't know how long it will be." He sounded disgusted, but not truly upset. St. John's words came back to her. *Ian is rarely tense....*

"Sometimes parts are hard to find," she said neutrally.

"I could make it myself faster."

Sam had to stifle a smile. With any other man, she would have laughed at the comment. With Ian, she knew he was probably right. But he didn't know she knew what he really did, so she kept quiet. And Ian wasn't done yet, anyway.

"When I had to have a fender repaired a while back, just because it's an older car they spent forever trying to match the paint. Like I cared. Henry Ford had it right."

"Henry Ford?"

"With the Model T. He said you could have it any color you wanted as long as it was black."

Ian was always tossing off bits of historical trivia like that, she thought yet again. He seemed steeped in history, and as he'd admitted, many of the nonwork-related books she'd seen him with had been historical in nature. She herself was very much of the present, and only cared about history in passing as it applied to her or her work, and given their similar ages the difference intrigued her.

"Everybody driving the same car, same color. Or rather, no color," she said. "Sounds kind of boring to me."

He looked at her for a long, silent moment during which she wondered what he was thinking.

"Yes," he said finally, slowly. "I imagine it would."

And suddenly the easy camaraderie in the car vanished. It was as if Ian, who'd seemed to finally relax around her, had thrown a wall up between them.

She managed to maneuver it so that they ate dinner at his place—hers was, as befitted a temporary home, minimally furnished, enough to appear curious—but the withdrawal she had sensed continued. The only good thing was that his silence gave her the opportunity to surreptitiously inspect his home further. The more she knew about him, the easier her job would be, she told herself.

"Nice set of pots," she commented, looking at the copper utensils hanging from a pot rack over the stove.

''My mother's,'' he said briefly. ''Cooking is a production with her.''

''But not you?''

''I never learned that kind of cooking. Can't afford the time.''

Which both answered and didn't answer her question—time to cook or to learn? Weary of pushing when she wasn't sure what she was pushing against, Sam finished her meal in a silence that matched his. She helped him clean up, then picked up her purse and keys.

She hadn't intended to, but at the doorway she stopped and looked back at him. ''If I said something to offend you, Ian, I'm sorry.''

To his credit he didn't deny it. But he didn't look at her when he answered. ''You didn't. It's not you.''

Her gut told her to push; her common sense told her to back off. She was here to protect him, after all, not probe his psyche.

As she made her way next door, she wondered why she was having trouble remembering that simple fact.


Ian sat alone in the dark for a very long time. His parents hadn't lived in this house for ten years, yet he could hear their voices as if they were here in the living room that now gave them heart palpitations to look at. As if he were still the child they didn't understand.

''Why didn't you invite your friend in?''

''Why didn't you go to the party?''

''Why don't you put that book down and go outside?''

He'd wanted to scream at them. *Because I'm not like you, I can't be like you, I'll never be like you!*

But it would only have hurt them, and he couldn't do that. He knew they loved him; they simply didn't understand that he was different. In so many ways. What was so simple for them, that easy, warm charm, just wasn't in him. He was a throwback or something, a changeling. It wasn't bad enough that he thought differently than they did, he had to be different in every other way, too.

*A misfit, that's you,* he told himself.

It was the only explanation he could think of for what had happened tonight. All Samantha had done was give a simple opinion, and he'd shut down.

*No color. Sounds kind of boring to me....*

He'd shut down because in that simple statement all the differences between them had leaped out at him, and he wondered what the hell he was doing. More than once over this past week he'd caught himself eagerly looking forward to seeing her. He'd had the thought that the timing on the breakdown of his car couldn't have been better. He'd even started to leave work at a regular time, and that was a real first.

And today, as much as he wanted to leave early, after a tension-filled day when he hadn't been able to shake himself free of either Rebecca or Stan, he'd hesitated. He hadn't wanted to miss riding home with Samantha.

He supposed it was only to be expected. He'd been alone for a long time, since Colleen had given up on him and walked out. Dump him into close proximity with a beauty like Samantha and it was inevitable he'd be drawn like an already singed moth to a new, even brighter flame.

But if he got singed again, he'd have no one but himself to blame.

He rubbed a hand over his eyes. For a while longer he sat there in the darkness. Finally, for the first time in longer than he could remember, he went to bed early, and without even cracking a book.

When the light in the converted living room never came on, Sam sat up straighter and watched the house intently. A short while later the upstairs light in the master bedroom came on, but only for a few minutes. When it went out, she expected the light downstairs to come on at last; he must have forgotten something upstairs.

The house stayed dark.

She looked at the clock on the bedside table. It was barely nine, and this time of year, barely dark. And Ian rarely went to bed before midnight.

Anybody had the right to a bad mood, she thought. And Ian certainly didn't owe her any explanation beyond what he'd given—that it wasn't because of her. But she couldn't help feeling that it was, that somehow she had sent him into this mood, whatever it was.

She frowned. Could simply disagreeing with his bit of Henry Ford trivia have done this? If he was that sensitive, then this, or something like it, would have inevitably happened sooner or later.

She got up and crossed to the box that held the files for this case—a copy of Ian's personnel records, along with some notes from Josh and Draven's background investigation. The box was locked, since it was a strict Redstone rule that such things be kept safe and confidential.

She got out the file, went back to the window seat and clicked on the floor lamp she'd set up next to the seat. She'd been through it all before she'd started this, but now that she had better than a week of contact with Ian under her belt, she wanted to read it again.

Nothing in particular jumped out at her anew. She did find herself looking at the rather stark entry that he had been married at age twenty-two, and that it had lasted for less than a year. It had ended, she realized, about the time he had moved back into this house. But that had been nearly ten years ago. Surely he wasn't still so gun-shy that he couldn't deal with a woman at all?

Perhaps it was just her, she thought.

She hadn't thought she would need to cultivate a different persona for this job, but perhaps she'd misjudged. Perhaps she should have acted less herself, and more…something. Someone else. Quieter. More reserved. Except that Ian was already so reserved himself that if she did the same they'd never get past it.

She sighed, and leaned back in the window seat, staring at the dark house next door. Maybe Josh should have had Rand do this. Maybe she was threatening to Ian somehow. It certainly wouldn't be the first time. But for all his reserve, for all his quietness, she just didn't get the feeling that he was the kind of man threatened by a competent, confident woman. She'd run into that kind often enough to know them, and she'd swear Ian didn't have the underlying insecurity and inherent double standards that caused that kind of reaction.

No, she thought. Whatever had made him back off, it wasn't that. And she had to trust that her boss knew what he was doing in sending her on this assignment. Josh had certainly earned that kind of faith.

So, she thought, she would take Ian's answer at face value and continue as she'd begun. Changing her tactics now would be too obvious. And she wasn't about to start playing games with him, acting hurt that he'd withdrawn. She was a stranger, nearly, after all. And he had the right to do…whatever it was he was doing.

And what she was going to do right now was take advantage of the situation and grab some extra sleep herself. Tomorrow was Saturday, and she had a busy day planned. Right in Ian Gamble's front yard. And if he didn't like it, he was going to have to come out and tell her to her face.

# *Chapter 5*

The faint sound of humming was the first thing Ian heard. For a moment he just lay there, a bit groggy after more sleep than he'd had in a long time—and after a series of jumbled dreams that he remembered in detail and, he admitted blearily, a few he did not. He had the feeling he was better off not remembering those; his new neighbor had figured prominently in most of them.

His new neighbor.

Samantha.

The humming was coming from his own yard.

It was Saturday.

Suddenly fully awake, he rolled out of bed. He went to the window where he could see toward the front yard, barely managing not to run. He couldn't see a thing past the overgrown passionflower vine. But he could hear that light, lilting voice humming bits of a tune he didn't recognize.

Instinctively, he glanced at his wrist before he realized he wasn't wearing his watch. He looked back over his shoulder at the alarm clock—the excessively loud one his mother had bought him when he'd started college, afraid he'd never get up without her to yank him out of bed— which read 7:20.

Hastily he pulled on some jeans and a T-shirt, finger combed the heavy mop of hair that had been a nuisance since childhood, and started downstairs. He paused half-way down when he realized he'd pulled on his most ragged jeans, with blowouts at both knees.

*Don't be an idiot,* he told himself, and continued down.

He pulled open the front door. She was beginning where she'd left off the other day. She was dressed in much the same way. And he was reacting the same way. For a moment he just stood there, marveling at the simple fact that she was there.

And then she did it again, straightened, turned and looked right at him, as if she had felt his gaze. And as before, it unnerved him slightly.

"Morning!" she called, pulling off her sunglasses. "Hope I didn't wake you."

So she was going to act as if nothing had happened, he thought. Either she'd taken his explanation to heart, or it didn't matter to her enough to worry about.

*If you're smart, you'll choose selection B,* he told himself firmly.

"I was awake," he said. He went down the porch steps. She'd already made considerable progress, at least another two feet of the perimeter flower bed. "You're doing it all at once."

She blinked, glanced at where she'd been working, then back at him. "All at once?"

"Weeding, clipping…" He paused, trying to remember what his mother had called it, pulling off the dead flowers. "Deadheading," he said as it came back to him, and he waved a hand rather vaguely at a couple of the more faded blooms.

She smiled. "Let me guess. You'd do the weeding all the way around, then go back to the beginning and do the clipping, then back again for the deadheading."

"Well...yeah."

"Not me," she said. "I need the sense of finishing a section as I go. Otherwise it seems too big a task."

He nodded. That made a certain amount of sense to him. And he was used to being the one who took a different approach from the rest of the world, anyway.

"I'll keep going, then, if you like how it's coming out," she said.

"I like it. I just feel guilty, you doing all this work here," he admitted.

"So take a break and dig in. It's good for the soul. And it helps you think," she added.

Now that was an aspect he'd never thought of before. His reaction must have shown, because she went on.

"You just throw your problem into the pot on the back burner and let it stew while you're working."

Even though he'd learned long ago that some of his clearest thinking happened when he was doing something totally unrelated to whatever problem he was working on, he usually did that while thinking about some other project. He'd never really tried something completely non-work-related. Even when walking or working out he was usually still concentrating on the puzzle at hand.

He wondered if it would work, if he could keep his mind occupied enough at a routine task to free up his subconscious to work on a pressing problem. If he could solve a problem by just not thinking about any problem at all.

He certainly couldn't do any worse than he had been doing.

After an hour of trying to settle into his indoor routine, he discovered that whether it would do him any good or not, he was going to be out there doing the garden tasks he'd always tried to avoid as a kid. He simply couldn't just sit inside, or even pace, as was his wont, while she was working so hard outside. And he didn't know if he was doing it out of guilt or because of some idiotic fantasy in his head about spending the morning with her.

*Didn't you learn your lesson last night?* he asked himself sourly.

"Doesn't mean you can't be friendly," he said out loud to the empty room. "Just get your mind out of places it doesn't belong."

*I'm not sure I trust people who don't talk to themselves....*

He couldn't help it; he laughed out loud.

And then he pulled on a pair of boots and headed outside to join in the clipfest.

"I didn't mean to force you into this," Samantha said when she saw him.

"You didn't. And maybe this will save me a lecture from Mom next time they drop in on their way to wherever, about letting the house go," he said.

"So, what work is it I'm keeping you from?" Sam asked after he'd begun the daunting task of tracking down the lengthy and tangled runners the wisteria had sent through every other shrub in the garden. "More research?"

He was beginning to regret that he hadn't just told her the truth in the beginning. And now that he knew her a little better, he had a feeling she just might understand. At least, he was fairly sure she wouldn't get that funny look on her face that others did, the look that said they equated the word *inventor* with *crackpot.*

He took a deep breath and then took the plunge. "Research is the socially acceptable term for what I do. Really I'm...an inventor."

She smiled. "Really? That must be a great job."

That simply, it was done. She knew, and there hadn't

been a trace of that look he'd come to expect from people. He smiled back at her.

"It is. Even when it's frustrating."

"Like now?" she asked.

He nodded. "We're trying to solve a problem with a new product, without much luck."

"What's the problem?"

"It needs to stick to specific metals, and it won't."

"Stick like glue, paint or like bubble gum?"

He laughed. "Right now I think we'd settle for any one of those. We've tried the paint and the glue, maybe we should try bubble gum. Or the equivalent."

"Desperation is the mother of invention," she said.

Ian just managed not to gape at her as she tossed off his mother's favorite misuse of the old cliché.

"That's why gardening is perfect," she went on. "You have to watch what you're doing, but it doesn't take much thinking, so it frees up a lot of brain cells to go work on, say, that nonstick problem."

He smiled, then dug into the honeysuckle. He soon discovered the long sucker he'd been tracking originated there rather than the wisteria, and was annoyed that he hadn't noticed the difference.

"Needs to be cut, anyway," Samantha said, reading his mood accurately. Which she seemed to do rather well, he thought as he took the clippers she offered, snipped the tough, woody stem and started to yank at the offending vegetation.

She was perceptive, that much was obvious. But he'd never met anyone who seemed so totally aware of what was going on all around her, even behind her. And suddenly he was curious, curious enough to overcome his innate shyness—which seemed oddly magnified around her—and ask. She'd asked him about his work, after all.

"So when you're not hacking through the jungle, what is it you do?"

For an instant she looked startled. Her gaze flicked to the overgrown honeysuckle, and her expression changed as if she'd just realized he meant the city jungle they were standing in. Wondering what other jungle she could have thought he meant, he waited.

"I'm a consultant of sorts," she said. "I run around a lot, picking up loose ends or trying to solve small problems before they become big ones."

*And I'll bet you're good at it,* he thought. "Sounds challenging," he said.

"I figure it's sort of like being a firefighter, without the heavy lifting."

He laughed. And when he heard it, he realized he'd laughed more since she'd moved in next door than he had in months. Maybe even years. His life, he thought, had truly become a glum, dry, humorless thing.

And he had better be very, very careful around the woman who had brought laughter back into his life.

Sam dropped the cordless phone receiver in her lap and lifted the binoculars to her eyes once more. The dark sedan still sat across the street. One of the first things she'd done was take an inventory of the cars normally on the block and make a note of make, model, color and what house they were connected with. Like any neighborhood, some strange vehicles had come and gone, temporary visitors to the various residences, but this was a new one.

It had arrived well after dark, unusual enough in itself in this quiet neighborhood. But when the driver didn't get out after five minutes, she'd grabbed her high-power binoculars and taken up a position to watch. Fifteen minutes passed, then twenty, and the driver still sat in the front seat. She wondered what he was waiting for, or if he was just watching. At half an hour she had picked up the phone and called Rand for a check on the license number.

She knew she could see the car from upstairs as well as

here. So she turned out the downstairs lights, ran upstairs, checked from the window seat that the car was still there, turned on the bedroom lights briefly, then turned them out. If the driver had been waiting for every house on the street to go dark, she'd do her part.

Moments later the light in the passenger compartment of the dark sedan came on as the driver finally opened the door. Sam leaned forward, focusing intently through the binoculars, wishing she'd checked out some of the spiffy infrareds Redstone Tech made.

It was a woman.

While she of all people wasn't one to assume being female meant being harmless, it did make her readjust her thoughts slightly.

The phone rang. She picked it up.

"It's a woman," she said without preamble. No one else had the number but Redstone.

"Yes. Rebecca Hollings."

Sam drew back slightly. "The assistant?"

"The same."

"Hang on."

Sam picked up the binoculars again. The woman below was standing next to the car, staring across the street. At Ian's house. She'd never seen Rebecca Hollings in person, but from the photo in the file, this woman could easily be her. The height and build were right, and although hair color was harder to tell in the faint glow that spilled over from a streetlight at the corner, it wasn't obviously wrong.

She freed one hand to pick up the phone again. "Could be," she told Rand.

"She could be our leak," Rand said.

"Nothing in her background check would indicate a high level of recruitability."

"Gamble says she's in a hurry to make her mark. And she's young," Rand said. "Who knows what she might have gotten herself convinced of."

So Ian did notice such things. She'd wondered if he was so focused on his work he missed the nuances, missed the subtle signals people sent. Perhaps he'd gotten more of his mother's people skills than he thought.

"Maybe," Sam said, still watching. "Maybe I'd better go for a walk."

"Your call. What's she doing?"

"Right now she's just watching his house. She's empty-handed and in light clothing, no place to really hide a weapon. I think I'll give it a minute or two."

She set down the binoculars and stretched. All that gardening had made itself felt in various tight spots. She was in good shape, but those were some muscles she didn't use on a regular basis.

"Josh had a little talk with the head of JetCal," Rand said.

"Poor guy."

She heard Rand chuckle. "Someday I'd really like to be there when he goes after somebody."

"Not me. I hate the sight of a grown man whimpering."

"I'd just like to see it happen. The guy must have felt like he'd tried to sneak past a puppy that morphed into a wolf on him."

"Sounds about right," Sam agreed. "So, what did the guy have to say?"

"Not much, according to Josh."

"Figures. They never do. But I'll bet they don't try slipping anybody in again."

"That's what Josh said. But he also said we have to figure they'll try something else."

"Keep me posted," she said, although she knew it was unnecessary. Rand was utterly, totally reliable when it came to being the base man for an operation like this. He thought of anything the operative missed, had information before you asked for it, often before you knew you wanted or needed it.

He was working the night shift on this because there were several people around during the day to take care of anything she needed. But at night, he was worth two or three all by himself.

"I will. If you need—"

"Hold it, she's moving." She grabbed the binoculars. "She's headed for the house. Later."

She hung up, knowing Rand would understand. She watched, waiting until Rebecca Hollings—if indeed it was her—got across the street and stopped on the sidewalk, still staring at Ian's home.

There was a narrow window at the top of the stairs, and she ran for it. A quick look told her the woman hadn't moved, and Sam kept going. She took another glance out a lower window as the woman moved along the side of the house, just beyond the half-trimmed honeysuckle.

Sam grabbed at the dark knit hat she'd hung near the door, and on the run shoved her gleaming pale hair undercover. Figuring the woman's wariness would be directed toward the street, she went out her back door.

She was thankful she'd cleared at least one path through the thick shrubbery. She was able to crouch there, out of sight, watching as the woman—it *was* Ian's young assistant, she could see that now—hovered along the side of the house, looking up at Ian's bedroom windows. Sam waited. She could be simply casing the house for a later action.

Or she could be a scout, Sam thought suddenly. A scout, with the real troops standing ready to move in the moment she gave the signal.

She swore at herself for not bringing her cell phone out with her. The built-in intercom feature was out of range of Redstone headquarters from here, but she could have speed dialed for help. If there were indeed troops in the wings, she couldn't take them on alone, especially with the two-inch revolver in her ankle holster her only weapon.

Her job was to protect Ian, and she couldn't do that if she got mowed down in the first offensive—one of the lessons Draven had thoroughly pounded home long ago.

But if Rand hadn't heard back from her in fifteen minutes, he'd be organizing backup, anyway. Unless she made contact within thirty minutes, they'd be on their way.

The woman let out an almost pained sound, then spun on her heel.

*Changed your mind?* Sam wondered.

Or was she really checking out the house for some later action?

She debated for a moment over confronting the woman, but decided against it. It was too early to tip their hand, to warn anyone that Ian was being guarded. And she hadn't really done anything, although if there was an innocent explanation for her appearance here in the dark of night, skulking around Ian's house, Sam couldn't think of one.

She watched until the woman got back in her car and drove off, then headed quickly for the phone. She got through two minutes before her time was up.

"All clear."

"Cut it close there, sis. What happened?"

"Nothing. Closest she came was a few feet between this house and his. She just stood there looking up at the windows for several minutes, then left."

"Casing?"

"Definitely possible," she said, although the pained sound she'd heard from the young woman nagged at her.

"I'll start digging, then. And we'll warn Gamble to watch out around her. If you think he can maintain, that is," Rand added.

"You mean can he lie with a straight face?" she asked.

"Exactly."

*He gave me a chance when no one else would, and I owe him everything....*

Ian's words echoed in her head. "If he had to for Josh, yes, I think he could."

"All right. You'll be up for a while?"

"Probably the night," she agreed. "Just in case."

"I'll be here."

She hung up, feeling for the first time that she might just be more than a precaution.

But it wasn't until Monday, after she'd gotten Ian safely to work and had returned to catch up on much-needed sleep, that it became more than just a feeling. The phone rang at a little after one in the afternoon. When she answered, the sound of St. John's voice woke her up in a hurry.

"Beckett?"

She sat up. "What's wrong?"

"They tried for him, right in front of Redstone."

## Chapter 6

It was absurd, Ian thought. Nothing had really happened, but he felt shaken. *The first time in ages you leave the building for lunch, and look what happens,* he thought.

He wondered if fate was trying to send him a message. He told himself he was feeling this way because everybody else—well, Josh and St. John, anyway—was reacting as if his near-miss accident out in the street was some kind of nefarious plot. Only he and Stan thought it was merely a distracted driver, probably on a cell phone, and that he'd come a lot closer to getting run down than any kind of public kidnapping.

The man simply hadn't been paying any attention, Ian thought, as he himself sometimes had to admit to, although never while driving.

Almost never, he amended, remembering when he'd nearly driven through his own garage door at the sight of Samantha in his yard.

Samantha.

Now there was the most absurd part of all. Nothing had

happened, he'd simply had a close call, as people did all the time on the busy, chaotic streets of southern California. Yet he'd had the urge to call Samantha. When they'd told him he should go home, he'd wanted to agree, to call the cell number she'd given him and ask if she could come get him, visions of another day spent with her forming teasingly in his mind. He just knew she'd find a way to prod him out of this weird mood, get him over this shaken feeling.

He didn't call, of course. He'd see her this afternoon when she picked him up at the regular time, he told himself. In the meantime, he did what he'd always done, turned to his work for solace and distraction.

But that wasn't working as well as it once had. And it wasn't merely that Josh had warned him they were watching Rebecca after some suspicious actions Josh wouldn't elaborate on in case they were wrong. Ian understood that that was Josh's way; if you were one of his, he'd protect you until it was clear you no longer deserved it. But knowing that they suspected Rebecca didn't make it very easy to act the same around her, as Josh had requested.

And it wasn't just what had happened this afternoon that had him so distracted, either, Ian admitted reluctantly. He was spending far too much time thinking of what a beautiful day it was outside—something he usually completely forgot about once he got into the windowless lab—and how much he had enjoyed working in his own garden.

With Samantha.

He sighed, realized that all the figures he'd entered in a results table were in the wrong column, deleted them and started again.

It was going to be a long afternoon.


"Could it have been coincidence?" Sam asked.

"Maybe," Rand said. "But we can't be sure."

She wanted to believe it had been, that the van that had

swerved perilously close to Ian as he crossed the street outside Redstone had been just a careless or reckless driver rather than an attempt to grab him. But they had at least one witness who swore the sliding side door of the van had been open, and added that he was fairly certain someone had been crouched there in the opening.

She shoved her hair back and grimaced. She picked up her glass of lemonade, then set it down again. She pushed her sandwich around on the plate a bit more.

Ian was now safely tucked away in his lab, insisting that he was fine. With Josh out of town, St. John was chewing on everyone in sight for letting Ian slip away, despite the fact that he almost never left Redstone to go to lunch as he had today. His explanation had simply been that he'd needed to get out, to think in the fresh air. Sam had felt a stab of guilt at that, wondering if her urging him out into the garden had somehow brought that on.

"This news shouldn't come as a great surprise," Rand said mildly.

"No," she said, "I'm not really surprised. It's just been so…routine until now that I was hoping maybe Josh was wrong about there being a threat."

"He's rarely wrong about much of anything," Rand said.

"I know that," Sam said, aware her voice sounded a bit snappish. Maybe more than a bit, judging by Rand's surprised expression.

"What's up with you? Bored with suburbia already?"

"No."

Actually, she was quite enjoying it. She'd settled into a routine that, while odd, seemed to work. Thanks to Josh, the shop that had Ian's car was awaiting a part that would take a considerable amount of time to find and install, so she was still taxiing him to Redstone. Even though she'd told Ian it was on her way, he'd been uncomfortable until she'd allowed him to fill the tank.

So each morning she would rise early—although not as early as Ian normally would, for fear he would back out altogether thinking he was making her get up earlier than she had to—dress in businesslike clothing and take him to Redstone. Then she would head over to spend the morning with Billy, who seemed vastly entertained by her new attire. But he was happy to see her so often, and excited to be planning their summer vacation together. After that she made her calls to or met with Josh or Rand for any updates, then she was free for the afternoon, often using it to catch up on sleep she missed while watching during the night.

At six she would head back to Redstone, knowing already that the chances of Ian being done earlier were slim and none, and as her father used to say, Slim just left town. Whatever high salary Josh was paying Ian, he got his money's worth. He worked hard, and—

"—so distracted."

Sam snapped out of her musings. "What?"

"Well, that proves my point," Rand said. "I said I've never seen you so distracted."

She opened her mouth to deny it, then shut it again. Rand knew her too well, they'd worked together too often, faced life-and-death situations together. Denial was not only useless, it was an insult to what they'd been through together. She *was* distracted.

"I think I'm just angry," she said, giving him the conclusion she'd arrived at during the long night she'd spent watching Ian's house every minute after Rebecca Hollings had left. "Ian's a good guy. He's trying to do a good thing with this explosives sensor, he shouldn't have to worry about crap like this."

"He doesn't," Rand pointed out. "We do."

She smiled then. "There is that."

Rand smiled back, but she caught a glimpse of something rather intent in his gaze as he looked at her—a speculative sort of expression that he rarely turned on her. But he said nothing more, just shoved a hand through the silken hair that was the same childlike shade of blond as hers and stood up, tossing down money for their lunch plus a generous tip for the long time they had taken up the table.

"We're sure of Hollings's whereabouts at the time of the incident?" Sam asked.

"She was signed into the lab. Gamble says he saw her there when he left." Before she could ask, Rand foresaw her questions and answered. "And no calls were made or e-mails sent from there after Gamble left."

"She could have used a cell, though."

"Yes."

"If it was a kidnap attempt, somebody had to tip them off. How else would they know he was leaving the building at that moment?"

"Reasonable deduction," he agreed as he held the door open. She accepted the gesture without comment; she was long past worrying about men holding doors for her. She did it as often for men, and figured it all evened out in the end. "Especially since it was a break from his usual routine."

"But who?"

"You answer that, and Josh might start sleeping at night."

"He does take this kind of thing personally, doesn't he?"

"Very. You want me to take over tonight?" Rand asked as they made their way out to their respective vehicles.

She shook her head. "I'm fine. Maybe tomorrow."

"Just let me know. It's tough sleeping with one eye and ear open all the time."

It was, and she knew he knew it. He'd done his own share of surveillance work for Redstone—more, in fact, than she had, since he'd been on the security team three years longer than she had. He was good at it, one of the best. She would—and had—trusted him with her life. But somehow she didn't want to turn Ian over to him. And that bothered her, because she'd never felt this way before. Bothered her almost as much as the fact that she didn't quite know why she felt that way now.

Sam hacked away at a wisteria stem as thick as her wrist. There were few things worse when out of control than these kinds of vines. She wondered what would happen when this was over. Would Ian let things run amok again, or would he remember the pleasure he seemed to have discovered in working out here and continue?

For some reason the thought of the garden returning to its neglected state—and Ian returning to his solitary hours holed up inside—depressed her on this lovely Sunday.

She glanced up as he hefted another full garbage bag and lugged it over to the ever-growing pile. They had taken to dividing the refuse for the trash pickup, a few bags in front of his house, a few in front of hers, so he didn't test the patience of the trash collectors quite so much.

He'd never said a word to her about what had happened on Monday. When she'd picked him up she'd asked if something had gone wrong, since he'd seemed a little preoccupied. He'd insisted nothing was wrong, and she wondered if he really felt that way, or if he was just trying very hard to convince himself.

All week she'd given him every opportunity, but he'd never even broached the subject, just told her not to worry. Then, in that oddly charming way of his, he added as a disingenuous afterthought, "But thanks, anyway."

She heard him coming back now. "I picked up a soaker hose," she said.

"A what?"

"A soaker hose." She gestured toward the flat hose with two rows of small holes punched along its length before she went back to her sawing. "It waters slow and deep, the best for this bed. Less water waste, too. It waters out both sides, so if you space it right, it will cover the whole bed."

"Is this garden stuff another one of those things women just know?"

She laughed but kept her eyes on what she was doing since she'd resorted to a rather lethal machete-type blade to try to cut through the rest of the woody stem.

"No. I learned from my dad. He had the proverbial green thumb. My mom used to say hers was brown. If she touched a plant, it died."

She heard his soft chuckle, the knife cut through the last of the stem, and she looked up.

She nearly dropped the blade. She was rarely caught completely off guard, but Ian Gamble had just done it. She was sure her jaw had literally dropped.

In the heat of the afternoon, he was pulling off his T-shirt. She had looked up just as he'd begun to tug it over his head. She'd seen only the graceful, sinuous movement of muscle on a fit, surprisingly broad chest, and strong arms. And that flat, taut belly, drawing her eyes unerringly to the gap between denim and skin....

He works out in the gym, Josh had said.

"No kidding," she muttered inwardly.

She fought to regain her composure, aided slightly by the fact that his glasses had caught on the neck of the shirt and he had to pause to save them from being pulled off. By the time he was done she had herself back together. She had even managed not to take that extra moment for another look at him. Instead when he got free of the shirt she was busily tugging at the vine again.

"Tell me about your brother."

The request was unexpected both in nature and that he had asked at all. She supposed it was a good sign that he was so much more relaxed around her than he'd been at first, enough to ask a personal question, anyway.

"Billy?" she said, carefully not looking up at him just yet. "He's great. He's in a new school, and he's doing really well."

It was the truth, but she was very aware of what she wasn't telling him. Stupid, that that bothered her. After all, this whole thing was a deception.

"How old is he?"

She couldn't help it, she tensed. It was instinctive, this protective urge, too long ingrained to be fought down.

"Almost fifteen." She glanced at him then, saw the faint crease between his brows. "I'll save you the guessing. Just over twelve years between us."

He had the grace to look abashed. "Am I really that obvious?"

She straightened up, making sure she looked only at his vivid-green eyes behind the glasses, not at his bare chest. "Sometimes," she said. "Sometimes I can't figure you out at all." And that, she thought, was the honest truth.

"He was only seven when your parents were killed?"

She nodded, the old, familiar pang tightening her lips just slightly. "I tried, but he doesn't remember them very well."

"You're the only mother he's really known, then."

"I tell him about them all the time. They were good people, good parents. They thought they couldn't have any more kids, so he was a gift. And they loved him."

"They must have been very proud of you," he said softly.

She plucked a leaf off the vine, curled it between her fingers. "I hope so."

"It can't have been easy, at that age, to convince the powers that be you could take care of a young child."

"I had to fight them every step of the way. Thankfully I had some help."

Josh, bless him. He'd given her the job she'd needed. Only later did she find out he'd also pulled some strings behind the scenes and told Child Services he would be responsible for Billy's care if she ran into trouble.

"Even so, it must have been tough."

"It was." She hesitated, and then it was coming out, despite the fact that she so rarely talked about it. "Especially because Billy is…challenged, I guess is the current word. They wanted to put him in a home, an institution. I knew it would destroy him, to lose me on top of Mom and Dad."

"Idiots." He said it flatly, angrily, and it startled her. "They're the ones with the handicap, if they couldn't see he was better off with a sister who loved him."

"That's how I felt."

"How did you convince them? Agencies like that aren't noted for listening to minors much."

"You sound like you've had some experience."

"I didn't. My best friend as a kid, Casey Blair, did. His folks divorced, then his mom started drinking. Instead of giving him to his dad, who wanted him but didn't make much money, they put him in foster care."

"What happened?"

He suddenly looked very uncomfortable. "Ancient history," he said.

Her instincts told her there was something here, something he was hiding, but they also told her it wasn't something he was going to talk about. At least not yet.

Or not to her.

Later that night, when she checked in with Rand, she asked him to poke around. If there was something Ian was hiding, they needed to know what it was. Needed to know if somewhere, buried farther back than even Redstone's thorough background checks went, was something that could be used against Ian, to turn him.

That the thought made her faintly ill was something she would deal with later.

* * *

Ian leaned back on the sofa, swirling the last of his wine in the glass. He didn't do this often; in fact, he rarely opened a bottle of wine at all, since he usually only wanted a glass at most. Nor did he often just sit here and mindlessly stare at the television, but tonight he needed the distraction. Not that it was working. Even his favorite History Channel show wasn't doing the trick tonight.

One part of him was savoring the day spent doing hard, physical work alongside a woman who wasn't afraid of it and who made him feel as if there was nothing on earth he'd rather be doing.

The other part of him was wary of her generosity and congeniality; women who looked like Samantha simply didn't hang out with guys like him. Not with the odd ones, the nerds, the ones who didn't fit in now and never had. He'd told himself to just take what he could get and be glad of it, that if he just kept his head on straight he'd be fine.

And then, long after the incident that had everybody but him convinced it was some sort of enemy move against him, it had abruptly occurred to him to wonder if perhaps there wasn't something suspicious to the Howards' abrupt sale of their lifetime home and Samantha's sudden appearance in his life. And no matter how much he told himself that all the warnings had just made him paranoid, he couldn't seem to stop thinking about it.

His gut protested mightily at the thought. She was just a warm, delightful woman making friends with a new neighbor. She was too open, too real to be playing that kind of game. But wouldn't she be, if that kind of game were her business? Weren't con artists successful mainly because they could make people think they would never be party to such a thing?

No, he didn't want to believe it of her, but neither was

he so naive—although he was sure some would argue that—as to discount the possibility entirely.

He sat there weighing the pain of being a fool against the pain of being wrong about her. The scale teetered back and forth, and by the time he finally went to bed, he still didn't have an answer.

He had, however, finished the entire bottle of wine.

## Chapter 7

"Worry, Sammy?"

Her towheaded little brother fixed those innocent brown eyes on her just as she was leaving, and she tried to smile. He might have trouble articulating words, but he was so sensitive to her moods it was almost eerie.

"A little bit, Billy," she said, speaking carefully and slowly. He had auditory problems that were at their worst on short words. "But it's okay. It will be over soon."

He smiled, and she wondered anew what it must be like in his mind, when problems were resolved simply on the assurance of someone you could trust.

Trust.

Just thinking the word made her grimace inwardly. She'd spent way too much time in the past few days pondering it. It wasn't as if she hadn't done undercover work before, so she didn't understand why it was bothering her so much this time. But it was. Lying to Ian, directly or by omission, bothered her. She'd had to deceive innocent people before in the course of an assignment, but it had never gotten to her the way lying to Ian did. Even the dancing around the truth she'd been doing bothered her, although she'd given him more of her real life than anyone else she'd ever been assigned to watch.

Perhaps it was because he was so fundamentally honest himself, she thought. Maybe that's why it went against the grain to lie to him. That and the fact that sometimes she caught him looking at her intently, as if he somehow knew she wasn't being honest with him.

That had to be it. It had nothing to do with the shock that had jolted through her when he'd peeled off his shirt in the garden and she'd found herself gaping at an unexpectedly beautiful male body.

*Absentminded professor my as—*

"Baseball tomorrow," Billy reminded her as he walked her dutifully to the door, cutting off her thoughts. And just as well, Sam thought. It was bad enough that that vivid image had taken over her dreams, without it taking over every waking moment, as well.

"I know." Rand was taking over so that she could take Billy to a game. He loved the sport and applied himself to understanding it as he did nothing else. "I'll pick you up here at noon. Do you remember what that looks like on the clock?"

"Both hands up!" he exclaimed excitedly.

Even though he seemed perfectly happy, she still felt odd about leaving him here. She'd fought so hard to keep him out of an institution for so long. But they'd told her the safe, happy home life she'd given him for ten years, and the way she'd worked to find ways to maximize his capabilities, gently pushing him to learn, had made it possible for them to do even more for him now. He'd been in the facility for over two years now, and it seemed to have done wonders for him.

It had been rough at first—he'd screamed every time she left, but the soft-spoken woman who ran the center told her that was normal, and he'd get over it. She'd been doubtful, had wanted more than anything to just take Billy back home again, but after Josh had gone through all that trouble to find—and to shore up financially—Mrs. Fortier's New Chances project, she didn't feel right quitting so soon.

And after three weeks Billy had suddenly turned a corner. He began to take an interest in the classes tailored to his interests and abilities. He responded to the social activities with the other kids in a way that made her realize that perhaps she had protected him too much, keeping him away from children his own age for fear they would tease or torment him for being different.

And most important, he had begun to learn to take care of himself, and it had given him a pride and confidence Sam knew she never could have instilled. He no longer got violently upset when she had to leave or when she was gone on assignment. He even took it with only a small tantrum when his beloved baseball team lost.

"On some level," Mrs. Fortier told her, "he was afraid of something happening to you, not just because he loves you, but because who would take care of him then? Now he knows he can take at least basic care of himself, with the proper reminders in place. It frees him from that worry."

She had been guilty, Sam realized, of the common misconception that because of his generally cheerful nature, Billy didn't have the capacity to worry. Get frustrated, yes, as he often did when he attempted something and failed repeatedly, but she had just never thought he would worry in the same sense she did. That realization alone made her wonder what else she was wrong about, and had made her determined to stick it out, to give Billy this chance, even though she missed him terribly. So she would just enjoy the time with him and be glad this assignment allowed her to see him often.

She called Rand as soon as she got back to the house, to confirm that he was coming on time to take over while she was gone.

"I'll be there at eleven-thirty. Don't want Billy to miss all the pregame fun."

"Thanks. He does love that."

"If I run into Gamble, I assume I'm your brother, as usual?"

*Oops,* Sam thought. "Uh, no. He knows I only have the one brother."

There was a fractional pause before Rand, his voice too neutral to be casual, asked, "He knows about Billy?"

"Yes."

"Does he know…your story? That there's no other family?"

"He knows I raised Billy alone, so it's been implied."

"I see."

She wasn't sure what Rand thought he saw, but she was positive she didn't like that too-interested undertone in his voice. Rand knew perfectly well her brother wasn't a topic of casual conversation with her, so it seemed an explanation was necessary.

"He's one of our own, so I've tried to keep what I've told him as truthful as possible."

"I suppose you do have a point," he agreed after a moment. "He isn't a bad guy we're staking out. So, who am I, then? The looks thing could be problematic if I try to say I'm just a friend."

She hadn't thought of that, either. Maybe Rand was right—she was too distracted. She should have thought about all of this. It had seemed so simple, just stick as much to the truth as possible, but now it was clear a bit more lying would have made things easier.

And if she was uncomfortable lying to Ian, that was her problem. Her job was to keep him safe, not keep herself comfortable.

"We'll use the looks, then," she improvised. "Bring it up front first thing. We met because of it. Friends got us together."

"Hmm. Okay, I'll be over...to do laundry or something. I think I can pull that off."

"You know you can," Sam said. She'd seen him bluff his way through much dicier situations than this, using that baby face and those big blue eyes. She'd done it herself, and it got easier with practice.

Which didn't explain why lately she'd been on edge as if this were one of those very dicey situations, even though there hadn't been a moment she'd been in real danger.

That the danger might not be physical wasn't an idea she was ready to deal with.

Ian backed away from the window, not wanting to get caught snooping.

There was a man in Samantha's house.

She'd told him she was taking her brother to a baseball game today, had even apologized that she wouldn't be working in the garden. He remembered that scene in the car with some embarrassment. He'd been half hoping she'd ask him to go with them. Then he'd felt silly; obviously she wanted this time alone with the boy. And he supposed she couldn't just drop a total stranger on the child, she probably had to be careful about such things.

He understood and admired that, just as he admired everything she'd done for the child. It would have been much easier, at nineteen, to simply hand over the boy and go on with her own life. But she'd put his welfare above her own, and no doubt given up a great deal in the process.

She had also mentioned, on the ride home, that a friend might stop by while she was gone, to use her washing machine since his was broken. He'd almost forgotten about it until he looked out and saw the same blue pickup truck he'd seen the day she moved parked at the curb. And shortly after Samantha left, a man came out, walked to the truck and retrieved two pillowcases apparently full of clothing to wash, hoisted them over his shoulder and returned to the house.

There was no reason for him to get involved, Ian told himself. Samantha had warned him someone might be here—thoughtful of her, really—and here that someone was. Just because from the glimpse Ian had gotten he was a young, good-looking guy was no reason to get himself in an uproar.

He returned to his computer and sat down. He nudged the mouse to bring his screen back up. He stared at the data there, wondering why he was having to force himself to concentrate on what usually came so easily.

He got up again and walked back to the window. He saw movement in the living room, only a shadow against the pleated shade. He stood there for a moment, realizing he'd never been in Samantha's house. He knew where things were because he'd been inside when the Howards had lived there, but he'd not set foot inside since she had moved in. But she'd been in his house several times now, usually when they got takeout food for dinner after a long day spent working in the wilderness of his yards.

He frowned, feeling his glasses shift slightly on his nose as he did so. He'd assumed she hadn't wanted anyone inside because she'd just moved in and the place was probably still pretty chaotic. Especially since she'd been spending so much time on his garden instead of her own house. But now that this guy was here, he wondered if maybe it was just him, specifically, that she didn't want in her house.

"Nothing like making yourself the center of the universe," he chided himself. "He's an old friend, and you've just met her."

He could, of course, go over there. Make sure the guy was legit, the one she said would be there. Just to be sure, for safety's sake. It would be a neighborly thing to do, after all.

He went back to the computer. When he had to give up for the third time, he knew he wasn't going to be able to concentrate until he did…something. Anything.

When he heard the sound of Samantha's front door again, he got up with a speed that made him laugh ruefully at himself. The man was heading out to his truck for something. Uncharacteristically, Ian thought for all of ten seconds before he went out his own front door in time to catch the man on his way back to the house.

He was holding a book, obviously what he'd gone back to the truck for. Ian saw that it was the latest techno-thriller by the leading author of the detail-laden books. He had a copy on his own shelf, as yet still unread. Ian cut through the honeysuckle. As he wouldn't have been able to do pre-Samantha, he thought.

"Hi," the blond man said, stopping on the walkway up to Samantha's door.

Ian nodded. He couldn't think of a thing to say, because the man looked so much like Samantha it was unsettling.

The man laughed. "Let me guess. You're thinking I'm Sam's secret twin or something, right? We get that a lot."

The easy way the man referred to her nagged at Ian. As did the "we." "She told me a friend might be over," he said, proud that his tone sounded fairly even.

"Yeah." The blonde grimaced. "Laundry. The machine at my building went south. Sam's a good guy, to let me use hers."

The mere thought of calling Samantha a guy made Ian want to laugh. But somehow that this man did it made him relax slightly. "You've been friends for a long time?"

"A few years. She's good people."

"Yes. She is."

He looked at Ian for a moment before he added, "You must be Ian."

She'd mentioned him? Ian thought, surprised. "I…yes. Ian Gamble."

"My name's Rand."

They shook hands. A strong, firm handclasp, Ian noted, but not excessive. Friendly, not challenging. But that didn't mitigate the fact that the man had only offered his first name.

"The resemblance really is remarkable," Ian said.

"I know. That's how we connected. People kept telling us we had to meet, because we had to be related. We thought they were crazy, until we came face-to-face."

"But you're not related?"

"Not that we know of. All my relatives seem accounted for, anyway."

Ian realized that the man must know Samantha didn't have any family left to ask. And then, almost involuntarily, he asked, "So, are you two…dating?"

It sounded so stupid he wanted to turn tail and run, go hide back among the safety of his papers and computers. But Rand answered so quickly and easily that he got over it.

"Sam and I? Lord, no. It would be like dating my sister."

Ian smiled, rather more broadly than the comment deserved. "I can see where it would be a bit disconcerting."

"Not to mention the looks we'd get," Rand added with a grin. Then he glanced at his watch. "My first load's probably done, I'd better get moving. Nice to meet you, Ian."

"You, too," Ian said, marveling once more at the resemblance as Rand went back into the house.

He went back to his own lair, sat back down in the computer chair, certain he would be able to work now.

He wasn't.

Still he sat staring at the screen, unable to focus. He rose and paced for a while, although it hadn't worked earlier. Nor did it work now, and with a sigh he walked through the entry and into the den.

He looked at the clock on the cable box atop the television—12:45. He picked up the remote, had a thought and reached for the newspaper. A quick glance sent him to the stereo instead, and he turned on the radio receiver. It took him a moment to find the station, tune it in and set the volume. Then he sat down on the sofa, wondering what the hell he was doing, sitting here listening to a baseball game he never would have thought of turning on, if his long-legged blond neighbor wasn't somewhere in the crowd.

And if he wasn't trying to convince himself Rand had seemed so familiar because he looked like Samantha, not because he'd seen him somewhere before.

When the ball game ended, he glanced at his watch. An hour and fifteen minutes later he heard her car. Almost involuntarily he walked to the window. After a few minutes he saw the two of them on the porch, saw how incredible the resemblance really was.

When Rand leaned over and gave her a distinctly brotherly peck on the cheek, he felt a spurt of satisfaction. When she gave the man a sour look, as if she were exasperated with him, that satisfaction grew. As did his chagrin as soon as he realized that was what he was feeling.

Samantha went back inside, and Ian watched Rand walk out to the truck. He was empty-handed. He must have taken the laundry and the book out earlier, while Ian had been listening to the game.

He watched the blue truck leave. Then he walked to the back patio where he had a comfortable patio chair and table, an arrangement he'd been taking advantage of on nights when he had thinking to do, which seemed to be happening a lot of late. He was still feeling a bit of satisfaction that Rand had clearly been telling the truth when he'd said they were only friends. And still feeling that chagrin that it had become so important to him.

But most of all he was feeling uneasy. Uneasy because he was now certain he'd seen Rand before, even if the man didn't seem aware of it. He couldn't remember exactly where, or when, but he knew the information was tucked away somewhere in his memory. And he knew he would find it eventually.

He wondered if, when he did, he would wish he hadn't.

"That," Sam said to the showerhead, "is the most ridiculous thing I've ever heard."

She nodded her head sharply for emphasis, and wound up with soap in her eyes. Another annoyance to chalk up to Rand's apparent loss of his tiny mind, she thought.

But his words came back to her yet again as she rinsed off.

*I don't believe it. You're falling for the professor.*

"You're an idiot, Singleton," she muttered to her absent partner as she stepped out of the shower and grabbed a towel. She dried off hastily, rubbing with an energy that reddened her skin, and pulled on a terry robe.

Grabbing up her detangling comb, she trotted over to the window to make sure nothing had changed next door, and breathed a sigh of relief when it hadn't. She'd been going to ask Rand to stay while she washed off the thick layer of sunscreen she'd had to use to avoid cooking in the full sun of a daytime baseball game, but he'd been in such a weird mood, with this craziness about her having a thing for the professor...

Funny, she never thought of him as the professor anymore. He was Ian, his own man, with his own strong personality. Different, perhaps, but certainly nothing like that nickname would make you think. A good man, as Josh had said. And a nice one. And certainly cuter than any professor she'd ever had, she thought with a grin.

And sexier.

The grin faded as that vivid image, a half-naked Ian in his wild garden, seared through her mind once more.

Fighting off the vision, she plopped down on the window seat and attacked her wet hair with the comb. Rand was totally, completely, utterly wrong, she insisted silently. He thought he knew her so well, but if he thought she would do something as stupid as falling for somebody on the job, he was nuts.

She could, she told herself firmly, appreciate that Ian was a sexy guy. Just as she could admire the depth of his intelligence. She could enjoy talking with him, be amazed at the way his agile mind worked. She could find his shyness endearing, and the way he came out of it admirable. She could envy his seemingly unflappable calm when the work he loved and possibly he himself was in danger. She could do all of that, had done all of that, without falling for the guy.

Yep, Rand was crazy. Had lost his mind. Didn't know what he was talking about. No way she was falling for anyone, let alone Ian Gamble.

No way.

## Chapter 8

"I met your friend," Ian said, sounding oddly neutral.

Sam wondered if he'd had to work up to it; he hadn't said a word about Rand's visit this morning. She'd been thankful for it, because talking about Rand would remind her of his assessment of her feelings for Ian, which would have made sitting here in her car with the man awkward at best. But now she was back in control, the silly idea quashed, and there was no problem.

"He told me you two had talked," she said as she changed lanes as they neared home. "He's a good guy. A bit of a pain sometimes, thinks he knows more than he does." She couldn't resist the jab. So maybe she wasn't totally back in control. "But he's okay."

"You didn't mention the resemblance."

Did he sound suspicious? She wasn't sure, only that some undertone had come into his voice. She didn't dare look at him now, in traffic.

"I guess I don't think about it that much anymore," she said, trying to keep her tone casual. "It is kind of amazing at first, though, isn't it? First time I saw him I started wondering about lost branches of the family tree.''

"I can see why."

He sounded better then, she thought, thankfully. "By the time we got done making sure we weren't related, we were friends."

"You are sure?"

He sounded nothing more than curious now, and Sam relaxed a little. "As sure as we can be, since I don't really have anyone to ask." Out of the corner of her eye she saw him look at her quickly, but before he could speak she assured him, "It's okay. Don't worry about reminding me. You don't have to walk on eggshells."

Her cell phone rang. She glanced at the screen and saw it was Billy's counselor at the center. She grabbed the earpiece she used while driving and answered quickly.

"Sam? It's Ellen Fortier."

"Billy?"

"Afraid so."

She sighed. "How bad?" she asked.

"Some agitation, but mostly withdrawal. Rocking. Refusal to eat."

"I'll be there as soon as I can."

"You know we wouldn't call you until we'd tried everything, but even Mario can't get through to him."

"It's okay. I'll be on my way in a few minutes."

When she disconnected and unhooked the headset from her ear, she saw Ian was watching her.

"Problem with your brother?" he asked.

"Yes. Outings like the ball game sometimes have aftereffects. Overstimulation or something. But I don't have the heart to deny him, he gets such joy from it."

"You need to go to him?"

"Yes. I'll drop you off and head over there."

"Go now, if you want. I don't mind."

That surprised her. "But it may take a while. Sometimes it's nearly an hour before I can get him calmed down."

"Maybe I can help."

She nearly gaped at him. He *wanted* to help her deal with Billy? "Are you sure about this?"

"Why not?"

She could think of lots of reasons, but one reason tilted her the other way; if he met Billy and reacted as most men did, she'd be safe. Nothing turned her off a guy faster than having him react with distaste to her brother. Meeting Billy had been the death knell for more than one relationship in her life. And, she realized with a little shock, if Ian was like the others who had run once they realized her little brother was part of the package, she didn't want to know it.

And she nearly drove off the road when she realized she was thinking of Ian in the way she thought of other men she'd been attracted to.

*No way,* she repeated to herself once again. She was *not* falling for the professor.

When they arrived and headed inside the center, Ian looked around with every evidence of sincere curiosity. He was quick to understand the functions of the different activity areas, and asked many of the same questions she had when she'd first been considering the center for her brother.

When they reached Billy's room, Mario, the boy's favorite aide, was outside the door. The young man looked troubled, but cheered when he saw Sam coming.

"Ah, Miss Sam, it is good you're here."

He looked at Ian curiously, and Sam quickly introduced them before asking, "How's Billy?"

"He is calmer, but still not right."

"I'll see what I can do."

She glanced at Ian. "Should I wait here?" he asked.

"For the moment," she said.

The boy barely looked up when she came in. He was huddled on his bed, backed against the wall, rocking gently back and forth. She sat down beside him. She reached out and touched his arm, carefully. The rocking continued, and he didn't look at her.

So she began to talk, softly, soothingly, about whatever came to mind. Gradually the rocking stopped, although he still didn't look at her. Finally she gestured Ian into the room, thinking he might be the distraction needed to draw Billy out of the chaos in his mind.

"This is my friend Ian," she said. "He wanted to meet you."

Not quite true, she thought, but it got the boy's attention.

"Hi, Billy." Ian knelt beside the bed.

Billy focused then, staring at Ian.

"Having a little trouble turning the brain off?" Ian asked gently. "That happens to me all the time."

Billy said nothing, just kept staring, but he didn't turn away as he often did when confronted with someone new.

"Sometimes," Ian said, still in that gentle tone, "I'm up all night because I just can't stop thinking."

Amazingly, Billy lifted himself up on one elbow to get a better look at this stranger.

"I wonder if rocking would help me?" Ian asked.

"Might," Billy said.

Sam's heart leaped. Rarely, so rarely did Billy interact with a new person. Somehow Ian had known exactly the right approach, the right combination of understanding and gentleness.

For a few minutes longer, they talked with the boy, until he was calm and alert. A buzzer on the bedside clock sounded, and Billy scrambled to the edge of the bed. "Dinner!" he said enthusiastically.

A moment later Mario stuck his head in and smiled at the boy. "Hungry, Billy?"

"Yes." He stood up and started toward Mario, then

stopped and turned back to Sam and gave her a hug. And after a moment's hesitation, he gave Ian a slightly less enthusiastic hug as well.

"Come back," he said.

"I will," Ian promised.

And when Billy had gone, his world back on its axis, Sam looked at Ian. "Thank you," she said, meaning it with all her heart. "You were wonderful with him."

Ian shrugged. "Different brains work in different ways."

The voice of experience, she thought. She supposed he knew exactly how people who thought differently were treated. But for him to look at Billy that way, simply as someone who thought differently than most, was a startling—and very pleasant—surprise.

She was silent as they left the center and continued their detoured trip home. As she negotiated the sometimes tricky left turn onto the street that led to their cul-de-sac, Sam noticed the Bergs' dog out in the yard as they passed and Mrs. Gerardi working in her garden.

They turned the corner onto their street. A moment later Ian groaned. "Oh, brother."

Sam had seen the same thing he had, but still she asked, "Something wrong?"

"Do me a favor, don't drop me in front like you usually do, just pull into your garage."

She didn't question him, just did as he asked. But she couldn't resist a glance over at the long, bright-red luxury touring car now parked in the driveway of his house.

When they were safely inside the garage, she stopped the car, turned off the motor, set the brake and turned in her seat to look at him.

"Ian?"

"I just need a minute. I wasn't ready for this."

His words and tone answered her question. "Your parents?" she asked.

He looked at her then. "Yeah. It has to be. That's just the kind of car dad would rent. 'Your mother,' he always says, 'deserves to ride in style.'"

Sam thought that sounded kind of sweet but decided this wasn't the time to say so. Ian was bracing himself, she could feel it. And for the first time, a heretical thought hit her.

"What was that?" he asked, clearly noticing some change in her expression.

"It just hit me that all my life I've thought how perfect my life would have been if my parents had lived. Now I'm seeing that we probably would have had moments like this, too."

"It happens," Ian said. "It's the nature of the relationship, I think. Especially when the child becomes an adult, but the parents still see their baby." He grimaced. "Even at thirty-two."

She hesitated, then asked, "Shall I go with you? Would it make it any easier to get over the initial hump?"

He looked startled. "I...yeah. I think it would." But then he shook his head. "No, maybe not. My mother would take one look at you and assume..."

"Assume what?"

"That you and I are..."

He lowered his gaze and seemed to be having trouble with the language all of a sudden. She thought she saw the faintest touch of color in his cheeks. She thought that was sweet, too. And wondered when shyness had become so attractive to her.

"That you and I are more than just neighbors?" she asked.

"Or that I'd want us to be."

Something in his voice kept her quiet. That, and the little jump her heart seemed to take.

After a moment he said, "I mean, what man wouldn't? You're...even nicer than you look."

To her it was the best kind of compliment. She had to take a quick, deep breath to steady herself before speaking. ''Thank you, Ian. That's probably the nicest thing anyone's ever said to me.''

''I find that hard to believe,'' he said, sounding wry now.

''Believe it,'' she said. ''Shall we tackle this?''

He looked doubtful, but when she got out of the car he did the same. He sucked in a deep breath and grimaced, as if in a last-minute plea for whatever it took to get him through these encounters, and then they turned to leave her garage.

Moments later she was introduced to a couple who matched even her vividly imagined vision of them.

''Mom, Dad, this is Samantha Harrison, my new neighbor in the Howards' old house. Samantha, Juliet and Hugh Gamble.''

Hugh Gamble had flair, it was clear: he was a thin, urbane-looking man dressed in a lightweight tan linen suit and wearing a Panama hat that should have looked silly but didn't, not on him. But Juliet surpassed him for pure style in a tailored summer suit that fitted her still-trim figure like a glove, hair worn in an elegant upsweep—hair she had passed on to her son, judging by the thickness and shine, Sam thought—and the kind of heavy, rich, artfully designed jewelry only someone with a forceful personality could carry off.

*They're exotic, sophisticated…two peacocks….*

If anything, Ian had understated, Sam thought.

''You're certainly a lovely addition to the neighborhood,'' Juliet said, with an openly assessing look that Sam couldn't mind because it was so honest. And when Juliet smiled, she felt enveloped in gracious warmth. ''And I have a feeling you'll contribute a bit of life this old house badly needs as well.''

''Indeed.'' Hugh took her hand, kissed it with continental dash. "My dear, if I wasn't already hopelessly in love with the most wonderful woman in the world, I'd be tempted to move back here just to see you every day."

Sam laughed; she couldn't help it. "Nicely done," she said. "Flirt outrageously but stay out of trouble at the same time."

Both Hugh and Juliet laughed, warm, genuine laughter that made Sam's smile widen.

"Come in, come in, sit down. We were just having some iced tea on this warm day, waiting for our too-hardworking son to come home. We didn't expect him to bring such delightful company with him."

"Told you they were charming," Ian said to her as they went inside, but without any rancor at all, with nothing but acknowledgment of fact in his voice and expression.

"That's our sweet boy," Juliet said, looking at her son with an expression that was as much bemused as loving as she led them into the dining area where a pitcher of tea and glasses were waiting. "Even if you have turned this house into one huge office."

"It works for me," Ian said mildly.

Juliet gestured Sam into a chair with a warm smile before she and her husband sat down. Ian waited until they were seated before he took his own chair, Sam noticed.

"Samantha's been helping—well, doing most of the work, really—in the garden," Ian told his parents.

"You've been working just as hard the last week or so," Sam pointed out.

"I noticed it was beginning to look quite nice again," Juliet said. "Thank you, dear, if you've gotten Ian out of the house long enough to do that."

"Guilt," Ian said with exaggerated glumness, "is a great motivator."

"Funny, we could never get it to work on you," Hugh observed. "We tried to get you to travel more, to take up an art of some kind, or at least to consider something more exciting as a career. But you weren't buying any of it.''

Juliet laughed. "But we're just his parents, after all.''

"I'm not like you. You know that. I have to be who and what I am.''

Ian's voice had the tone of an old refrain, and she wondered how many times he'd said it. Sam began to see what it must have been like for Ian, growing up with these two. And what it must have taken for him to stand fast in the face of their efforts to change him. There was steel beneath that shy exterior and a kind of courage that was no less strong for being quiet.

"Samantha, I'm so glad we decided to stop by before we catch the red-eye for Monte Carlo, or we might have missed the chance to meet you," Juliet said effusively, but with such warmth Sam couldn't doubt the enthusiasm was genuine.

"Thank you," Sam said, marveling more than a little at this couple's Old World charm despite Ian's advance description. They really, truly liked people, she thought. "Ian's told me about all your travels.''

"While he's the complete homebody," Hugh said.

"I seem to recall a few stamps in my passport during my misspent youth," Ian said dryly.

"Well, that's true," his father agreed. "We did drag you hither and yon a bit, didn't we?''

"For all the good it did." Juliet smiled indulgently at Ian.

"You were always happier to get home than to go.''

It was clear that while they might not understand their very different son, they loved him dearly and accepted him the way he was. She wondered if Ian realized how precious that was.

"Of course, you could always come with us this trip. Bring Samantha," Hugh added with a devilish glint in his eye.

Ian opened his mouth and then shut it again, as if biting off whatever he'd been about to say. And Sam thought she saw that faintest brush of color again. She couldn't blame him, the attack was coming as predicted, just from a different quarter than he'd expected.

"Oh, darling, you know Ian doesn't want to go to Monte Carlo."

Hmm, not only was his mother not joining in the attack, Sam thought, she seemed to be interceding for her son. Juliet glanced at Ian before looking at Sam. "He simply refuses to live up to our name," she said, her tone teasingly dramatic. "He doesn't gamble with anything. Money, time…or emotions."

*Spoken too soon,* Sam realized as Ian's mother fired that round with motherly accuracy, judging by Ian's wince. Then Juliet went on before Ian could say a word.

"Can you believe he's ours? Or is it that we're his?"

"They say things skip a generation," Sam said, trying for tact as they all sat down.

Juliet laughed again. "Yes, they do, and he is a bit like his grandfather."

"We adore him," Hugh put in, "we even admire him, but how we ever had such a staid, methodical child I'll never understand."

"There's lots to admire," Sam said. She sensed Ian go very still but went on without pause. "And while his process maybe be methodical, the way his mind works, the leaps of intuition he can make, is anything but. It takes an…eccentric mind to do what he does. He must have gotten that from you."

Both his mother and father looked startled, then thoughtful, and then, finally, with smiles that fairly warmed the whole room, they nodded.

"You're absolutely right," Hugh said, clearly delighted.

"I'd never thought of that," Juliet said, equally cheered.

If possible, Ian's parents were even more charming as

they spent a pleasant evening. Juliet put together an elaborate meal—they'd stopped at the market, she told Sam, knowing all too well their son's idea of preparing a meal—and insisted that Sam stay and join them. After a glance at Ian netted her a flatteringly pleading look and a quick nod, Sam confessed that cooking wasn't in her repertoire, either, and accepted gratefully on condition that she be allowed to clean up.

She was glad she had, the dinner of luscious lemon and dill-buttered salmon, fresh asparagus and crusty bread, with a tart, fruity sorbet for dessert, was the best thing she'd had in ages. She made certain she told Juliet so repeatedly and refused to let the woman even pick up a dish when the meal was over.

Maybe she really should learn how to cook.

At an hour when most people their age would be thinking about going to bed, Hugh and Juliet were getting ready to leave for the airport. And Ian couldn't help feeling a bit relieved; as parental visits went, this one had been fairly painless.

*Because of Samantha,* he thought.

"You have some long flights ahead of you," Samantha said with a note of concern.

"We'll sleep on the plane," Juliet assured her with a smile.

"We're quite used to it," Hugh put in.

Ian loaded his mother's bag—she couldn't stop for even a few hours without unpacking a bag, he told Samantha—into the trunk. Hugh and Juliet drove off in a long flash of red car, waving gaily, with a goodbye toot of the horn as they went.

"They're quite something," she said as she and Ian stood in the driveway, watching the taillights fade. "Everything you said and more."

"Yes."

"Not to mention rather exhausting," she added.

Gladness rippled through him; he should have trusted she would see that there was more to it than just their charm. She was too perceptive, too sharp to miss the undercurrents. He grinned at her. "That they can be."

She grinned back. "Let's go finish cleaning up the disaster area. Is there a pot or pan she didn't use?"

"That's my mom," he said, holding the front door for her. "Leave no utensil unturned."

"But it was worth it," Samantha said, almost prayerfully.

He laughed. They worked companionably together, until the mess was cleaned, the pots and pans shining and re-hung on the rack and the dishes in the dishwasher. Then a glance at the kitchen clock made Ian grimace.

"It is late, isn't it?" Samantha said.

"And it feels later," Ian admitted while rubbing at his neck; he always tensed up around his parents, but this, too, wasn't as bad this time.

*Because of Samantha,* he thought again.

And as he walked her to her door, he knew he had to tell her.

"Thanks," he said.

She unlocked her door, reached in to flip on a light, then turned to look at him. "I should be thanking you," she said. "I haven't eaten like that in ages."

"But I haven't been so relaxed with my parents around in longer than that."

She smiled. "I enjoyed it. Even the buffer zone part."

That she knew exactly what he'd meant came as no surprise.

"What you said to them tonight, about what I got from them," he began, then hesitated. At the time he'd felt oddly comforted by the quickness and the earnestness of her intervention. Now he was simply very aware of the powerful feelings her words had roused in him. Especially the words that had so stunned him. *There's a lot to admire....*

At last he stumbled on.

"They've never looked at me like that before. Like they didn't just love me because I'm their son, but like they were proud of me."

*God, how pitiful can you get,* he thought. *Thirty-two years old and you're still trying to make your parents proud.*

"I'm sure they always have been, but if tonight's the first time you've been sure, you've had a long wait," Samantha said softly.

She was looking at him, something so warm and understanding in her eyes that he couldn't help himself. He took a step toward her, expecting her to pull back. She didn't, she just kept looking at him in that same way, her mouth curved in a slight smile. Holding his breath, he lowered his head.

He kissed her. Gently, tentatively, but in no way the same kind of peck on the cheek Rand had given her. No, he had her lips beneath his, soft, warm, sweet. He could taste her, could feel the heat of her, and his body came to alert in a rush.

Like a man awakening after a long illness, the new awareness was almost painful. Yet it was a sweet, aching pain, one he wanted more of, as if it would shock him into being alive, really alive, for the first time in longer than he could remember.

Samantha shifted slightly, not really pulling away, but yet enough to make him realize he was getting too lost in this, that he was asking for too much too soon. He drew back, wanting to look away yet knowing it would be cowardly.

He struggled for something, anything to say that wouldn't sound inane. He couldn't think of a thing, not when his body was demanding he return to this delightful activity he'd too long neglected.

And then, again Samantha saved him.

"Good night, Ian," she said, rescuing him from having to say a thing. "See you in the morning."

He nodded mutely, and when she went in and closed the door, he stood there for a moment, lost in a tangle of emotions. And in his head rang his mother's words to him, spoken while Samantha was safely in the kitchen.

"Hang on to this one, Ian. She's special."

He knew that all too well.

But he also knew she wasn't his to hang on to.


"You," Sam said to herself as she paced the bedroom floor, "have lost your mind."

What the hell had she been thinking? It wasn't like she hadn't had practice turning away unwanted good-night kisses, albeit not much lately, since she'd been working for Draven. But she'd done it countless times before, managing on occasion to even do it gracefully. So was a great home-cooked meal all it took to sap her defenses?

She shoved her hands into the back pockets of the jeans she'd changed into, turned on her heel and started back across the room, trying not to focus on the one word that explained everything. The one word that made it all clear, including just how much trouble she was in. She tried, but she wasn't very successful in ignoring that the operative word here was *unwanted*.

Unwanted kisses.

Those were the ones she turned away. She did it instinctively, automatically, without even having to think about it. But with Ian she hadn't. And it had been just as instinctive. She hadn't deflected that tentative, almost shy kiss she'd had more than enough time to dodge, hadn't even thought about it. Even though she sensed Ian wouldn't have persisted had she done so.

*And I would never have felt that lovely heat,* she thought.

She spun around once more, unable to quite believe it, but less able to deny that she had felt that rush of sensation when Ian had kissed her.

When she realized her pace had increased almost to a run, she stopped dead in the center of the room. She made herself walk sedately to the window seat and take up her familiar post. She drew her legs up and crossed them in front of her. It had been a long time since she'd used the meditation technique Draven had taught her—it had been a long time since she'd needed it—but she needed it now.

She consciously tightened every muscle in her body, then relaxed them. Then she started again, working from her feet upward. Tighten, relax, tighten, relax....

Okay. So she'd made a mistake, allowing that to happen. So she should have rebuffed him, as gently as possible.

She hadn't. As Draven said, you can't go back, it's the here and now you have to deal with.

*So deal with it.*

She lost track of her progress and had to start at her feet again.

She would treat it as if it had been a friendly, casual, good-night kiss, a thank-you kiss even, brought on only by his gratitude for her being there while his parents visited. She would treat it like that and go on as if nothing had happened, as if—

Her own thoughts brought her up sharp, her exercises forgotten.

What if nothing *had* happened? What if the reaction had been all one-sided? On her side? What if he'd felt nothing more than what she was proposing to pretend? What if that was all he'd meant to do, thank her for a few hours' moral support?

Sam shook her head at the sickly feeling this idea gave her. Then her sense of humor reasserted itself, and in a bemused tone she asked rhetorically, "So, just when did you become so irresistible that any man must fall in love with one kiss?"

She laughed aloud, then glanced out the window, to send Ian a silent apology.

There was someone breaking into his house.

She hadn't heard a vehicle. A quick glance told her there wasn't a strange one within sight on the street. There appeared to be only one person. Dressed in dark clothing. At the downstairs front window that led directly into the living room Ian used as an office.

She ran halfway down the first set of stairs, then went over the rail and dropped down to the lower landing. Two steps more and she was running toward the back of her house and the slider onto the patio.

She nudged the door open until she could squeeze through. Moving as fast as she could while staying silent she headed toward Ian's home.

*Stay upstairs, Ian. Stay safe.*

In the darkness she crouched in the even darker shadow of the honeysuckle. She'd never turned on any lights inside, so her eyes didn't need a lot of adjustment time, and she quickly spotted the figure still working at the window. He had the screen down, and was going at the window itself with a pry bar of some kind.

Thankful Ian had at least been wary enough to apparently lock the windows to his office, Sam inched forward carefully. She heard a sound, and the dark figure began to make movements that told Sam he was giving up on prying and had taken to cutting the glass itself.

*Prepared,* she thought. Not just an impulse break-in. Not that she'd thought for a moment it was.

She held her breath, waiting. It would be better if she caught him actually in the act of entering the house. Made the case more solid. Not that she'd be calling the police until after she'd gotten some information out of the guy.

Josh would want to know who exactly was behind this, and she intended to find out for him. But most important, she would stop him before he got anywhere near Ian; the thought of Ian hurt or worse spurred her heart rate into high gear.

She saw the man's arm move, saw him stretch, and knew he had gotten through and was reaching for the lock. She moved forward, gauging the distance between them, planning her move for the moment he was awkwardly straddling the windowsill. Barely a dozen feet between them, she could cover that in—

Some finely honed sixth sense warned her. She spun. Saw the dark shape coming at her. Dodged right. She wasn't fast enough, or he was faster than she'd expected. A heavy, strong arm came around her, holding her fast, then pulling her back in the shelter of the honeysuckle.

She struggled, knowing from the sound of wood sliding over wood that the man at the window had gained entry. And this had to be his accomplice, holding her back until he got what he was after. She was letting Josh down, letting Redstone down. She'd been so worried about Ian's safety that she'd become *too* focused.

Ian's safety. If she was taken out of the game, he was a sitting duck.

So she would just have to make sure that didn't happen.

She drove back with an elbow. Connected with a solid wall of flesh. Heard a grunt.

"Take it easy!"

A familiar voice, impossibly, coming from the man who had stopped her. She shook her head, certain she'd been thinking of him so much she'd somehow manufactured that sound in her mind.

She twisted to one side. Looked up at the man holding her back.

It was Ian.

She went still for a moment in disbelief. Then the need

for action rushed back in. She was standing here while the very thing she'd been waiting for happened. Doing nothing. Watching as the man climbed into his office, seeing his shadow as he spent several minutes at each computer and then began to search each desk and table, rifle every drawer.

She twisted against his grasp once more. "Let me go!" Her voice was harsh with the effort to keep it low.

"Just wait," Ian whispered back, never loosening his surprisingly strong grip.

She could break free. Easily, in fact. But to do it she would have to risk injuring him. And while at this moment she wasn't sure what he was up to, she knew she didn't want to hurt him.

So instead she stood doing nothing as the burglar came back to the window, slipping a small box into his pocket before swinging a leg over the sill and sliding back to the ground outside. Then he was out of sight, and moments later they heard a car at some distance, leaving the area with a squeal of tires.

She pulled free at last and whirled on him. "What was that for?"

"You looked like you were going to tackle that guy."

He said it so calmly, as if a thief hadn't just made off with work that was, from what she knew, irreplaceable.

"I was. I could have stopped him. Did you *want* him to get away with your work?"

He drew back slightly, frowning. "He didn't."

"But that was a box of disks he stuffed in his pocket."

"Yes. But it wasn't my work. It was a dummy set of disks. I put them in a locked box on the computer desk. Only thing locked up in the room."

Which would naturally lead the thief to assume that was the important thing and grab it.

"Lots of data," Ian added, "and it looks real, but it's not. They won't find out until they get fairly deep into it."

"And the real disks are…?"

"Under the kitchen sink, in the dishwasher soap box."

She blinked. And couldn't think of a single thing to say. For all her admiration for him, she realized she had underestimated Ian Gamble. Not only was he tougher—he'd absorbed her struggles without an ounce of give—but he was also less naive and more clever than she'd given him credit for.

A lot more clever, she thought as he took a step back from her, an expression of shock dawning on his face.

Shock, and realization. Her heart sank.

He knew.

# Chapter 9

Ian felt himself shiver slightly, even though the night was warm.

He'd been puzzled, first by her reaction to the burglary, and then by her assumption it was his work the thief had been after; he didn't think an ordinary neighbor would have assumed that. But it wasn't until she had turned to look at him, until even in the faint light he'd seen once more the incredible resemblance to her friend Rand, that it hit him. And he suddenly knew exactly where he'd seen the man before.

As vividly as if it had been yesterday a scene from several weeks ago played through his mind again. He and Stan had been waiting to fly to Denver for a meeting with some researchers there. One of the Redstone fleet of jets was being readied for them as Josh's personal jet returned from the Redstone Bay Resort, where Ian had heard there had been a tense hostage situation involving some children.

It wasn't until their pilot had come in to announce the

plane they were taking was ready that Ian had once more glanced out the window.

Just in time to see Rand, dressed in all black and carrying a duffel bag, jump off the bottom step of Josh's plane's stairs and disappear into the hangar. The memory was painfully vivid now.

"You work for Redstone."

His voice came out flat, emotionless. Which was a good thing, considering how he was feeling just now. If she lied, if she denied it, he didn't know what he was going to do.

"I what?"

"Your friend Rand does, too. I finally remembered where I've seen him before. You both work for Redstone, don't you?"

She didn't lie. She didn't look happy, but she looked him in the eye and told him the truth.

"Yes."

The way his gut flinched told him how much he'd been hoping this was somehow all a mistake. He wanted to turn away, to run, hide, pretend this hadn't happened, that he hadn't remembered, pretend that Samantha was still just the warm, lovely woman next door who had inexplicably taken him into her life.

But it had happened, he had remembered, and it wasn't inexplicable any longer. He'd been right all along to suspect her motives for befriending him so quickly and completely.

"Ian—"

"Josh sent you, didn't he?"

"Yes."

"I told him no."

"He's worried about you."

"I told him I didn't want a baby-sitter."

He knew he was focusing on the wrong thing—Josh going against his expressed wishes. He even knew why he was doing it. Knew he couldn't let himself come face-to-face with the real betrayal, that Samantha had been lying to him from day one, that his suspicions of her had been right.

"And you can tell him just what I think of his clandestine methods."

"He did what he had to. Josh doesn't take any chances with his people. If you don't know that, there are a lot of people who do."

He did know. He'd heard the stories before. The rescued hostages, the airlifted earthquake victims, even the family Josh had himself rescued from a burning car. Real hero stuff. The kind of stuff he himself wouldn't have a clue about. That it was all true only made him feel worse.

"He's even helped Redstone people with personal things," Sam added, "up to and including using Draven."

Even he, tucked away in his lab, had heard of John Draven, the legendary head of Redstone security. The man who had rescued the employees caught up in that Asian drug war, the one to go in and get the Redstone exec who'd been held hostage by extremists in Eastern Europe, and countless others. His name was spoken in tones of awe, admiration and respect.

As Samantha had just spoken it.

"I've heard of Draven. He sounds intimidating."

"He can be, if you're on the wrong side."

"So you're tight with him."

"We're all tight, on the team. But yes. He's a leader in the best sense. Only Josh is more important to me," she said.

He'd never heard her sound like that. Of course he'd only known her...could it really be only three weeks? But he'd heard women who sounded like that before. Women in love. Which would figure. A woman like Samantha could only love a dangerous man like Draven, as far removed from he himself as any man could be.

"Of course Draven would gag if you told him that,"

she added, with a note in her voice that sounded almost wistful. The longing of a woman who knows she can't have the man she loves? he wondered.

"It must be hard on his family, the work he does. His wife, especially." It wasn't subtle, but he wanted to know. Wanted to know just how big a fool he'd been.

"He's not married. I doubt he ever will be, for that reason and others. But if you need help, he's your man."

He heard that undertone again, and was even more certain he was right. The knowledge sharpened the edge in his voice. "I am not helpless, nor am I a hostage who needs rescuing."

"I know that." Her voice was gentle now, and he thought he heard a trace of pain in it, but he wasn't sure. He didn't want to hear it, anyway; she'd been here under orders, had approached him under orders, become his friend under orders.

Had she let him kiss her under orders, too?

His mind shied violently away from that thought and retreated to the safety of his anger.

"I don't need a damned bodyguard."

She winced on the curse, and he wondered if she thought he meant the adjective to apply to her specifically. Right now, he wasn't sure he didn't. But she recovered quickly.

"I think what just happened here proves you do need one."

"He was only after my work, not me."

He knew it was weak, that had he been inside instead of sitting out on his back patio—pondering the shock of his body's response to kissing her—he could well have gotten hurt or worse. But he hadn't been, and he was angry enough to use that fact.

To his surprise she didn't make that obvious point. Instead, she smiled. "And you protected it rather cleverly."

For an instant his heart took that same old leap it always

had when she smiled at him like that. It took him a moment to quash it with the reminder of what she'd done. That it had been a lie, all of it.

"So you can tell Josh his precautions aren't— Never mind. I'll tell him. I've got a few other things to say to him."

"Don't be mad at Josh. He was only looking out for you."

"So, I should be mad at you instead?" He couldn't help the edge of taut emotion that came into his voice. It was his own fault, for half convincing himself that her interest in him, however unlikely, was genuine. "You were only following orders, right? Was that up to and including kissing me? Just how far would you have gone?"

She winced again. "Ian—"

"Have you done this before? How far did it go then? How much do you…sacrifice for your job?"

Samantha drew herself up. "I know you're angry at me, but that was below the belt."

It was, and he knew it. For a long moment he simply looked at her. Finally he spoke.

"I am angry with Josh. I told him in no uncertain terms I did not want him to do this. I'm angry at you, too." He took in a deep breath before adding softly, "But I'm angriest at myself. I've felt like a misfit before, I've even felt stupid before. But I've never in my life felt like such a fool."

Sorry he'd even said that much, he turned on his heel and walked away from her.

His words echoed in Sam's head as she stood there, her stomach churning, her heart pounding as it never had when she'd been planning her attack on a burglar. Too much of what Ian had been feeling had shown in his face, even in the faint light. This had hurt him much more than she'd feared it would.

And she was beginning to realize it had hurt her, too. She had the feeling it was going to be a while before she knew just how much.

*I've never in my life felt like such a fool.*

The implications of those particular words took her breath away. They were so much worse than his anger, so much worse than simple embarrassment at having been deceived.

She shivered slightly, much as Ian had. She'd seen it ripple through him and wondered if he'd been feeling the same chill she had.

She had to get moving. Josh needed to know about the break-in. And that her cover had just been blown to bits. She should call him, tell him herself. It was late, but she knew if he didn't answer, St. John would. Everybody at Redstone knew that; there were rumors that the man never slept, since no matter when you called, he appeared to be awake and alert. And she needed to ask if Josh wanted the police called, now that an actual crime had been committed.

But the last thing she wanted to do was talk to Josh— or St. John—now, when she was so shaken herself. Her disjointed, jumping thoughts told her too well what she'd probably sound like.

She would call Rand. He was running the show on the inside. He could decide what to do next.

Just making that decision calmed her somewhat. Enough, at least, to realize she was still standing in Ian's yard.

*You are a wreck,* she told herself as she retreated to the other side of the honeysuckle barrier.

She went inside and then up the stairs. She grabbed the cordless telephone handset and headed for her usual spot on the cushioned window seat. It was doubtful Ian would have any more trouble tonight, but she couldn't take any chances. He was still her job.

When she finally sat down, she felt an odd weakness in her legs and arms. She felt faintly nauseous. But most of all she felt horribly guilty, more than she'd ever felt in her life. She tried to tell herself it was simply from lying to one of the good guys, that she'd had to do it, she'd had no choice, that it had been for his own good. She told herself all those things, and it didn't alleviate her guilt one bit.

She'd lied to him from the first day she'd met him, and no amount of rationalization could change that fact. But she'd lied before when it was necessary to get the job done, she'd even lied to Redstone people before, if she'd been undercover inside a Redstone operation, and it hadn't bothered her.

So why now? The only thing different in this situation was...Ian.

She wrapped her arms around herself and sat staring at the phone she had yet to dial. She had to do it, had to call Rand and let him know what had happened, but she simply couldn't reach for that phone.

*You're falling for the professor.*

Had Rand been right? She liked Ian, had liked him from the beginning, but what Rand was suggesting was something entirely different from casual liking. And he did know her better than most people did.

She could admit she'd grown to more than just like Ian. But...

Slowly, using Draven's technique, she regained control. And with returning calm came one simple fact: it didn't matter how she felt about Ian. He was still her assignment, and the fact that now he knew it made no difference. Her job was still to protect him. No matter how angry he was, no matter how justified that anger might be, he was stuck with her until this was over, until Josh called her off. And that would happen when Josh was certain he was safe and not before.

And she was going to have to tell him that.

With a smothered sigh she at last dialed the phone.

He didn't come out as he usually did when she pulled into his driveway to pick him up the next morning. She took a deep breath and got out of the car. She marched up to his door. She'd been awake most of the night preparing for this, so she was now, as Rand would say, loaded for bear.

She didn't even give him a chance to speak when he pulled the door open.

"I know you're mad at me and you have the right to be, but it doesn't change a thing. It's still my job to keep you safe, and I intend to do just that. So you might as well resign yourself to it, because you're stuck with me for the duration. Now let's go."

To her surprise he didn't protest, he didn't say a word. He picked up the briefcase that was sitting just inside the door and stepped outside, pulling the front door securely closed behind him, even checking to make sure it was locked. She'd heard hammering this morning, and had looked out to see that he'd nailed a board of some kind over the window the burglar had cut through, so the house was as secure as it could be for the moment.

The silence held as he got into her car and fastened his seat belt. He sat staring straight ahead. And stayed that way until they were halfway there. She doubted anything would change the second half of the drive. Except that, she thought as her cell rang.

"Sam? It's Josh."

"Yes, sir."

"Is he with you?"

"Yes, sir."

She heard Josh sigh. "It's that bad?"

"If not, then very close."

"Let me talk to him."

She silently held the phone out to Ian. He looked at it, glanced at her face, and she saw that he knew perfectly well who it was. After another silent moment, he took the phone and put it to his ear.

"Yes, sir?" he said, with emphasis on the second word.

Whether the tight repetition of her words was a jab at her or the most anger he would allow himself to show his boss she didn't know. Didn't want to know. He listened silently for nearly a full minute.

"I realize that," he said. "I see. That's…nice to know, I suppose." And then, after a moment, even more stiffly, "That's not an issue, sir."

Sam stifled an inward sigh.

"Yes, sir."

Without a goodbye, Ian snapped her small phone shut and handed it back to her. Her fingers brushed his as she took it, and he yanked his hand back.

"Ian," she said.

"I understand you were just doing your job, *Miss Beckett*." Josh must have told him her real name, Sam realized, so he knew she'd lied about that, too. "Let's leave it at that. My problem is with Josh."

"But you're angry with me."

"Yes. But that's my problem, not Josh's."

"I told the truth as much as I could," she told him. He didn't react. "Everything except my name and that I work for Redstone."

"And why you moved in next door and decided to make your odd neighbor your new best friend."

She'd been better off when he wasn't speaking to her, she thought wearily.

"I never thought you were odd. And that's why it was easy. It's easy to…befriend somebody you like anyway."

He made a low sound she couldn't interpret other than to be sure she was far from forgiven. And when he spoke again, his tone made that even clearer.

"So tell me, where did you go when I thought you were at work?"

"To see Billy."

That startled him. "You mean he's real? You really have a brother?"

"I told you I gave you truth as much as I could. More than I ever have on a job like this before."

"And the story about your parents, and you nobly raising your handicapped little brother?"

She flinched. "The story's true. You're the one who hung the noble tag on it."

To her relief, he lapsed back into silence after that. Until the moment the Redstone building came into sight.

"At least you don't have to hide anymore. You can come right in, instead of sneaking off as if you'd never set foot in the place."

"I never have." He stared at her. She could see he thought she was lying. Again. "I haven't. Josh believes in keeping the security team completely separate from the rest of his operations."

She wasn't telling him anything everyone at Redstone didn't know already. But his expression told her she'd still surprised him.

"I didn't realize…of course you're security." He gave his head a slight shake. "The famous Redstone Security team. I should have known. And I should be flattered, I guess."

"Ian—"

"I can see why he does it. Makes it easier to fool people if they've never seen you, doesn't it?"

She gave up. She wasn't going to talk him out of his anger now. And she couldn't blame him. "We rarely have to work inside, the personnel people are very good at screening, but when we do, it's usually very important. So Josh keeps us as low profile as possible."

"You work for the famous Draven."

She nodded. "He trained me."

Oddly, Ian seemed to give up then. He leaned back in the seat, head against the headrest, and closed his eyes. She wondered if his night had been as sleepless as hers. She thought it probably had been.

He didn't move until she stopped in front of the Redstone building. He picked up the briefcase and opened the door. Put one foot out and then stopped.

"Josh wants to see me first thing. I'll be sure and tell him you didn't screw up. If I hadn't figured out where I'd seen Rand before, I never would have guessed."

As reassurance, it failed miserably. As indictment, it succeeded all too well.

Sam watched him go, the ache in her chest growing with his every step.

She wished she could—

She wasn't sure what she wished. She hadn't been this confused since she'd been nineteen and facing trying to raise Billy on her own, with what seemed like the entire world lined up against her.

But that was when Josh had stepped in, fixing everything. For everything he'd done for them, she owed him a lot more than just some emotional pain she'd brought on herself by getting too personally involved. It was her own fault, so she would have to live with it. In the meantime she would continue to do the job Josh had asked of her.

And if it hurt even more now, so be it.

# Chapter 10

"It was my decision, Ian. Sam was only doing what I told her to do."

"And well, I might add. Or perhaps I'm just easy to fool."

Josh studied Ian for a moment. Ian guessed he was analyzing the tone as much as, if not more than, the words. He couldn't help the sourness in his voice; it was all still too raw. Plus, he was uneasy here in the throne room of the Redstone domain. He hadn't set foot here since Josh had hired him.

He had to admit the office hadn't changed much since then. It was still comfortably unpretentious, almost spare, Ian was sure, compared to other executive offices. The furnishings were of high quality, with the rich sheen of oak and the soft gleam of leather, but they were chosen for function rather than show.

Josh leaned back in his chair, and Ian heard the faint sound of leather creaking.

"I'm sorry, Ian. I appear to have misjudged things," Josh said.

"So you agree I don't need a bodyguard?" *A little late,* he added silently.

"No. You do, more now than ever. I won't have my people at risk. But I misjudged how to go about it. I see now that I should simply have told you what I was going to do."

And there, Ian thought, was the essence of Joshua Redstone. He cared, deeply, about his people. He would go to extremes to help or protect, and he wasn't above apologizing. But when it came down to the bottom line, he made the decision and he stood his ground.

Ian closed his eyes for a moment, dreading the answer before he even asked the question.

"I gather that means this will continue?"

"Until I'm certain you're safe."

"Josh—"

He stopped when his boss held up a hand. "No, Ian. I have to ask you to put up with this. I'll instruct Sam to keep her distance, if that will help, but she stays."

*Keep her distance...*

No more days spent in his garden, working side by side. No more evening meals amid the litter of Chinese takeout cartons or pizza boxes. No more companionable chats on the rides to and from work. No more—

It hit him suddenly. He nearly groaned aloud. "My car. I should have realized right away."

"That's the time you're most vulnerable. We had to do something."

"And I suppose you're behind the delay in repairing it?"

"I pulled a string," Josh admitted, but he didn't sound particularly guilt-ridden about it.

"Great," Ian muttered.

"I've apologized for how it was done, but I will not

apologize for doing it. If it makes you feel any better, my first instinct was to slap you in a safe house somewhere until we found out exactly who's behind all this.''

Ian drew back slightly, his eyes widening at that grim prospect. "I could never work like that."

"Your work isn't the priority here. As important as it is, it isn't nearly as important as you are."

For the kid who'd never felt quite right about himself, those words from a man like Josh would have been balm to the soul. For the man who was feeling like the largest kind of lamebrain just now, they bounced off the shell of his anger. And, he admitted reluctantly, his hurt feelings.

He thought of asking Josh to assign someone else. But he quickly realized the first choice would probably be Rand, who obviously was in on this whole thing, and that wasn't going to help much. The man who looked enough like Samantha to be her twin wasn't going to help him forget what had happened.

So maybe he shouldn't forget. Maybe he should remember, as insurance that he never be so stupid again.

Or maybe he should remember because nothing like it would ever happen again, no woman would ever make him feel as Samantha had.

But it had all been lies.

"You like her, don't you?"

Josh's soft question snapped him out of his reverie. "Liked," he answered, emphasizing the past tense.

"She's the same person she was before you found out she was working for me."

"She's a little too good a liar for me."

"And motive doesn't count? It doesn't matter that your welfare was her only goal?"

It should matter, shouldn't it? Ian thought. How many times had he read about somebody doing something that made no sense to him—until he found out why they'd done it.

"She did what she had to, Ian. If you blame anyone, blame me. I'm the one who put her in the position of having to lie to you."

*But I wanted it to be* real!

God, you're whining, Ian thought in disgust. For distraction he asked the first thing that popped into his head. "How did she end up on the security team?"

"She was working at the resort in Alaska. She'd turned in her notice, and I didn't want to lose her, so I went to talk to her."

Only Josh would fly halfway up the world to try to talk a single hotel employee out of quitting, Ian thought.

"Why was she leaving?"

"The main reason was she wanted to bring her brother back to California."

"I suppose there are more resources here than in Alaska for children like Billy."

Josh's brows rose. "She told you about him?" He nodded. "Well, well. She doesn't usually talk about him much. If she told you, she trusted you."

The irony of that bit deep, and he wondered if Josh had meant it to.

"The other reason," Josh went on, "was that she was feeling stifled. The security job there was pretty much a nine-to-five, paper-pushing situation, and she's not that type of person."

"I noticed."

"She's turned out to be one of our best operatives. She was the linchpin for the Colombian situation, and probably saved a dozen lives in the process."

"I thought Draven was behind that one." He hadn't really heard that, just assumed it, as most people did; Draven's reputation, if not his face, was known throughout Redstone.

Josh shook his head. "Draven planned it, but Sam carried it out." He leaned forward abruptly. "Cut her some slack, Ian. She's good people. She's got guts, smarts and a streak of integrity a mile wide.''

"Integrity," Ian repeated. Odd thing to say about a woman who probably spent a lot of her on-duty time lying to people.

"Yes," Josh said firmly, as if he knew exactly what Ian had been thinking. "You think about what she's done for her brother and tell me if the kind of woman you've got yourself convinced she is would do that."

Josh let him go then, but Ian pondered his words for the rest of the day. On the surface he appeared to be working busily. He dealt with finding Stan sitting in his office waiting for him, and Stan's anger at not having been informed Ian was with Josh. He handled two phone messages from suppliers. He input some data, but he was only giving it half his attention. Rebecca was hovering again, but for once what irritated him about it was not her constant presence but the fact that thanks to the warning he'd gotten about her, she reminded him of the supposed threat to him, which reminded him of Samantha.

At last he gave up and left the lab. He walked toward the window alcove that looked out on the courtyard. He plopped down in one of the comfortable chairs, then wondered if he should have; he felt as if he could fall asleep at any moment.

"Where was this sleepiness when I needed it last night?" he muttered to himself. Last night, when he'd spent the hours staring into the darkness, thinking not of the burglary to his home but of the unmasking of the woman next door.

The gardeners were at work on the plants around the pond below. That made him think of Samantha, which made this a doubly bad idea. He was leaning forward, preparing to leave when one of the men started coiling a long, flat hose. He wondered if it was one of her soaker hoses, or if they even had to worry about such things with the pond right there. The image of Samantha laying out that hose in an even, snakelike pattern for full coverage came back to him vividly.

*It waters out both sides, so if you space it right, it will cover the whole bed.*

*Space it right...cover the whole...*

His mind suddenly kicked into high gear.

"Of course!"

He leaped up and headed back to the lab at a run.


"You okay? You look pretty grim," Rand said.

"I'm not happy, but yes, I'm okay," Sam answered honestly.

"It happens. At least he's not a *bad* guy who made you."

That, Samantha decided, didn't help much.

They were in the security team's office, which took up the back upstairs section of one of Redstone Aviation's hangars at the county airport. The layout included a communications center, a bunk room and a sizable, securely locked room they called the equipment locker, that contained everything from makeup to explosives. It was not only private, with low traffic even from Redstone personnel, who came through the other end of the hangar nearer the airfield, it was easily securable and regularly patrolled by the airport police. And with all their gear stowed there, it was convenient for quick departures when necessary.

"We got Hollings's cell phone records," Rand said. "She made a call the day Gamble was almost grabbed, but it was well before he left the building. According to the time in Gamble's statement, it was before he'd even decided to leave."

"Who did she call?"

"A restaurant on Pacific Street. Or rather, a pay phone there."

"A pay phone?" Suspicious, she thought.

"Yeah. But from what I was able to find out, it's used a lot for overflow orders around lunchtime."

"So it's suspicious, with an innocent explanation."

"Something like that, yeah."

"What about her computer?"

"The techies didn't turn up any unauthorized files," he said. "But there are signs that several files were recently deleted. It'll take a while for them to retrieve what they can."

"She doesn't know she's under observation, right?"

He shook his head. "Nobody's approached her for explanations yet, and they're working on the computer at night. She hasn't been back to his house, has she?"

"Not while I've been there."

"And her time here is accounted for."

"I still don't like it."

"Neither do I." He pulled another piece of paper out of his pile of notes. "You still want that info on Gamble?"

In her funk, she didn't remember what he was talking about. Figuring the safest answer was yes, she told him to go ahead.

"Seems that childhood friend of his vanished, along with his father."

Ian's words came back to her then, along with the feeling she'd had that he was hiding something. *My best friend… Instead of giving him to his dad, who wanted him but didn't make much money, they put him in foster care.*

"Vanished?" she asked.

"Blair and his father just dropped off the planet, as far as the cops could see. Not a trace of them anywhere. And I wasn't able to find anything, either. Of course, as a case it's a bit cold after eighteen years."

"I wonder if Ian knows where they went? If that's what he's hiding?" It didn't seem like enough to make him so uneasy about the topic, Sam thought, but maybe it had seemed like a big deal when he'd been a kid.

"I don't think so," Rand said. "At least, that's not all."

"What do you mean?"

"The night they disappeared, the father's house blew up. Completely. There wasn't a shred left to give the cops any clue to where they might be headed."

Rand waited silently for her reaction. It only took her a moment. "You think Ian did it?"

"He'd gotten suspended from school a month before for nearly blowing up the chem lab. Although that was pretty clearly an accident. Another kid messed with some experiment he was running, and pow."

"Was he a suspect in the house incident?"

"Formally? No. But I'm not sure the cops knew about the friendship."

She eyed her friend. "Do they now?"

He grinned. "No. I didn't burn him. Didn't seem to be any point at this late date. And I got my info from several different sources, anyway."

"Thanks," she said, before she realized how odd it sounded, for her to be thanking him for not causing trouble for Ian.

But Rand, if he noticed, was mindful enough of her mood not to mention it.

"Seems he was quite the odd one out in school," Rand said. "He tested nearly off the charts on IQ but got lousy grades."

"Josh says he thinks outside the box," Samantha said. "Kids like that don't always do well trying to fit in standardized school formats."

"Didn't Einstein flunk algebra?"

"Something like that," Samantha said. "Maybe it's the same for Ian."

Rand looked at her consideringly. "It's going to be tougher now, isn't it?" he said.

She didn't bother to deny it. "Yes."

"Want me to take over?"

"No," she said, so quickly she startled herself.

For a long moment Rand just looked at her. Finally, softly, he said, "Keep your head on straight, kiddo. I've got a nasty feeling about this."

So did she, she thought as she headed back to her car and made her way out of the airport. The problem was, she wasn't sure how much of it was that gut instinct she'd developed since coming to the team and how much of it was simply that gut still churning after what had happened with Ian.

By the time she got back to Redstone to pick Ian up, she had steadied herself. She had no choice but to continue, and if keeping him safe had become a personal thing, that was her problem and she'd deal with it. She stopped in her usual place, and as she waited, worked on steeling herself for a silent, tense ride home.

When he didn't come out by six-thirty, she wondered if he'd decided to avoid her completely. But she didn't think he would. Josh had told her he'd grudgingly accepted that nothing was going to change until this was over.

When her watch hit a quarter to seven, she gave in and called.

"St. John."

She didn't bother identifying herself, she knew he'd know the instant she spoke. "Is he still in the lab?"

"Wait."

She heard a click, silence, and then in less than ten seconds he was back. "Yes. Hollings, as well."

"All right." She wanted to ask if he was working or simply avoiding leaving and facing her, but St. John would have no way of knowing that.

"He appears to have had one of his brainstorms," St. John said, as if he'd read her mind. Which wouldn't surprise her.

"So it could be a while."

"Yes. I'll call you when he appears to be leaving."

"I'll be close."

But the time rolled by and Ian still didn't come. At eight o'clock, her stomach growling, she moved a block farther away and went through a fast-food drive-through. She barely tasted the burger, but it quieted her stomach, so she settled for that.

At nine her phone rang.

"Beckett."

"He's showing no sign of stopping," St. John's voice said. "From past patterns, he may stay the night."

"What about Hollings?" She hadn't seen the girl leave, but there were parking lots she couldn't see.

"He finally sent her home. She stalled around for a while, but finally left. She went straight home."

She didn't bother to ask if he was sure or how he knew. You simply didn't question St. John.

"Go home," St. John said. "If he does leave, I'll handle it and let you know."

"I'll stick it out a bit longer. I'll notify Rand when I pack it in."

"Up to you," he said. "But have him keep me posted."

By ten o'clock she was wishing she'd taken St. John up on his suggestion. At least at the house she could read or something. Sitting here in the dark in her car, having to keep alert in case somehow Ian slipped out unnoticed, was leaving her with little to do but think. And inevitably her thoughts were about the one thing she could do nothing about.

Under the existing circumstances she'd had to do what she'd done. It was the only way to get the job done in the way Josh wanted it done. She'd had no choice. So why did she feel so lousy about it?

The only answer she could come up with was the one Rand had already given her. And she didn't much like it. Especially since, if it were true and she'd somehow managed to fall for Ian, what she'd had to do had likely destroyed any feelings he might have had in return. He was a good man, but this was a lot to forgive.

Besides, she had no business getting involved—or even wanting to get involved, which she still wasn't convinced she did—with somebody on an assignment. With somebody who *was* her assignment.

At midnight Rand called her.

"St. John just let me know Gamble has now started a whole new research prospectus. Gamble's here for the duration, I'd say. Go get some sleep."

"All right."

"Sam?"

"What?"

"Are you okay?"

She opened her mouth to say yes. Instead, out came "No. But I'll get over it."

She was half braced for one of his usual teasing comments, but all he said was, "If you need to talk, you know I'm here."

"Offering me a shoulder to cry on?" she said, not completely comfortable with the sudden sensitivity of the always wisecracking Rand.

"If that's what you need," he said. "I'm no relationship expert, but—"

"Well, that's an understatement," Sam said with a chuckle.

"Hey, at least I got you to laugh."

"Yes, you did," she said with a smile. "Good night, big brother."

But the moment she disconnected, her smile faded away. And she realized she wasn't at all sure that she would get over this.

Ian shifted in the chair, only aware when his muscles protested that he'd been sitting in one position far too long. But he couldn't help it. This was the first new idea he'd had on this in weeks, and it might, it just might work. And that possibility grabbed him as it always did, until everything else slipped away.

Well, almost everything.

He told himself it was because Samantha had indirectly inspired the idea that she kept popping into his mind. He surely had no other reason to keep thinking about her. Not now that he knew the truth.

He smothered an echo of the qualm he'd felt around seven o'clock, at the thought of her outside waiting for him as usual. It was her job, after all. It wasn't like he was keeping her from the work he'd thought she was doing.

*I run around a lot, picking up loose ends or trying to solve small problems before they become big ones....*

He supposed he fit in the small-problem category.

He'd reached a certain amount of calm during the distraction provided by this new idea. He understood that Josh had done what he felt he had to do. He could even, grudgingly, accept that in the position she'd been put in, Samantha had had little choice but to lie.

What he couldn't accept was his own idiocy. The very idea that a woman like Samantha would be interested in a man like him was ludicrous. That for a short while he'd believed it was even more so.

Shaking off the unwelcome thoughts he stood up for a moment, stretching cramped muscles. He would finish the section delineating the procedure he planned to implement, he thought, and then he would grab a nap. He thought briefly about going home but decided against it. Only, he assured himself, because it would be inconvenient, when he could sack out right here and be back to work in a couple of hours.

He sat back down and started where he'd left off, at stage three. The excitement began to build again as his mind raced, looking for reasons this wouldn't work and not finding any.

Much later he thought he heard something but finished his sentence before looking around. The lab should be empty. Stan had left shortly after obtaining the data Ian had needed from Redstone Aviation. He'd seemed a bit peeved that Ian had asked him to make the call, but he hadn't wanted to stop his work just then. Then Ian had realized it was Stan's golf Tuesday, and apologized for keeping his boss from his standing 2:00 p.m. tee-off time. Stan was very aware of appearances, and the ability to get away to play golf was part of that, Ian knew. He didn't understand it, but he knew.

An explanation of the new idea seemed to placate the man, and he'd asked if there was anything else he could do. At Ian's negative response, Stan had encouraged him to get as far as he could tonight and had left him to work, exactly as Ian preferred.

Ian glanced up at the clock now, and for a moment stared at it, confused. He was certain he'd been working longer than four hours since Stan had left at two-thirty, yet the clock read six-thirty. It took him a moment to realize the entire evening and night had passed, and he was looking at six-thirty in the morning.

No wonder he was stiff, he thought as he stood up. He needed to walk around. And so much for his nap; the building would start waking up itself in an hour or so. Knowing Josh, he was probably already here, and knowing St. John, he probably had never left.

He'd take a walk outside instead, he decided. Some cool, fresh air would do the trick, maybe a cup of coffee, and then he could come back ready to go again.

He locked the lab after him, since no one else was here yet. He yawned as he got into the elevator. He'd walk the perimeter of the building, he thought, and go by the coffee stand across the street that was open early, his usual stop on the frequent occasions when he pulled an all-nighter.

He stepped outside and took a deep breath of unprocessed air, already warm enough to hint at how hot the day would be. He hadn't done this since Samantha had moved in. He hadn't wanted to keep her waiting. His mouth curled sourly at the thought that she would have, in fact, waited as long as it took. It was her job, after all.

He saw a blue car parked down from the coffee place and marveled at the way his heart took a little leap at just the sight of a car that resembled hers.

He forced himself to look the other way as he headed toward the street, not bothering this early to go all the way down to the crosswalk. He would cut across midblock where his desperately needed coffee waited, and if he got arrested for jaywalking, at least nobody could say he wouldn't be safe, sitting in jail.

He stepped off the curb. Heard a car door slam somewhere to his right. Where the blue car had been. He tensed, all the while telling himself it couldn't be her. He kept going. Heard an engine start. Hoped it was the blue car, leaving. The bark of tires told him whoever it was, was leaving almost fast enough to suit him. At the last second he couldn't resist a glance.

It wasn't the blue car.

It was a black van.

It was almost on top of him.

Something grabbed him. Yanked. Hard. He saw the asphalt seemingly rising toward him.

The morning sun blinked out.

# Chapter 11

"Sam?" She looked up to see Josh striding across the hospital waiting room toward her. "How is he?"

"They say he'll be fine."

Josh let out an audible breath. He'd obviously rushed. She wondered how many movers and shakers he dealt with would even recognize him in the worn jeans and faded sweatshirt he'd pulled on to rush to the hospital.

"What's the status?"

"They did X rays, a CT scan and an EEG. The diagnosis is a very mild concussion, incurred when his head hit the curb. He's in good physical shape, which they say will help him bounce back. But they want to keep him a day for observation, just in case something develops later."

"Good. Can't be too careful with that kind of injury, even if it's mild."

"That's what the doctor said, that 'There are no minor brain injuries.'"

She didn't mention that the phrase had chilled her even after they'd assured her Ian would recover.

"Is he conscious?" Josh asked.

"Yes. He never went out completely. He was a little dizzy and disoriented immediately after." She gave her boss a crooked smile. "And cranky, I might add, when the medics kept asking him to repeat the same words every five minutes. But by the time we got here, he was almost back to normal. They said that's a good sign, too, when the symptoms clear up that fast."

Josh smiled back, but it was fleeting. "If you hadn't been there to pull him out of the way…"

She grimaced. "If I'd been there ten seconds sooner, he wouldn't be lying in there at all."

"If you'd been ten seconds later, he could well be dead and we'd be notifying his family."

Josh's quiet words made a chill ripple through her. The image of Ian lying motionless in the street was bad enough. The thought of him never getting up again was hideously worse. That it would have been while she was right there would have been unbearable, and she was honest enough to admit it would only be in part because she was responsible for his safety.

"Any word on the van?" she asked.

"No. But the police have it down as a felony hit-and-run, so you can bet they'll be looking for it seriously."

Yes, with Josh's name involved, she would bet they'd be looking seriously.

Josh gripped her shoulder comfortingly. "You did your job, Sam. He's alive, and he's going to be fine."

She couldn't quite discard the idea that if she'd really been doing her job properly, he wouldn't have been hurt at all. But she also knew there hadn't been much else she could do beyond being there and ready. She'd had no way of knowing they'd try something again, after they'd successfully stolen what they thought were the right disks. And certainly no way of knowing it would happen the first time Ian stepped out of the building in more than twenty-four hours.

"It wasn't a kidnap attempt this time, Josh."

"I know."

It was only two words, but Sam felt the ice in them. She looked at her boss's face and thought that she was very, very glad not to be whoever turned out to be the mole in Redstone. The outsiders after Ian's work would be in enough trouble when Josh found them; the insider who had betrayed them and nearly cost Ian his life would be much worse off.

"Do we have any idea who it is yet?"

"We have suspects. I've put everyone on the team who's in the country to work on it. In the meantime, everybody in the lab is suspect. I haven't even told Stan Chilton what's going on."

Sam couldn't picture the rather fussy man as involved in industrial espionage, but she nodded. And was still puzzled. "Why? Why would they suddenly change and try to kill him? Without him, the project is dead in the water, isn't it?"

"Unless they think they got all they needed when they stole those disks from his house."

She frowned. "He did say they'd get pretty deep into them before they'd figure out they were fake."

"If I know Ian, they'd have to be as smart as he is, too."

"So if they think they have the real deal, why would they…"

Her voice trailed off as the realization hit. She raised troubled eyes to Josh. "Would somebody really do that? Kill him now that they think they have the data, just to stop Redstone from getting there first?"

"When they say business is cutthroat, sometimes it's meant literally," Josh said.

His voice was inflectionless, but Sam wasn't fooled. "You're furious, aren't you?"

"I am," he said calmly, "outraged. Until now I was satisfied with protecting Ian until he succeeded, making their efforts pointless."

"And now?"

"Now," he said in a voice that was all the more frightening for its lack of emotion, "I will bring them down."

"Still don't remember what happened, Mr. Jones?"

Ian grimaced. "Can we stop with the 'Let's see if I can catch him' stuff? And no, I don't remember what happened. I was heading for a cup of coffee, and the next thing I remember is being in an ambulance with a paramedic asking me questions like that."

The young man in the white coat that, with the pockets stuffed full and sagging crookedly, looked rather like his own lab coat, actually laughed.

"You're going to be fine, Mr. Gamble. You may have some occasional residual dizziness or headaches, but if it lasts longer than twenty-four hours I'd be surprised. You're going to be one of the lucky ones."

He opened his mouth to say, If he was one of the lucky ones, he wouldn't be here in the first place, but a shrieking wail made him shut it again. The nurse who had been in to take his blood pressure—every few minutes, it seemed—had explained the woman making the haunting sound had suffered a serious brain trauma. *Lucky* might be the word after all.

"Of course, having your friend around to save your life was pretty lucky, too."

"My friend?"

"The very attractive blonde in the waiting room. She's been quite concerned about you."

Samantha.

It came back to him now, sort of, a fuzzy memory of

her face as she crouched beside him, saying his name over and over.

"She's here?"

"Yes. I'll send her in in a moment, as soon as the doctor says you're okay for a visitor."

Before Ian could think of a good reason to protest, the young man was gone. Ian couldn't blame him. What man in his right mind wouldn't think a woman like Samantha would be very welcome?

A few moments later he heard footsteps and tried to brace himself. And then thought his vision was acting up again when a man walked in. A split second later he realized it was Josh and started to breathe again. Then he stopped when he realized Samantha was on Josh's heels. But he realized this would probably make it easier. They could hardly get into any uncomfortable discussions with Josh right here.

After assuring his boss that he was fine, Ian asked him wryly if he had any pull around here.

"I want out of here," Ian said. "I need to get back to work, while things are still clear in my mind."

Josh smiled. "And you'll get out—" Ian brightened until Josh added "—*when* the doctor says so."

Ian grimaced, but he recognized finality when he heard it.

"Besides," Josh said, "you can't be sure your mind *is* clear just now."

Grumbling, Ian had to concede that point.

"And you'll be safe here," Josh said. "Until we track them down."

Ian blinked. "Safe?"

"It was no accident, Ian." Josh's voice was soft but resolute. "Just like the earlier incident was no accident. Only this time, they didn't intend to kidnap you."

"Then what—" He broke off as the obvious meaning

penetrated his still slightly foggy brain. "You think they meant to kill me?"

"And would have, if not for Sam."

He didn't turn his head, remembering how nauseous that had made him in the ambulance, but Ian's gaze flicked to Samantha. She wasn't looking at him.

"But why?" The only reason he could think of was retaliation for the useless disks they'd stolen, but that didn't make sense. "They couldn't have gotten through the fake data so soon," he said.

"Exactly."

It took him a moment to get there in his current state. That now that they had what they thought was the real data on the Safe Transit Project, their next logical step had been to eliminate the one man who could possibly reproduce it and still beat them to the final product.

"I buried it too deep," Ian said as the logic of it got through.

He'd apparently given them too much good data—albeit from an approach Redstone had abandoned as unworkable a few weeks ago—before he'd inserted the contradictory data that made the whole thing fall apart.

"More likely, you overestimated their intelligence," Samantha said, speaking for the first time. "Brilliant people tend to do that."

"You may have masked it better than you had to," Josh agreed, "but it worked just as you hoped."

"I didn't hope they'd try and run me down," he said wryly, deciding he was better off with that little gap in his memory. Too bad he couldn't have lost a chunk of Samantha memories while he was at it.

"They'll pay for it, Ian. I promise you that. As soon as we find out who's behind this, they'll—"

"But we will know soon," Ian said, brow furrowing. "Or we should."

Josh looked puzzled. "We should?"

"Yes." Ian had to think a tiny bit harder to make sure his words came out right. "I had a Trojan horse put on the disks."

"Have mercy on me, Ian," Josh said. "I can use a computer, but that tech-head stuff isn't my thing."

"Programming isn't mine, either," Ian said. "Stan was busy—he's the best in the lab on computers—so I had Mike in info systems do it."

"What," Samantha asked, "does the Trojan horse do?"

"I don't even know what a Trojan horse is, in computer talk," Josh protested. "Some kind of virus?"

"It's like a virus, but it gives the newly infected computer orders to do something specific," Samantha explained. "Usually something the computer owner wouldn't want it to do."

"Exactly." Ian was a little surprised at her knowledge but wasn't about to say anything now. "In this case it's supposed to notify me when the data on the disk was run through any computer but mine."

"Notify you? You mean, send you an e-mail or something?" Josh asked.

Ian nodded, and was pleased when it didn't bother him. "And send me a...fingerprint of sorts of the computer it's being run on."

Josh went still. "You mean you'll be able to identify where it was sent from?"

"I won't, but Mike should be. It may take him a while, but he says he can figure it out."

Josh let out a long breath. "I take back anything bad I ever said about my computer."

"Get me out of here, and I can see if it's come yet."

"No, Ian. I want to know, but you're not getting out of that bed until you're cleared. I'll have somebody else go to the lab and check."

"It's not at the lab. If you were right about the leak there, I figured it was safer to have it notify me at home."

"Good idea," Josh said approvingly. "And here I thought you weren't taking this seriously."

"I wasn't," Ian admitted, a bit sheepish now. "But I knew you were, and that was enough to make me take some precautions."

Josh's mouth quirked up at one corner. "I appreciate that. I know what a compliment that is."

Ian wondered if he'd ever get used to Josh's easy way of dealing with his employees and acknowledging openly when they'd pleased him.

"I'll have somebody go by the house, then. Sam, you want to handle that?"

"All right." Her voice was inflectionless, but her glance at Ian told him she knew perfectly well this wasn't the solution he would want. "I'll need a password, I assume?"

"I—"

Ian broke off suddenly. Dear God. This couldn't happen. He'd never live down the embarrassment. As clearly as if it had been five minutes ago, he remembered that day last week when he sat down as he always did on Sunday and changed his password for the next week. It had been the day of the baseball game, the day Rand had appeared next door. He'd been in the middle of all those tangled emotions when he'd sat down at the computer. And instead of his usual choice of an alpha-numeric mix, he'd instead picked a name.

Samantha.

"Ian?" Josh asked.

"I...can't remember just now," he said, for the first time grateful for the cover of that knock on the head, knowing neither of them would push because of it. "I change it every week."

"Is it written down anywhere?" Samantha asked.

*It's etched into my brain,* he told her silently. "No. But I'll remember, as soon as I sit down at my computer. I always do."

"Ian," Josh began warningly.

"No, I'm not trying to get out early, I just...can't remember."

"It'll have to wait, then," Josh said, not sounding too happy about it.

"It's armored," Ian said. "The Trojan horse, I mean. They shouldn't find it."

"I'm not worried about that. I'm worried about giving them another shot at you." Josh straightened up, his jaw set. "I'll have a guard posted outside your room."

"Josh—"

"I don't want any argument from you," Josh snapped. "I've had it up to here with this dance. It's over, as of now."

Ian couldn't stop himself from glancing at Samantha. He'd never seen Josh stirred to full anger, and he could tell by her expression that neither had she. This was not the charming, easygoing boss they all knew, this was the hard-nosed, steel-spined man who had built Redstone into a worldwide powerhouse.

"I need a direct connection, not just suspicions. If JetCal is behind this, I want irrefutable proof. And then I'm going to destroy them. *Nobody* hurts one of my people and walks away."

"Now what?" Ian asked, more than a little warily.

Josh looked at him consideringly. "We could put it out that they were successful. Announce your death. That would protect you, at least."

"And risk my parents hearing scmehow? And I do what, go into hiding until you track them down, hoping they don't find me?"

"There are risks," Josh acknowledged.

Ian's mouth tightened. "No, thanks. I'd just as soon help you nail them, thank you."

"Good. Because I'll need your help and cooperation."

Ian didn't like the sound of that last part, but he didn't say it. "What are you going to do?"

"First," Josh said, "I'm going to call Draven."

## Chapter 12

This wasn't the first time Sam had been in someone's home without their knowledge. It wasn't even the first time she'd been digging through someone's belongings.

It was, however, the first time it had ever troubled her overmuch.

Her reason for being here was utterly innocent—to pick up some clean clothing for Ian to wear home, since his shirt had been ripped and his pants muddied yesterday—but still she felt guilty, knowing how angry he was at her. As she went past the cluttered office, and the near-spotless kitchen, a memory of that evening spent with his parents shot through her mind. She'd enjoyed that so much. They'd been so different from anything she'd expected or experienced. She'd found the bemused acceptance they had for Ian, and he for them, the very definition of family at its best.

With a smothered sigh she turned to go down the hall, remembering from the floor plan that the master bedroom was to the left. She passed a spare bedroom that was full of exercise equipment; his fitness clearly wasn't just a lucky gift from Mother Nature. A second bedroom was set up as a guest room. She thought she sensed Juliet's fine touch there, and wondered if that was where they stayed when they were in town for longer than a few hours.

If they ever were, she thought with a smile.

She continued to the end of the hall. The door was half-closed, and she nudged it open. She expected much the same kind of room as the den, a mixture of function and more work, most likely with papers and books piled up as they were elsewhere.

For a moment she just stood and stared. And then she smiled. The smile became a grin as she stepped into another world. She wouldn't have thought Ian's touch would be recognizable, not the way Juliet's had been in the guest room, but it was. From the huge four-poster bed to the bright, cheerful colors in the quilt that covered it, to the equally bright colors in the large painting on the wall, it was a surprise.

Yet it fit him, somehow. Not only was there no trace of the clutter he lived with elsewhere—only a single hardback book on the nightstand, one of the historical books he'd mentioned—but the room was in its own way as charming as his parents. Whimsical, almost, and that was something she never would have guessed at.

Instinctively she was drawn to the painting, which was apparently of a young, rather dashing-looking wizard, decidedly un-Merlin-like. Done in oils or acrylic, she didn't know enough to be sure. But even she couldn't miss the energy and enthusiasm of the style; the brush strokes were powerful and quick, giving the subtle impression that so was the wizard of the painting. The background was in a softer focus, a laboratory of some sort. The figure wore a cloak, of course, but it lacked the traditional stars and moons, and looked more modern somehow. As did the setting, and the man himself, she thought, stepping closer. There was something in those green eyes that—

She cut off her own thoughts abruptly. Took a step back. And realized, belatedly, that the wizard was Ian. It was the glasses, she thought, that had thrown her off. She'd never seen him without them.

For a long, very still time she stood there, just looking. Gradually, something on the edge of her vision drew her gaze downward, to the scrawled signature of the artist in the lower right corner of the painting. Gamble.

She knew instantly it wasn't Ian himself; he didn't have the ego necessary to paint himself like this. Hugh? Juliet? Could be either one, she thought, the style fit their energetic personalities. But if he had this from them, why would he ever doubt their understanding of what he was?

She backed up a couple of steps, to change her view of the painting, to better get the effect of the whole. She sensed she'd reached the bed and leaned back against it. After a moment her attention shifted as something else crept into her awareness. She turned around to look at the bed she was leaning against.

She hadn't realized it was so high. Even at her height she'd have to use the step to get in it comfortably.

The moment the thought formed in her mind she groaned aloud.

"Where is your head, Beckett?"

She stopped short of answering her own question aloud, but she thought it. She didn't think about climbing into any man's bed, but least of all a man who despised her. At least for the moment, she added silently, refusing to acknowledge how much she hoped that feeling was only temporary.

"Get to the job you came for," she ordered herself.

She found the large and only partially full walk-in closet and grabbed the first pair of jeans she saw, refusing to take the opportunity to snoop any further. She took a green shirt

she'd seen him wear before—and remembered because of
how it brought out the color of his eyes—off a hanger and
put it with the jeans. His shoes were still at the hospital
and wearable, but he'd need new socks. There was a small
dresser against one wall, and she pulled open the top
drawer, figuring it to be the most logical. Not that she
expected logic to apply with Ian, but—

Silk boxers.

She stood staring into a drawer full of boxer shorts with
the undeniable sheen of pure silk. And color. Blue, green,
even, back in one corner, red. She reached out with a tentative finger and touched the luscious fabric. It was like
touching soft air, like what she'd thought of as a child
when she'd read about magical beings with gossamer
wings. It was delicate yet incredibly strong, and was warming even under her slight touch.

A barrage of erotic images hit her in a rush. Silk, soft
and delicate, warmed by hot, solid male flesh. The idea
that all this time, the quiet, studious Ian had been indulging
himself in something so sensuous, the feel of silk on naked
skin. That hidden beneath his often staid clothes was
this…

The seeming contradiction stunned her. And suddenly
she understood the male fascination with women's linge-
rie, because the thought of Ian in nothing more than a pair
of these was heating her up in a big hurry. Her silly
thought about the bed had embarrassed her; these thoughts
took her breath away.

In a swift, short grab that was almost desperate she
yanked out a pair of the boxers and stuffed them in the
pocket of the jeans. She dug out a pair of socks, then
shoved the drawer shut, wishing she could shut off the
stream of images as easily.

She headed for the door as fast as she could walk, refusing to admit that what she really wanted to do was run.
At the door she paused, unable to resist a last look at the

painting. But somehow even it looked different now, as if discovering this one secret about Ian had changed her perception of him completely.

She made it out to her car but didn't move to start the engine. With the discipline Draven's long, hard training had instilled, she forced the vivid images out of her mind. If she betrayed herself to Ian, she'd be embarrassed beyond belief.

It was several minutes before she finally turned the key.

Sam had expected the reaction she got when she walked in and announced to Ian she was his ride home. As anxious as he was to leave the hospital, she thought he'd probably rather stay than go with her. He made clear the accuracy of her guess with his first words, spoken as he sat upright in the hospital bed.

"I'll take a cab. Or walk."

"Right. It's only four or five miles."

"I'll go back to Redstone, then," he said. "It's practically around the corner."

"Josh wouldn't let you in the building. Besides, did you forget you need to check your computer at home?"

"No," he said sharply.

Sam took in a breath and turned to face him head-on, her hands on her hips. "Look, I know you don't like this, but neither of us has a choice. It's Josh's orders. And if you don't like this, you're going to like the rest even less."

He drew back slightly. "The rest?"

"I'll tell you when we're in the car. And moving."

Sarcasm tinged his voice. "Afraid I'll jump out and run?"

"Exactly," she said, dead serious.

His wariness increased, but she didn't give him a chance to dwell on what could be that bad. She grabbed up the small bag of items she guessed the hospital was letting him take home, since they'd already added the exorbitant price to the bill.

"Here," she said, handing him the clothes she'd brought, proud that only for a fleeting moment did the image of silk on skin gain a hold in her imagination. "If you want out of here, get dressed."

He looked down at the clothes, then back at her. "You raided my closet."

It was more an observation than an accusation. "I figured you'd want to get out of here more than you would mind my intruding on your space."

If he had differing thoughts on the matter, he didn't voice them.

"Do you need a nurse to help?" No way she was going to help him, not with her suddenly overactive imagination.

"I can do it."

No way was she going to stay here while he got out of the bed in one of those hospital gowns, either.

"I'll wait outside the door," she said.

Still, she stayed close, and kept the door open so she could hear if he had a problem or fell or worse. But a few minutes later he was at the door, looking much as he always did.

"Ready?" she asked.

"Don't I have to ride out in a wheelchair or something?"

"I asked. They said no, they don't do that anymore. That if you couldn't make it under your own steam, you probably shouldn't be released in the first place."

"I'll make it," he said, sounding rather fierce.

"I've got the instruction sheet. And your discharge papers," she said, gesturing with the paper that included a list of symptoms to watch out for, like headaches that refused to go away or blurred vision, and instructions not to drive until cleared by the doctor. A moot point,

Ian observed aloud sourly, since his car was still being held hostage.

Sam chose not to answer that one. "Let's go."

He did make it, although Sam thought he was concentrating so intensely he could have scaled Everest if he'd set that prodigious mind to the task. He insisted on getting into the car by himself and truly didn't appear to need any help.

He belted himself in without reminder. She thought about asking if he'd remembered the password, but decided since they were going there first, she'd know soon enough.

And then, she thought, would come the big explosion.

He couldn't, she told herself philosophically, be any madder at her than he already was. And Rand would be there. That should help. He wouldn't blow up completely in front of somebody else. At least, she didn't think he would. But after this morning, she was no longer sure just how well she could predict the behavior of Ian Gamble.

Deciding he couldn't get any quieter, she said, "I saw the painting of you. It's wonderful."

To her surprise he smiled, an inward-turned smile that looked almost wistful. "It is, isn't it?"

"I saw the artist's name."

"Yes." His voice had that same wistful note.

"Was it one of your parents?"

He looked at her then. "My wife."

Sam barely managed to keep from gaping at him. She had quite literally forgotten the woman existed. Ian never mentioned her, and the file had indicated the marriage was both hasty and short. For an instant she dug through her memory, because he'd not said "my ex-wife" or "former wife." But no, she was sure, there had been a divorce.

"I'm sure you must have known about her." His tone had turned sour now. "Redstone wouldn't send you on a job unprepared."

She recovered herself. "According to the file, you were divorced some time ago."

If he'd been trying to snipe at her, he gave up then. "Yes. What had seemed to her…like that painting at first, soon became dull and boring."

"So she left?"

"We agreed it was a mistake," he corrected. "She was a free spirit, and I was…who I was. I wasn't any better at it than she was, after the novelty wore off. Having somebody around all the time made me crazy."

"You were young," Sam said neutrally.

"Very. We were crazy about each other, but it just wasn't working."

"And now?"

He shrugged. "She's in Europe. Painting. Living with another artist. And happy. I'm glad for her."

"What about you?"

"I'm not carrying a torch, if that's what you mean."

"But you still hang that painting."

He smiled again, that same smile. "Yes. The fact that once, somebody actually saw me like that is not something I want to forget, no matter how inaccurate the perception."

"It's not inaccurate."

She said it before she thought, and when his smile vanished with the tightening of his mouth, she wished she could take it back.

"Infatuated eyes don't always see reality," he said.

Was that aimed at her, personally? Her hands tightened on the steering wheel. She didn't dare look at him. Not when she wasn't sure if she wanted the answer to that question to be no…or yes.

"Are you going to tell me what's hanging over my head now?"

She gave him a sideways look as she made the last turn. He didn't look particularly tense, so she said, "We're almost there. It will keep."

He didn't react when she pulled into his driveway, but then that's what she usually did when she brought him home. But when she got out when he did, he looked at her across the roof of the car.

"I'll be fine, thank you," he said.

"Let's go see if that notification is on your computer. Josh will want to know ASAP whether it worked or not."

"Oh. Sure."

He went straight to the computer next to the window the burglar had broken into—Josh had had it fixed already, she noticed—as soon as they were inside. It came to life the moment he touched the keyboard. She'd noticed before that he left it on all the time. She guessed it was because when an idea struck, he didn't want to waste time booting up.

With a few quick mouse clicks an e-mail program opened, and then he glanced over his shoulder at her.

*Great. He doesn't even trust you to watch him do this, in case you try to snag his password.*

With a smothered sigh she turned away. The moment she did, she heard him type something so quickly she couldn't even be sure how many letters it was.

A knock came from the front door. Ian looked startled, but Sam knew who it was; Rand must have seen them arrive from next door.

"I'll get it," she told him, and Ian turned back to the screen. He seemed immediately engrossed, because when Rand came in he didn't even look up.

"It's here," he said a moment later.

She walked to look over his shoulder then, and he let her, as if he hadn't cared in the first place. Not that it mattered. What she saw made no sense to her, anyway.

"Does it tell you anything?"

"Other than that they got this far? No, nothing that I understand," he said, making her feel a bit better. "But Mike encoded it, so he should be able to get something out of it. May take a couple of days, but at least we know someone is running the data and the program from my disks.''

Only then did he seem to realize they had company. His face went expressionless as he saw Rand, his only reaction to look from her face to Rand's, as if comparing them now that they were here together.

''Let me reintroduce myself, for real this time,'' Rand said, holding out a hand. ''Rand Singleton. The other half of the team that tried to pull a fast one on you. Although you should have known Josh wouldn't just let it go,'' he added, in an almost teasing tone.

His easy acknowledgment of the situation seemed to defuse the tension. At least Ian shook his hand.

''I won't introduce myself, since you probably know more about me than I do,'' Ian said.

*Well, maybe not,* Sam thought.

''What I do know about you tells me you're not one to blame somebody for something they had no choice about,'' Rand said.

For a moment Ian looked chagrinned, and then he said in a wry tone, ''What makes you think I'm blaming somebody else?''

Rand considered that for a moment, his brow furrowed. Then slowly he smiled. ''Ah.''

*Ah, what?* Sam wondered. *What was that supposed to mean? Men! Half the time you can't get them to talk, but then when they do, they don't make much sense.*

''So, is that what we needed?'' Rand asked, gesturing at the computer screen.

''It's what we were waiting for,'' Ian said. ''Whether it's what we need I don't know. Mike will have to tell you that.''

''I'll take it in to him, if you like, while you guys get settled in,'' Rand said.

"Settled in?" Ian's gaze flicked from Rand to Sam, then back.

"Nice job." Sam nearly snarled it at her loose-lipped partner.

"Uh-oh," Rand said, looking at Sam. "You haven't told him yet?"

"Told me what?" He focused on Sam, his entire demeanor suddenly wary. "Is this what you wouldn't tell me before?"

"I think I'll just take this and—"

"Oh, no, you don't," Sam said, cutting Rand off. "You did it, you stick around for the fallout."

Rand drew back with a deep sigh. Sam took an equally deep breath and turned to face Ian. "They know where you live, Ian. And it's already been in the news that you were released from the hospital today."

That startled him. "It was? Why on earth would I be in the news?"

"You were a hit-and-run victim, and you work for Redstone. That's enough to make the papers in this town," Rand said.

Sam frowned as Rand tap-danced around the truth, just as she had done with Ian for so long now. But she didn't see any other way to do it; her perceptions may have been rattled, but she was still fairly sure Ian wouldn't stand for what had really been arranged.

"Josh thinks, and we agree, it's not safe for you to stay here," she told Ian. "Especially now that they know they didn't kill you or even seriously incapacitate you."

Somewhat to her surprise, he took that part well.

"Oh. I guess that's true."

"Good," Rand said briskly. "You want to put that thing on disk, or print it out? Maybe you should do both, just to expedite things."

Ian did as Rand asked, quickly. Rand took the disk and the rather lengthy printout from him.

"Don't get mugged for it," Ian said dryly.

Rand grinned. "I'll try not to."

*Well, great,* Sam thought. *Now they're joking buddies, but I'm still persona non grata. How'd that happen?*

She shoved the rather whiny sounding thought aside. "You want to pack a few things?" she suggested.

"Okay."

He said it with resignation. But Sam knew there was one more hurdle coming. And despite his apparent capitulation about not staying here, Sam doubted the rest was going to go down as easily.

"Some inconspicuous grocery bags would be best," Rand put in. "And now, I think, since we're fairly certain you're not under observation at the moment. You should be able to get next door without being seen."

*Well,* that *did it,* Sam thought as Ian's expression froze.

"Next door?

He enunciated the words carefully, as if to make sure he'd heard correctly. And then he turned his gaze on Sam, like the business end of a laser.

"With you?"

She braced herself, knowing he would probably hate her even more before this was over.

Knowing it would be a small price to pay for keeping him safe.

# Chapter 13

Ian thought he hid his emotions fairly well when Samantha answered him in an expressionless voice.

"That was Josh's plan, yes." She dodged his gaze, as if she felt a bit of a coward invoking the boss's name. "Time is a factor here, and we don't have time to discuss this."

"Make sure you take all you need," Rand told him, "because you can't be running back just because you forgot something. You might be spotted."

He was feeling a bit beleaguered. In fact, he felt like telling them both to get the hell out of his house. But he didn't. Because deep down he knew, no matter how much he wished otherwise, that they were right. So he fought down the urge, and quashed the roiling, confused feelings he couldn't even begin to sort out just now.

"What about my work?" he asked instead.

"You get a vacation," Samantha said.

Ian frowned. "I can't take a vacation now. I just started work on what could be the answer to our whole problem."

"Then we'll hook you up to the lab from next door, with your laptop," Samantha said. "We'll tell your boss you're working from home. It'll have to do."

For a long, silent and rather strained moment Ian just looked at her. "I suppose it will," he said at last.

Rand and Samantha exchanged glances, and he thought he saw her give him a barely perceptible nod. And knew it when Rand said, "I'll get this off to Redstone. I'll be in touch later to see if you need anything."

"You can come cook for us," Samantha said.

"Be nice to me and I might," Rand said with a grin.

And then he was gone, leaving them alone together.

"He cooks?" Ian asked.

"Exquisitely," Samantha answered.

"Useful."

"Rand is useful in many ways. It almost makes up for the times when he's a total idiot."

He didn't pretend not to understand. "When were you going to tell me, Samantha? After you were sure you had the coded message?"

She drew back as if he'd swung at her. "Is that what you think?"

"I don't know what to think. So tell me."

"I waited," she said tightly, "because I'm a coward."

He blinked. "What?"

"I knew you weren't going to like the idea, and I didn't want to get into a nasty confrontation with you."

"Now there's an understatement."

He purposely didn't clarify which part of her statement he was referring to. She hesitated a moment, and he thought he saw pain flicker in her eyes. But then she was all business, as he would have expected from a member of the vaunted Redstone security team.

"Start gathering what you need. I'll get a couple of grocery bags."

She turned on her heel and walked toward his kitchen.

He watched her go, with that leggy stride that made his pulse quicken. With a silent curse at a body that responded despite his confused emotions, he began to gather some essentials.

"I've got three bags here," Samantha said as she came back from the kitchen. "Will that be enough?"

Thankful for her neutral tone, he turned to look at the pile he'd built so far. "I think so," he said. "That's it."

She glanced from his face to the pile of books, folders, computer printouts and disks, then back to his face. "Do you think you might want to pack some clothes? Maybe even a toothbrush?"

He felt himself start to flush. "I was getting to that."

He paid little attention to what he did grab in the way of clothing, barely remembered to toss in a razor and a spare pair of glasses. Then he grabbed the laptop he only rarely used, made sure he had the power cord and stuffed it into a carrying case. By the time he was done with that, he had himself under control.

At first, when they stepped inside the house next door, he was startled. Mrs. Howard had been a collector, and her home had shown it, with shelves and display cases full of figurines and knickknacks. It had all been far too cluttered and loud for his taste. The living room had held so much floral furniture and so many little tables that he'd always felt like the proverbial bull in a china shop. Now the sight of a room with bare walls and only a sofa, a single table and a lamp startled him.

*Of course,* he realized. *Why furnish a place that's only a front for your undercover assignment?*

That sour feeling knotted his stomach once more, and when Samantha brushed past him with the bags she'd been carrying and set them on the back of the sofa, he grimaced. He didn't think she'd seen, but then she turned on him.

"Look," she said sharply, "I don't care how angry you are at me—" She stopped abruptly, grimaced herself and started again. "That's not true. I do care. But right now it doesn't matter. The only thing that matters to me is that you be all right. And I'll do what I have to to ensure that."

He wanted to ask why it mattered to her, but he wasn't sure he wanted to hear her answer. He gave himself an inward, scornful smile when he realized it was because he was afraid of being a fool again, afraid of believing she meant what she'd said in the way he would like her to mean it.

He would not be a fool again.

Sam saw Ian's expression harden, as if he were steeling himself against her. And it dug into her gut in a way she'd never felt before. In some small part of her mind she realized that in order for her to hurt him, he had to have cared, but that didn't make her feel any better.

How could she explain to him that she'd meant what she'd said literally, that it had become so very important to her that he be all right? She felt…centered when she was with him. She could talk to him as she never could to anyone else, even Rand. Perhaps especially Rand, with his near-constant teasing.

But she'd hurt him, simply by doing her job.

"I'm sorry, Ian," she said softly.

He shrugged, not looking at her. "It's my fault as much as yours. I should have known better."

She frowned. "Known better?"

"Women like you don't hang with guys like me. Not by choice, anyway."

"Guys like you?"

"Geeks. Nerds. You know."

Sam drew back slightly. That's how he saw himself? "We call them propeller heads," she said.

His head snapped around as he stared at her; she had his full attention now.

"Let me tell you a story," she said, her voice tight,

"about a misfit. A gawky, gangly girl who was a foot taller than any girl in her class, and most of the boys. Who had hair so white kids taunted her, calling her 'ghost,' or 'albino.'" She saw by his expression he knew what she meant. "A girl who had the additional burden of being smart enough to intimidate most of the boys. A girl who was, in a word, a freak."

Ian winced, but she went on doggedly.

"When she grew up, things changed. That same girl found that the boys who had laughed at her had become men who flattered her. Men who seemed to think she should forget how cruel they had been, just because they were being nice now."

"I'm sorry, Samantha," Ian said, with a note of quiet pain in his voice that gave her pause. But she had to finish, now that she'd begun.

"Don't be. It taught me that most of the men who flatter me now would have been among those who'd laughed at me then. They'd never have given that kid a second glance." She shook her head, lowered her eyes. There was no way he could understand the way she'd felt. "Sorry. I'm not even making any sense."

"Yes, you are," he said vehemently. So vehemently that her gaze snapped back to his face. "I spent my life being the weird one. The one who scored high on IQ tests but flunked basic courses. The one who always got in trouble because my school projects were too off center."

He took a gulping breath before going on.

"The one who had no friends because I was seen as too studious, too smart, too shy, too quiet. Now that it's a buzz phrase, I get praised for being able to think outside the box. Then it was hell."

He understood, Sam thought, staring. He truly understood. He'd seemed infinitely comfortable in his own skin, but she realized now that he'd had to fight his way to that peace just as she had. That he bore his own scars, no less deep and painful than her own.

The blurting out of such personal revelations made her feel both closer to him and more awkward around him. And it seemed to affect him, too; as if by tacit consent, they both backed away from the high emotions.

They busied themselves getting him settled in, both seemingly relieved to keep the conversation on the surface. She tried to think of it as if he were a roommate moving in temporarily, but that didn't work; she'd never had a roommate who'd made her pulse jump the way Ian could. So she tried instead to play it as if it were Rand moving in to complete a job. That, too, was a miserable failure; the sisterly warmth she felt for her old friend bore no resemblance to what she felt for Ian.

Whatever that was. It seemed she could only think about it in terms of what it wasn't. And it wasn't like anything she'd ever felt before.

*Lord, you can't make sense even to yourself,* she thought.

With renewed effort she quashed her rebellious thoughts and concentrated on acting as if this were just business. She bustled around, showing him where things were, a notepad in her hand as she made a list of things he might need that she didn't have.

"I'll make Rand pick them up," she said, hoping her cheerful tone didn't sound too forced.

Ian blinked. "I'm not even allowed to go out?"

She stifled a sigh. "For the moment, no. Until we know exactly who's behind this, it's for your own—"

"—good. Right. Sure." He eyed her rather balefully. "Aren't you good enough to keep me alive on the outside?"

It was Sam's turn to blink at the surprise attack. But before she could respond, Ian shook his head and let out a compressed breath.

"Sorry. That was…pointless."

Interesting choice of words, Sam thought.

"I'm sure Josh wouldn't have hired you if you weren't good." He looked suddenly thoughtful, much as she imagined he must look when something unexpected happened in his laboratory. "I suppose that explains it," he murmured.

She wasn't sure she was supposed to respond, but did anyway. "Explains what?"

He blinked and rejoined her plane. "Why you seem to sense things you couldn't possibly see."

"Such as?"

He looked momentarily discomfited but said only, "Things going on behind you, or out of your range of vision."

*Like you watching me?* she thought. But she knew better than to ask just now.

"That bothers you?"

"It offends my scientific sensibilities, to believe in that kind of instinct."

"It could get me—and possibly you—killed not to believe in that kind of instinct." He drew back slightly. Sam shrugged. "Like it or not, that's the way it is, Ian. This was not an accident."

"But it's so insane."

"Yes. But still fact. I know you're upset with me. And I'm the first to admit you have the right. So you can make this a pain from beginning to end, or you can make the best of it, knowing it's only temporary. Your choice."

For a long, silent moment he just looked at her. She could almost feel that prodigious intellect working, and she wondered what he was thinking, what facets of this complex turn his life had taken that he was turning over in his mind.

"I believe," he said finally, "a truce is in order."

Sam suppressed the urge to let out an audible sigh of

relief. "I think that would be wise, if we're going to get through this without going crazy."

*Not that I won't, anyway,* she admitted ruefully to herself.

Maybe Rand was right. He was always saying she needed to address her dearth of social life. Maybe if she had, she wouldn't have been so quick to be fascinated by the decidedly unusual Redstone inventor.

Then again, she thought as she watched Ian jam a hand into that thick, gleaming mop of hair, maybe she still would have.

This time the sigh escaped, but it was one of disgust. And aimed solely at herself. Ian gave her a sideways look, as if he were pondering the wisdom of having offered that truce.

"I'll get my stack of menus," she said abruptly. "For tonight, we might as well order in."

Ian nodded. "Anything but pizza, please. That cold piece I had…whenever it was…didn't sit too well."

For a moment Sam wondered if he was having residual effects of the rap on the head, but he seemed fine. Then she realized the cold pizza had probably come some time in the middle of his work marathon, and he simply didn't remember when.

"I'll handle it," she promised.

But when she went to pick up the receiver of the cordless phone, she wondered if she was going to survive this job. And for the first time in her career with the team, she didn't mean physically.


Ian felt a little bit like a puppy, waiting for his food bowl to be set down in front of him. He was hungry, and whatever Samantha had ordered smelled great.

"We're going to have to do something else," she said rather fretfully. "I don't want to draw too much attention to us, and having food delivered every night is going to do just that.''

"It's only been two nights. Besides, I have it delivered all the time,'' he said.

"My point, exactly,'' she said. "If the deliveries stop at your place and start up here, anybody who's been watching wouldn't have to be a genius to guess you might just have relocated.''

He couldn't really argue with that logic, so didn't. Instead he followed her into the living room, where she'd flipped on the small TV Rand had brought this afternoon. She plopped down on one end of the sofa, the only seating in the sparsely furnished room. That left him only the other end, which put a scant two feet between them, hardly far enough for his comfort.

"You didn't have a TV before?'' he asked, more for something to say than out of real curiosity.

"No.''

It took him a moment to figure out that she'd been too busy watching him to be watching television. But now that he was under her nose constantly, that had changed. The realization brought back all the painful memories, and he lapsed into silence as they ate, letting the news be the grim soundtrack for their meal.

After the news they settled on a documentary on extreme weather, something he was surprised to find she had a real interest in. He made himself focus on it, conscious of the effort he had to make not to steal glances at her. Conscious, and annoyed.

How could he still be so fascinated with her, after what she'd done? How could he still be so drawn to her that it was a battle not to sneak looks at her, like a schoolkid with a secret crush?

He tried to tell himself it was simply that she was a fascinating woman, that any man would be curious about her, that any man would want to know more about a woman who looked like Samantha and was a part of one of the best, most lauded corporate security teams in the country. It was natural, he thought. Women were fascinated by men who held dangerous jobs, so why shouldn't it work the other way around?

He almost had himself convinced that was all it was when, his guard lowered by his musings, he took that glance at her.

She was asleep. Her head pillowed on her arm, her long legs drawn up on the sofa beneath her, she was by all appearances sound asleep.

She was also beautiful. Not that she wasn't always, but there was something about her in this vulnerable moment...

*Vulnerable.* A word he would never, ever apply to Samantha in a waking moment. She was too strong, too competent, too alert—

Alert.

Well, not at the moment. If he wanted to slip the leash, this was obviously the time. But did he?

He jerked his gaze away, feeling suddenly on the wrong end of a conundrum. If he didn't believe there had been an attempt on his life, why was he wary about walking out the door right now? And if he did believe it—as he grudgingly admitted he should—then what right did he have to be angry at Samantha for trying to protect him? Especially when she'd been under orders from a man he himself would find very difficult to disobey.

It wasn't what she'd done, he argued with himself, it was how she'd done it. It was the lying, the sneaking...again done at Josh's behest.

*You should have known Josh wouldn't just let it go.*

He supposed Singleton had been right. He should have known. Anybody who knew Josh's reputation for protecting his people should have realized the man wouldn't stop doing that simply because one of those people didn't like it.

And really, Josh hadn't gone completely against his wishes. He'd accommodated them as best he could, Ian supposed. Keeping the protection at a distance, instead of hovering over his shoulder at every moment.

The protection.

His gaze slid back to Samantha. He tried to think of one man he knew, had ever known, who would resent having Samantha in his life, even under deceitful circumstances. He couldn't think of a single one.

As he looked at her, he even felt a qualm at how tired she must be. She had probably been watching over him all night and grabbing sleep when she could, he guessed, when he was in the lab at Redstone. Besides, it probably took energy to maintain the false front....

Agitation rippled through him. Maybe he should slip that leash Josh had fastened him to. Maybe he should take advantage of her weariness instead of feeling sorry for her.

He got to his feet. Maybe he should—

Too late.

The moment he'd stood up, she'd awakened. And not just sleepily opened her eyes, she'd come awake totally alert and ready to move. He could tell by the way her body went instantly taut, the way her legs uncurled from under her. And he was certain he'd barely made a sound.

"Light sleeper?" he asked wryly.

"I'm used to sleeping with one ear open," she answered.

"Handy in your line of work," he said, careful to keep his voice neutral.

"Yes," she agreed, equally neutral. She waited, and he wondered if she was expecting him to say something else. When he realized she was still slightly tense, it irritated him. "I agreed to a truce, so you don't need to act like I'm going to snap at you."

"Maybe I think I deserve it."

Something in her voice told him she meant it. She felt guilty for what she'd done. He wasn't sure how that made him feel. It should make him feel better, shouldn't it, to know that she felt badly about lying to him? Then why did he still have that sense of loss? As if he'd really had something to lose, instead of just an illusion?

Samantha let out a long sigh. "I'm going to say this once more, Ian, and then it's a closed subject for me. I'm sorry I had to lie to you."

"Josh said you had no choice in the matter."

"He sent me in undercover, yes. But still, Josh is... understanding. If I'd thought about that, I could have gone to him and told him I couldn't lie anymore. Not to you."

Ian's breath caught in his throat at her emphasis on that last word. He told himself not to be a fool again, not to assume she meant what his heart wanted to hear.

*Ask her.*

He could almost hear his mother chivvying him, as she had so often when his innate reserve and shyness silenced him.

*Ask her.*

"Josh is..." he began, then stopped and had to try again. "Wouldn't he ask...why?" It was as close as he could get to flat out asking her why this case was different from any other she'd handled. He was afraid, he guessed, that she'd say it wasn't any different.

Samantha grimaced slightly. "He's very perceptive. He probably wouldn't have to ask."

He wasn't going to escape, he realized. It took him a moment to gather his nerve and take the plunge. "I guess I'm not very perceptive then, because I have to ask. Why not to me?"

For a long moment she just looked at him. Her eyes seemed to bore into him, as if she were seeing to the very core of him. Then she said softly, "I think you know the answer. You just don't trust me enough to believe it."

His breath caught once more.

"If it's any help," she added, "It's never mattered before. I've done my job, and never cared about what anyone thought, because I knew I was doing the right thing."

"And now?" he barely managed to ask.

"I still know I'm doing the right thing. But I do care about what you think. I care a lot. And nobody's more surprised about that than I am."

*Except me,* Ian said silently. And when she looked away, he was almost relieved.

## Chapter 14

It should have been easier.

Sam rolled her shoulders, aware of the tension that had settled at the back of her neck. It should have been easier with Ian here under the same roof. She didn't have to watch for him, didn't have to sit up for hours spying on his house, didn't have to worry about timing trips to pick him up. She was able to simply lounge here in the living room and keep an eye on him as he sat at the table they'd set up in the dining room for him to work on. The only thing she had to worry about was her daily sweep of the house and phone lines for bugs; it was much safer for them to use scrambled landlines rather than too-easily monitored cell phones for regular communications with Redstone. Yet she was more tense now, on the third day of his residence here, than she'd ever been while watching him from a distance.

*You just don't like the feeling of being watched yourself,* she admitted ruefully.

And he *was* watching. Intently. And it unsettled her, to

feel that itchy sensation and look up and find those unwavering green eyes fastened on her. Once she caught him with his glasses off, looking at her, and wondered what he saw. Wondered if she looked different to him that way, unfocused perhaps. And if he liked it better that way....

Sam sat up straight, resting her elbows on her knees and her head in her hands. She was losing her mind. That's all there was to it. She'd never wanted to bail in the middle of a job before, but she wanted to now. Wanted just a few hours alone, to think, to sort out the chaos cascading around inside her.

"Are you all right?"

Her head snapped up at the sound of Ian's voice, very near. "Fine," she muttered, hiding her surprise that he'd been able to get so close without her hearing or sensing his approach.

"You don't look fine," he said frankly.

"Thanks for the observation." *Especially since it's your fault,* she added snappishly to herself.

"Cabin fever?" he asked, sounding almost genuinely sympathetic. "I know you'd normally be outside in the garden today, since it's Saturday."

She gave him a sideways look. "Where'd all the cheer come from?"

He shrugged. "Work always takes my mind off my problems."

*My problem* is *my work,* she thought sourly. Which made her say aloud as she leaned back on the couch, "I thought work was your problem."

"No. Answers are my problem. Work is...satisfying."

"Even when you hit a dead end?" She asked with a curiosity that had been growing since she realized how much of his work was truly trial and error.

"It's worth it, for the times when it all comes together." Unexpectedly, he sat down beside her. "I've been meaning to thank you."

Thank her? He'd agreed to a truce, not to forgiveness, so what was this? "For what?" she asked cautiously.

"Solving my problem."

She blinked. It took her a moment to remember the problem he'd told her about, that the explosives-sensitive material wouldn't stick to metal.

"How did I do that?" she asked, mystified.

"Your soaker hose."

She blinked again. "Okay, now I'm totally confused. What does my soaker hose have to do with your adhesion problem?"

He grinned at her, and for a moment she forgot to breathe. "Do you remember I said the sensor material sticks okay to lead?"

She nodded. "And lead is too heavy and toxic to line a plane."

"Yes. But the *ribs* in the plane could be coated with lead without adding a prohibitive amount of weight, or presenting danger of its own."

"Okay. But what does that have to do with—" She broke off suddenly as an image formed in her mind, of the evenly spaced ribs of an airplane and the evenly spaced folds of the soaker hose. "You mean it can react to the space in between?"

"Looks that way, so far. It takes a slightly more concentrated application, but I think it's going to work. We were just too focused on lining an entire plane with it. We never thought about using more of the sensor and spacing it out."

She stared at him. "And you got this from just looking at a garden hose?"

"Ideas are where you find them."

It amazed her, that kind of leap from an everyday object to the solution of a totally unrelated problem.

"Outside the box," she said, almost to herself. "I could

never do that.'' She knew she was bright, but her mind was logical, and for the most part linear.

"I could never do what you do."

She winced inwardly, thinking he was once more referring to her having deceived him. As if he'd read her thoughts, he said, "I meant the bodyguard thing. The security thing in general. Any more than I could be a cop."

"I couldn't be a cop, either. Working for Redstone is much better."

Ian smiled. "Working for Redstone is better than just about any other job."

On this, at least, they could agree.

"Josh told me he pulled you out of Alaska."

She nodded. "I was working in the resort division. Redstone Sitka," she said, and went on to explain how Josh had rescued both her and her brother.

"Tell me about Alaska," he said. "I've always wondered if it's as wild as they say."

"It is. And not, in the bigger cities. But you still get from nonwild to wild faster there than anyplace I've ever been."

"I've seen photos and documentaries, and it all seems so incredible."

"It's all true, and they don't capture the half of it. It's vast, beautiful and awesome in the original sense of the word."

"You sound sorry to have left."

"I am, a little. But not sorry to have left the job there, or to have brought Billy here. I do want to go back, someday. With enough time to see what I want to see."

"You mean with all your traveling for your job, you'd still do it for fun?"

"Sure. I love seeing different places and people. Didn't you like it, when you traveled with your folks?"

"I suppose when they were dragging me all over, I was too young to appreciate it."

This was nice, Sam thought as they talked. The strain she'd been feeling just slipped away. She snuggled deeper into the cushions of the sofa, feeling herself slowly unwind. He was right here, she didn't have to be watchful, to worry, she could relax a little, just for a moment or two....

She awoke slowly, wondering why nobody had ever thought of a heated pillow before. This was wonderful.

The inanity of her own thought brought her awake enough to realize that the heat she was feeling was indeed beneath her cheek, but it was not a pillow.

She went very still, suddenly aware of the slightest of movements, as if someone were stroking her hair. In the moment of her realization the movement stopped. A tiny sigh escaped her at the loss, surprising her.

"That was nice," she murmured, wishing she could go back to that sleepy state, and only half-aware she was speaking out loud.

"Yes, it was."

Ian's voice was soft and husky above her, and the sound of it made her shiver. She tried to sit up, wondering how on earth she had ended up in this position. He moved at the same moment, and she had to stop to avoid smashing her head into his chin. They wound up face-to-face, Sam in an awkward, uncomfortable position that she barely noticed. The room was nearly dark; he'd also apparently turned out the lamp, and the only light was spillover from the dining room.

Ian had taken off his glasses. She'd seen him so rarely without them that it always stopped her breath to see those vivid green eyes with no barrier of glass. And now those eyes simply took her breath away, because they were hot with a look she couldn't mistake.

"Samantha," he said, his voice barely a whisper this time.

"Yes," she said simply, unable to stop the answer her

heart, mind and blood wanted to give him. All the reasons why this was insane, all the reasons why it was stupid, all the reasons why it was reckless vanished in the heat created in her by that look.

"Samantha," he said again, and suddenly it was the most beautiful name she'd ever heard, so much better than the "Sam" everyone else called her.

He moved closer, then hesitated. Afraid he would change his mind, afraid he would remember he was angry with her and pull away, Sam lifted her head to close the last little gap between them.

She had barely a moment to think about how warm and firm his lips were before fire erupted in her. She heard a soft, needy sound she thought was him, but that could have been her. In fact, it must have been her, because it sounded exactly the way she felt—hungry and wanting more of the rich, male taste of him.

He might have hesitated in the beginning, but there was no indecision left in him now. He deepened the kiss, probing, tasting, teasing her tongue with his until she was dizzy with it. She felt her fingers digging into his shoulders, and the feel of the taut muscles there reminded her of that day in the garden when he'd blown any last remnants of her preconceptions about "the professor" to bits by pulling off his shirt.

That image in her mind made it suddenly imperative that she feel that bare skin, and she moved her hands down to his waist to tug his shirt free. Then she slid them up under the cloth, stroking satin skin stretched over hot, taut muscle. Memories of a drawerful of silk boxers seared through her mind, and she wondered if her fantasy of those moments was about to be fulfilled. The thought made her heart begin to hammer even faster.

He murmured something against her mouth she didn't catch, but it didn't matter. His voice, heavy and thick with desire, was all she needed to hear. She kissed him back harder, deeper, reveling in his response, in the way he groaned low and harsh, in the shiver she felt ripple through his body. He pressed her back onto the couch, and she welcomed the solid feel of his weight.

And then they were clawing at each other's clothes, or maybe their own, desperate to be rid of them. Ian's shirt went flying, Sam's followed, then the rest. Sam only paused long enough to fulfill that fantasy thought, to touch him through silk warmed by his own heat. It was as erotic as she'd imagined and then some.

Skin to skin now, it still didn't seem enough to her. She wanted him closer yet, and opened her mouth to ask, but the only thing that came out was a whimper of need.

For a moment Ian stopped. When he sat up and simply stared down at her, Sam was afraid he was having second thoughts. But when he said in an awed tone, "God, you're beautiful!" the tension faded as quickly as it had arisen. She looked at him hovering over her, at the solid shape of his chest, the ridged abdomen and flat belly, and below, where she couldn't help shivering at the jutting flesh mere silk couldn't have restrained any longer.

"So are you," she whispered fervently, making him color slightly.

He moved then, slowly, much slower than he had been, as if with great purpose. And it didn't take her long to realize what that purpose was; to drive her utterly mad. Methodical, his father had called him. She'd never thought at the time how that word could be applied to other things; but now, as he lingered over every inch of her, kissing, tasting, caressing, stroking, until she was wild with aching, pulsing need, she thought that methodical could be a very good thing.

And then she stopped thinking much at all as Ian found and caressed that center point that sent heat billowing out in waves. She cried out his name, heard him suck in a breath, then mutter an apology. Before she could gather herself to ask what on earth he was apologizing for, he was sliding into her, showing her just how ready her body was by the ease of his entry. At the same time she had the most wonderful sense of fullness, of being stretched by his rigid flesh, so wonderful she couldn't hold still, but lifted her hips, demanding more, then more.

Ian shivered in her arms as he slid home. For a long moment he didn't move, just held her hips tight against his as he groaned low and deep in his chest. She shifted slightly, spreading her legs wider, and he slipped another fraction of an inch into her, just enough to make her cry out his name once more.

He called her name in turn then, and began to move. Slowly at first, in long, smooth strokes, but then, as his control began to shatter, in harder, fiercer thrusts. Sam thrilled to the sight and feel of him, her studious, brilliant, shy professor, driven to this.

It was her last coherent thought. Her own formidable control deserted her as her body drew tighter and tighter, until she thought her nerves must be fairly humming. And then Ian shifted slightly upward, and the first sliding caress of his body over hers from that new angle sent her flying. She convulsed almost violently, every muscle seeming to tighten as wave after wave of incredible sensation swept through her. She grabbed at Ian, as if only he, who had brought her to this, could save her from flying into a million pieces.

In the next moment she heard him cry out her name, felt him pulsing inside her, felt the shudders that rocked him. He collapsed atop her, gasping.

Naked and still entwined, they lay for a very long time, and eventually Sam wondered if he was as afraid to speak as she was. She had no idea what to say, nor had she any illusions that what had just happened made things any easier. The opposite, in fact, she was fairly certain.

"Ian?" she finally said.

"Could we," he said, confirming her guess, "just not talk yet?"

"Gladly," she agreed. And simply lay there, savoring what could never last, the weight and feel of him both on her and in her. And all the while knowing she was only postponing the inevitable.

## Chapter 15

Worrying about Draven, Sam thought, was an exercise in uselessness.

*It's Draven,* she told herself. *The man can take care of himself. And then some.*

She knew what was really wrong. Knew she was focusing on Draven to avoid thinking about what had happened between her and Ian. If there was anything messier than sleeping with the subject of a job, she couldn't think of it.

If there was anything sweeter than what she'd found in Ian's arms, she couldn't imagine it.

With a sigh she glanced through the lowered, translucent shades at Ian's house next door. Ian hadn't noticed, at least not yet, that his home wasn't vacant anymore. That someone had arrived much as he himself always had, in a car that looked suspiciously like Ian's own.

Sam had. But then, she'd known it was coming. She'd known the plan. And for the first time she wondered if Draven could pull it off. She knew it was hardly the first time he'd masqueraded as someone who was a target, putting himself in the line of fire. She knew he'd dealt with much worse, but she was still edgy, because the disguise part didn't seem to be as good this time. He was driving Ian's car, he would be keeping Ian's erratic hours. He was dressed as Ian dressed—minus, she guessed with a rush of heat, the silk boxers.

She fought down her body's reaction and forced herself to concentrate. Draven was even wearing a wig that was a fair simulation of Ian's hair over his own short, dark hair, yet something didn't work.

She played back the scene in her head, when Draven had arrived at the house next door this evening—thankfully while Ian was getting coffee in the kitchen. She couldn't pinpoint what was wrong. All she knew for sure was that it had been too obvious that the man wasn't Ian.

It was odd. Draven was usually better than that, adopting even the smallest mannerisms of the person he was pretending to be. And now that she thought of it, he did have Ian's easy, loping kind of stride and his habit of pushing back that thick hair down pretty well. So why wasn't he as convincing as he usually was?

She pondered it for a moment, wondering what she should do. Finally she went to the phone and called Rand.

"I'm on my way," he said, answering his cell.

"Fine," Sam answered. "Tell Draven to be careful."

"He always is," Rand said. "Anything in particular?"

"Just…something off. I don't know what."

"Off?"

"Not as convincing as usual. I'm worried."

For a long moment Rand didn't answer, then, softly, he said, "Maybe you're just a bit too familiar with the subject?"

"That's…" Her voice trailed off. Could he be right? *Too familiar?*

Visions of last night—and this morning—flashed through

her head, like some erotic movie stuck on fast forward. Oh, yes. Very familiar.

"Sam?" Rand said.

"Forget it," she muttered. She hung up, not caring what she was giving away to her perceptive partner. And turned around to see Ian there, watching her.

Her mind raced, wondering if she'd said anything betraying. Or humiliating, she added to herself ruefully.

"Did you want some?" he asked, gesturing with the mug of coffee he held.

"No, thanks."

She wondered if she sounded as awkward as she felt. And it only got worse as Ian stood there looking at her. After a long moment during which she got the strangest feeling he was withdrawing, he turned and walked without a word to the table where his computer was set up. It was as if the man she'd spent that long, passionate night with no longer existed.

There was no doubt about what he'd heard. Samantha was worried, to the point of distress. And he couldn't imagine what it would take to distress the usually unflappable Samantha.

*Tell Draven to be careful. I'm worried.*

Or maybe he could imagine, he thought grimly.

It came back to him with the power of a kick in the stomach, what he'd completely forgotten in the heat of the passion that had erupted between them. He'd forgotten the moment when he'd heard her talk about the legendary Draven. The awe, admiration and respect that had rung in her voice. The sound of a woman in love.

His own thoughts then haunted him now.

*A woman like Samantha could only love a dangerous man like Draven, as far removed from he himself as any man could be.*

If she loved Draven, why had she turned to him? Was

he just a temporary, convenient substitute for a man she, for whatever reason, couldn't have?

He stole a glance at her from where he was sitting at the dining room table. He fought down the gut reaction he had to her, the welling up of a fierce need he'd never thought himself capable of feeling. The need that had so stunned him last night, sweeping over him until he was out of control, until even his strength of mind was no match for it.

She was pacing the living room. He'd never pictured her as a pacer. It only seemed to emphasize the accuracy of his guesses. He stifled a sound that would have been half laugh, half groan. He'd actually been nervous about tonight, with the awkwardness of any man wondering if the huge step taken in their relationship last night would be repeated tonight. He had his answer now, it seemed.

A bitter sort of pain welled up inside him. He'd been a fool to think anything else. As sweet, as hot, as incredible as it had been, it had been an illusion. Perhaps she'd only been able to turn to him when Draven was out of sight, off to wherever the man was this week.

If he'd been his father, or more like his mother, he'd go confront her. Ask her exactly what last night had meant to her. But he wasn't like them. Nor was sure he wanted to know.

Maybe she'd just lie, he thought. She was certainly good enough at it.

But the moment he thought it, he discarded the idea. She'd meant what she'd said last night, about never lying to him again. He couldn't doubt that. If he was wrong about that, then he was even more obtuse about people than he thought.

He tried to focus on the computer screen before him. He'd received yet another e-mail memo from Stan, pushing for details he didn't have yet, but thankfully Rand had told him not to answer anything work-related, that everyone had been told he was ill.

*How like Stan, to pester somebody even when told they're sick,* he thought wryly.

He switched over to his latest data entries and tried to concentrate. But the work that had always been his refuge failed him now, and he found himself repeatedly staring into space—or at Samantha. And for once that spooky radar of hers didn't seem to be working; she never looked up.

Or maybe she was just avoiding meeting his gaze. Maybe she regretted last night so much she couldn't bear to even look at him.

Even as he thought it he had a hard time reconciling the idea with Samantha. He couldn't picture her wasting time with regrets. Not that he didn't think she could feel them, she simply wouldn't waste time dwelling on them. Nor would she take the fainthearted way out of avoiding the issue—and looking at him. Samantha was nothing if not straightforward....

Except when she was lying.

The reality slammed into him once more, and he got to his feet in a reaction he couldn't control. He couldn't go on like this. Not only was it wearing, and distracting him from his work, it was making him crazy. And he wasn't sure who he was angrier at, Samantha or himself.

Determined now, he strode into the living room. He didn't know what he was going to say, or how to say it, he only knew this had to be faced.

When she saw him, her pacing came to a halt. He thought he saw her eyes flick toward a window, then she turned away, continuing her traverse of the room. Instinctively he looked at the same window, wondering what she'd seen.

He'd never realized what a good view this house had of his own. And it never would have occurred to him to think of it now, had he not known that Samantha had been placed here exactly for that reason. The thought of her sitting here, watching him, sent his already confused emotions into free fall again. He turned to confront her, then stopped dead as something caught the edge of his vision.

There was someone in his house.

He whirled back to the window. He hadn't been wrong; there was someone there. A man, moving through the living room office as if he belonged, casually, unconcernedly. As Ian watched, he sat down at one of the computers. There was something odd about the man, something familiar....

Why wasn't Samantha doing something? She had to have seen him—that had to have been why she'd glanced that way. Shouldn't she be calling Redstone, or rather, knowing her, charging over there herself as she had the night of the burglary? Yet she simply paced, restlessly, as if under stress, but did no more. Was she waiting for someone else to do something? She hadn't called anyone; he would have heard.

He frowned. There was the distinct possibility that the ever-active Samantha wasn't doing anything because she'd been ordered not to. Which meant she likely knew what was going on in his house. Likely knew who it was over there.

It hit him then, with an almost palpable force.

*Tell Draven to be careful.*

Slowly he turned once more. Samantha was watching him. No longer pacing.

"It's Draven, isn't it?"

He waited, knowing on some level that a great deal depended on her answer. She hesitated. Then, with a barely perceptible sigh, she nodded.

"He's pretending to be me, isn't he? That's why he seemed familiar. He's dressed like me, in my house...and is that some kind of wig he's wearing?"

"Your hair is fairly distinctive," Samantha said, her tone so neutral it was impossible for him to read anything at all into it.

"Tell me about it," he muttered. "I've had to live with this mop all my life."

"Your hair," she said, not so neutral this time, "is great."

That distracted him for a moment, because there was no doubting the sincerity of the unexpected sentiment. But he didn't let himself get sidetracked.

"What's going on over there?"

"He's not messing with your work," she said. "He's just…"

"Trying to act like me," Ian said. "That's obvious. But why is—" He stopped, wondering why the obvious hadn't occurred to him before now. "Bait," he said softly. "He's acting as bait, isn't he? To lure out the people after me?"

Her lack of an answer was an answer in itself. The man she loved—or at least longed for—was setting himself up, putting himself in danger, for his sake. That it was his job mattered little to Ian; the idea of another man, any man, dying to protect him while he waited safely on the sidelines, didn't sit well with him.

He'd never thought much about having any kind of code of honor. There hadn't been much call for such a thing in his quiet, rather staid life. But if he had one, he thought, this would most definitely go against it.

"It's the best way, Ian," Samantha said quietly.

"Oh? Then why are you so worried? I thought the great Draven could take care of himself."

"He can."

Ian thought he saw a faint touch of color rise in her cheeks. His stomach plummeted. So he'd been right about her feelings for the chief of the Redstone security team. And now that he was next door, was she no longer able to deny that Ian was merely a poor substitute? Was that what was behind her seeming withdrawal?

"Why did you sleep with me?"

Samantha blinked, clearly startled by the abrupt change of subject. Or by the volatility of the new topic; he wasn't sure which.

"For starters," she said after a moment, "because I wanted to."

"Why?"

Recovered now, she studied him for a moment. "Fishing for compliments?"

"No," he said, "I don't expect that. But if I'm…pinch-hitting, I'd like to know it."

She frowned. "Pinch-hitting?"

"For who you really want to be with."

She drew back slightly, her eyes narrowing. "Ian, I don't know what you—"

A rap on the door made Ian start, and cut off Samantha's words.

"It's Rand," she said, heading for the door.

"What's he doing here?" Ian asked, turning to follow.

"Since he's already established to the neighbors as a visitor, he's visiting."

"But in reality he's…?"

"Backup. Just in case."

"For Draven?"

She nodded. "Josh isn't taking any chances. He doesn't like how this has gone down so far."

"I'm not overly fond of it myself," he muttered, drawing a sharp glance from her in the moment before she pulled open the door.

It was indeed Rand Singleton, looking as cheerful and casual as any real guest. He had a duffel bag over his shoulder, was carrying a paper bag that looked as if it held a bottle of wine, and a plastic grocery sack.

"Food?" Samantha asked, brightening at the sight of his burdens. "You're going to cook?"

"Hello, Ian. For Draven's sake," Rand added to Samantha teasingly as he stepped inside. "You won't do him much good if you keel over from malnutrition or food poisoning."

"Yeah, yeah," Samantha muttered, grabbing the plastic bag and immediately inspecting the contents. "Oh, heaven," she sighed. "You're going to do your garlic pork chops?"

"If you stay out of my way," her partner said as they headed for the kitchen. "Have you discovered, Ian, that she's not just helpless but a liability in the kitchen?"

"I wouldn't know. However bad she is, I'm probably worse."

"Children, children," Rand said with mock parental concern. "How will you ever survive when you grow up?"

"I plan to avoid growing up, period," Samantha retorted without missing a beat.

"So far, so good, then," Rand returned. It was clearly an old routine with them, this verbal jabbing back and forth. Ian didn't think there was anyone he felt that comfortable with, and he envied them their friendly ease with each other.

"How do you stand it, Ian?" Rand asked with an exaggerated roll of his eyes.

"I try not to think about it," he answered truthfully. For a moment Rand looked at him steadily, with an intensity that made Ian wonder just how much he knew, just how much Samantha might have told him.

Or perhaps he was just perceptive enough to realize something was going on beneath the surface. Perhaps he had that same sort of odd sixth sense Samantha seemed to have about things, that sense that made him uneasy because he didn't understand it.

Maybe it was a requirement for the kind of work they did. He could see where a strong sense of…intuition would be useful. Perhaps it was something they learned by long experience in that kind of work. He thought he could accept that. At least, he could accept it better than the idea that they were born with that kind of intuition. To his logical mind it seemed too inexplicable otherwise.

*His process may be methodical, but the way his mind works—the leaps of intuition he can make—is anything but.*

Samantha's words to his parents echoed suddenly in his head. He'd been too gratified at the time to really dwell on the sense of what she'd said. Intuition? Was that what she thought it was, the, to him, utterly logical thought process he went through?

Was that what it *was?*

Leaps, she had called them. He'd interpreted that as a jump to a conclusion without the necessary logical steps. He had no patience for that kind of thinking, figuring when people who indulged in it happened to be right, it was by chance. But could it be that they had simply gone through those logical steps as he sometimes did, at such a speed that it seemed they'd been skipped altogether?

Yet he couldn't forget those times when Samantha had apparently been aware of his gaze when she couldn't possibly be. He couldn't think of a single train of thought that could explain it. And that still bothered him.

"—like garlic?"

It took him an instant to tune in to Rand's query. "What? Oh. Yes. Yes, I like garlic."

It seemed utterly ridiculous to Ian to be discussing something so mundane, when next door a man had set himself up as a target for his sake.

A man Samantha clearly had very strong feelings for.

Ian tried to quash his recalcitrant thoughts as Rand went back to unloading his bags.

"Anything from Mike?" Samantha asked her look-alike.

"Not yet. He said they have a lot of security on their system, so it's taking a bit longer to dig through the garbage to the real source of the message. But I told him that was his priority now, everything else could wait."

"Good thing you work for Josh Redstone," Samantha said with a grin.

Rand chuckled. "Yeah. Not many places where a mere security peon can give orders."

Ian couldn't think of anybody who would dare term the much-vaunted Redstone security team as mere peons, but he didn't say so. Instead he asked, "Is that suspicious? That they have that much security on their computers?"

Rand shrugged. "Not necessarily. Some corporate systems are really tight, others are Swiss cheese."

He was aware of Rand and Samantha trying to include him in their easy repartee over the meal but couldn't make himself join in. And for once it wasn't only a sense of his own social awkwardness that stopped him; he simply had too much on his mind. His work, the man next door and Samantha, all three combined to draw all of his attention.

It wasn't until after the meal, when Rand picked up his duffel bag and disappeared into the up-to-now unused third bedroom, then reappeared sans the bag, that he realized the significance of it. Rand was moving in.

It made sense. If he was going to be backup, he would need to be close by.

It also made the question of what would—or would not—happen tonight moot. If Rand was anything like Samantha, and he had to assume he was, he would never miss what was going on.

He felt a strange combination of frustration and relief. Frustration at the removal of any chance at experiencing that wonder again, relief at the removal of the chance of rejection. A chance that had increased exponentially, it seemed, with the arrival of Draven. The irony of the fact that Draven was impersonating the man Samantha had turned to because she couldn't have him wasn't lost on Ian.

When coupled with the subtle yet unmistakable edge of tension in both Samantha and Rand—he was seeing the Redstone security team on alert, he realized—it made for a long and relatively sleepless night for Ian. Which was followed by yet another night just like it, even though he was exhausted from his efforts to concentrate on his work despite the constant, overpowering presence of two trained operatives ready to move at any sign of trouble.

He couldn't imagine living like that, he thought as he lay staring at the ceiling in the bedroom he'd been using. It was hard enough being on the periphery.

He wondered who had the shift tonight. He'd heard them discussing it that first night. Since they had both been handling the night shift before this, it was a split as to who got the break of sleeping at night. They ended up doing something so ordinary it took him by surprise; they flipped a coin.

He shifted position, pounded at his pillow, even knowing it would make little difference. He hadn't thought about how difficult Samantha's job must have been, staying awake all night to watch him.

To watch over him.

Somehow when he put it like that, it didn't seem quite so distasteful. More…protective, less like spying. Still, he surprised himself with his uncertainty about how he felt about a woman protecting him. He'd never thought of himself as a traditionalist, but still, he wasn't quite comfortable with the idea. Which was ridiculous; it only made sense. She was the one with the training, the experience. And the idea of reversing their roles was absurd; he was hardly qualified.

It suddenly struck him that perhaps he was uneasy because the woman in question was Samantha. That, at least, made sense to him. He didn't like it, but it made sense. What he felt for her—whatever it was—was something so new to him he had no idea how to deal with its existence, let alone how to turn it off. So naturally he was concerned, and he didn't like the idea of her risking herself for him.

Then again, he didn't like the idea of Draven, a man he'd never even met, risking himself for him, either. So maybe it was more complicated than that, maybe—

"Sam! This is it!"

Rand's shout cut through Ian's thoughts like a razor-sharp blade. He sat up. Reached to flip on a light, then stopped himself, afraid he might alert someone they didn't want alerted. Heard running footsteps go past his door then down the stairs.

By the time he'd pulled on some jeans and shoes, it was quiet upstairs. He raced down the stairs, stopping at the bottom to listen. He heard nothing but silence.

It had to be something at his house. He ran to the window he'd looked out before, when he'd first seen Draven. The house was dark and quiet.

A movement caught the corner of his eye. He looked to the left, saw two darker shadows in the shadow of the honeysuckle between here and his house. The honeysuckle Samantha had no doubt trimmed to give her better access, he realized suddenly. Shaking off the irrelevant thought, he peered at his house once more. And heard the faint sound of breaking glass.

This was indeed it.

## Chapter 16

The target should be most vulnerable with his hand through the hole he'd made in the glass, right...about... now, Sam thought.

"Now," Rand whispered, on the same beat with her thoughts.

They had taken the first step when Rand suddenly grabbed her arm and held her back.

"A number two. Up front," he whispered. "I'll take him."

Sam merely nodded, keeping the chance of being heard to a minimum. Rand moved quickly, yet in utter silence. She paid him scant attention, knowing he could handle whatever he found.

They'd alerted Draven, not that it had been necessary; he'd already known. And now she used the small walkie-talkie she carried to let Draven know there were two attackers.

He didn't acknowledge.

Her instincts, already humming, now kicked into high

gear. She could hear sounds from the back of Ian's house, and concentrated on her own man, edging forward with exquisite care. She knew Rand would be monitoring and would have heard Draven's silence, so she didn't use the little radio again; she was too close. She rounded the corner of the house and went quickly to the rear slider, which had been pried open.

She heard a thud from inside, then a grunt. Something crashed, like a pile of something knocked over. She stepped inside, crouched for a moment, peering around the shadowy room. Another thud, and now she could tell it came from the front of the house. Rand's man, she guessed, being taken out of the picture.

Then she spotted a large, bulky shape in the corner near the stairway. A harsh, muttered curse in an unfamiliar voice issued from it. The shape seemed to split, then recombine. The curse came again, laced with pain this time. Draven, she thought, making it clear to the intruder the folly of his life choices.

"The stairs!"

Draven, yelling, just as a sudden movement above spun her around. A third man? She started to move quickly. But before she could get there the figure leaped over the stair rail, down onto the two men struggling below.

Sam ran; as good as Draven was, this could distract him for a crucial second or two. In the darkened room it was hard to tell exactly—

Light flooded the room. For a split second everyone, even the combatants, froze.

"You've got the wrong man, idiots!"

Sam's heart leaped to her throat. Ian. And for the first time in her career with Redstone security, she was paralyzed, unable to act.

But Ian's unexpected intrusion gave Draven the distraction he needed. He moved with quick, efficient skill. In moments his original attacker was facedown with Draven's

knee on his kidneys, and the man who had swooped down
from the stairs was jammed against the wall with an iron-
strong forearm a fraction away from crushing his wind-
pipe.

"What in the *hell* do you think you're doing?" Samantha snapped at Ian, finding her voice at last.

"I may not be Redstone security," he snapped back,
"but if you think I'm going to sit back and let somebody
else risk their life for me without doing a thing, you're
wrong."

"That's what we're trained to do. You're not!"

"Stick to my lab, is that what you mean?"

"I mean stay safe and let us do our job!"

An audible clearing of a throat finally drew Sam's attention. Draven. And the moment she looked at his face
she realized both that this wasn't the first time he'd tried
to get her attention and that he was intrigued by her reaction to Ian's unanticipated, but in the end helpful, inter-
ruption.

"Want to take one of these problem children off my
hands?" Draven suggested mildly to Sam.

"Sure," she muttered, hideously embarrassed that she
had so lost track of the real crisis here. "Sorry."

She went about the familiar task of taking custody of a
culprit stunned by Draven's moves. She barely noticed the
man pinned to the wall looking from Draven to Ian with
puzzlement.

But the man on the floor was quicker. "A decoy," he
said with disgust.

"Sit," Draven said as the man moved as if to rise. The
man glared but did as he was told.

Draven glanced once more at Ian. "Mr. Gamble, I presume?" he asked, reaching up to tug off the wig, revealing
his own close-cropped dark hair. "John Draven."

"I gathered." Ian's voice was stiff, formal. He was
looking at Draven with the same intensity Sam had seen

him turn on some problem in his work, and she wasn't sure what that meant.

Draven seemed to notice it, as well. Sam saw the faintest of creases between his brows before he turned back to the business at hand.

As she had better do, she realized. On some level Sam knew it was a good thing this had become routine, because her mind wasn't focused on the job. Her thoughts were in a tangle. The moment when she'd whipped around, expecting yet another threat and instead seeing Ian directly in the path of danger, was scorched into her mind. It struck terror deep inside her, in a place she hadn't even known existed.

"Gee," Rand said from the entryway as he brought in his own captive, "funny how they always deny everything, isn't it? This guy says he's got nothing to do with JetCal."

*Thank God Rand wasn't in here before, when I had my lapse,* Sam thought, as Rand directed the man he held to sit on the floor beside the others. Draven, at least, was unlikely to tease her about her reaction. His sense of humor was far too subtle for that.

"They always start out that way," Draven agreed mildly.

"I know my rights," the man Sam was holding began.

"Save it for the police," Draven said. Then, with a small smile that was anything but reassuring, he added, "When you finally get to them, of course."

"What's that mean?" Draven's man asked warily.

"Don't worry about it," Rand put in jovially. "Now and then we just rejoice in not having to follow all the rules the police do."

Sam would have laughed aloud at the expression on the men's faces, had she not been so distracted. More often than not, just the realization that they weren't dealing with rule-bound cops was enough to get amateurs like this to buckle.

But she was distracted and more than anything wanted to simply get Ian out of here. At the same time, she didn't want to be alone with him, not until she'd dealt with the tumult he'd caused in her when he'd burst in, putting himself at risk.

"Why don't you and Mr. Gamble go back next door until we get this cleaned up?" Draven said.

It wasn't phrased as an order, but Sam knew it was one just the same. Apparently Ian did, too, because although he hesitated, when Draven looked directly at him he grimaced, nodded and walked out the way he had come in, through the same back slider Sam had followed the first man through.

Sam gave Draven a last look herself. If it had been somebody else, she might have suspected this was a case of get the female out of the way, but she knew better. Draven didn't think like that. This was nothing more than the fact that Ian was her job, and until they were certain the threat to him was over, she had to stay on that job.

Sam went after Ian at a trot, caught up with him at the honeysuckle, but said nothing as they went back to her false-front of a house.

When they were inside, Ian turned around to face her.

"Going to chew me out again?"

"I should," she muttered. "Do you have any idea what a disaster that could have become?" She didn't want to think of what could have happened if that third man had broken free, or worse, come in behind Ian.

"It worked out."

"Only because Draven's as good as he is," she said.

For a moment he did nothing but look at her, studying her much as he had studied Draven. Something, some instinct she'd learned to trust, told her to stay silent.

At last Ian smiled, almost sadly. "He is, isn't he?"

"What?"

"Draven. He's as good as they say."

"He's the best," she said, puzzled by the undertone in his voice. "But that doesn't mean he can't get hurt by the unexpected."

"I'm sorry," he said, and there it was again, that almost sad note. "I was trying to keep him from getting hurt because of me, and instead I just made it worse, didn't I?"

"You were trying to keep Draven from getting hurt?" Sam asked, a touch of astonishment creeping into her voice despite her efforts.

Ian smiled ruefully. "Stupid, huh, the thought of me trying to do that? But my intentions were good. And I see why now."

She was feeling a bit at sea here. "Why what?"

"Why you…feel the way you do about him. A woman like you should be with a man like that."

It finally hit her. And took her breath away. "Ian Gamble," she said slowly, "are you telling me you pulled that stunt because you've got it in your head that I *love* Draven?"

"It's all right, Samantha. I understand now."

She stared at him. She was sure her mouth was gaping open, but it was beyond her at the moment to do a thing about it. She wanted to yell "Are you nuts?" but bit it back. Her, in love with Draven? Hardly. It would take a crazier woman than she to make that mistake.

"I'll start packing up," he said, turning to go. Then he stopped. "I will be able to go home now, won't I?"

"Not until we get the all-clear from…Draven," she finished awkwardly. Ian's assumption made it hard for her to even say his name.

"Oh. Then I guess I'll wait."

He walked into the dining room, and she saw him reach to turn on his laptop computer. Only when he sat down, obviously intending to work, did she give in to the urge to retreat. She ran up to the master bedroom and sank down on the window seat, staring out toward Ian's house but seeing nothing. Nothing except that instant when the light had flared and she'd seen Ian standing there, drawing attention to himself, and giving Draven that precious moment of distraction he'd needed. In essence, he *had* protected Draven, even though he hadn't really needed it.

*You pulled that stunt because you've got it in your head that I love Draven?*

*It's all right, Samantha. I understand....*

This was insane. Beyond insane. Ian, the quiet, studious professor, on a mission to sacrifice himself, to offer himself up as prey to killers in an effort to protect a man he thought she loved?

It made no sense. Men like Ian just didn't do things like that.

*Women like you don't hang with guys like me.*

She drew her knees up and clasped her arms around them as his words, spoken what seemed like eons ago now, came back to her. He thought himself a geek, a nerd. Sam had never seen him like that. She might have thought it before, but once she'd laid eyes on him, that image had been blasted out of her mind forever. He was brilliant, no doubt about that, albeit in his own unique way. He was quiet, almost reserved, but also a man of strong principles.

And however misguidedly, he'd just shown he was certainly no coward.

So why had he done it?

She tried putting herself in his position, which was difficult. It was often her job to protect others. But she tried, tried to imagine why someone not in her position would do what he'd done, and she could only come up with one answer.

The only reason she could think of was caring so much for someone you didn't want them hurt. Like she cared for Billy. Or Josh. Or the team, over and above the job.

Caring so much you did what you could, even if it meant you were protecting the competition.

Her breath caught anew at the implications. And hastily she shoved the door shut on that line of thought. She wasn't going to make that mistake, letting wishful thinking convince her Ian felt something he didn't.

Wishful thinking? Did she *want* Ian to feel that way about her? For that matter, how exactly did she feel about him?

Judging by the way her heart had slammed into her throat when Ian had stepped into harm's way, she was afraid she already knew.

"I'm not in love with John Draven."

Ian froze in the act of slipping off his other shoe as Samantha's voice came from the doorway.

"I'm probably in awe of him, I admire him, respect him, and won't deny he's sexy in a dark and dangerous sort of way, but I don't love him."

What she'd just described sounded to him like every woman's dream man. Or, at least, it was what he'd always heard he wasn't, as some woman explained how he was a nice guy, but...

At last he kicked off the left shoe and looked over at her, standing in the doorway to the bedroom he'd been using. He sucked in a breath and tried to ignore that she was in only a silky-looking shirt that ended midthigh on those long legs. She looked wide awake and unmussed, and he wondered if she'd pretended to go to bed early just as he'd pretended to keep working late, just to keep a floor of the house between them.

"I just thought you should know," she said then, as if his silence had torn it out of her. She turned away, and before he could stop himself he called her name.

"Samantha?" She stopped, but didn't turn back. "Why? Why did you tell me that?"

He thought he heard a soft sigh escape her. "Maybe because I got this crazy idea you were comparing yourself to Draven and coming up short." She turned then, facing him in the doorway, her hands on her hips as if daring him to disagree with her. "Don't ever think that, Ian. Draven's damned good at what he does. But so are you."

"It's hardly the same," he said, although her words pleased him.

"Should it be? What you do takes something special, something that neither Draven, nor I, nor anybody else I know has."

He thought of what she'd told his parents. She'd meant it, he thought with not a little wonder. She hadn't just been placating them.

"Besides," she added, "Draven's also the most alone man I know, except for maybe St. John. It would take more woman than I am to change that."

Ian looked at her for a long moment. "More woman? I don't think so." He wanted to tell her there was no one who was more woman, not in his view, but he didn't dare. And as she looked at him, he had the oddest feeling she wanted to ask what he'd meant, but also didn't dare. And the thought that there was anything this woman wouldn't dare to do surprised him.

He became suddenly aware of where they were, in his bedroom. Aware of the fact that he was barefoot and shirtless. Aware that their chaperon, Rand, wasn't in the house tonight.

Aware that what had happened likely meant the threat was over, and there would be no reason for Samantha to be with him any longer.

The thought made him ache. It made no sense to him, that he could feel this way when he wasn't even sure yet how he felt about her deception. He was working his way through it, realizing she'd had no choice, but still not sure he could accept how easily she'd done it. Practice, he supposed, but that she'd used her skills on him seemed to taint everything that had happened between them.

Everything. Including the hot, passionate night they'd spent together.

The memories swamped him, and he felt an incredible urge to go to her, to begin again, to have at least one more night to remember. At the same time he shied away from the idea, thinking it would only make it more painful when, as was inevitable, she went away. Off to her next assignment, to the next job.

"Ian?"

Her voice was soft, warm, and he abruptly snapped out of the haze, focusing on her as she took a step toward him. One single breath-stealing step.

One more night of memories?

Should he? Did he dare?

He stood up. Samantha stopped. She simply stood there, this beautiful, exotic woman he never would have dared think about as he was thinking now had they not been thrown together by circumstance.

"Ian?" she repeated, her voice husky, as if she were feeling the same inner tightness he was.

"Go or stay," he said hoarsely. "But if you stay..."

"I know," she whispered, and held her hand out to him.

He still couldn't quite believe it, but she was clearly stating her choice, and he wasn't about to try to change her mind. Not now, not when he doubted there would ever be another night for them.

A new determination was born in him then; if this was to be the end, it would be the most spectacular he could manage. And he set about making it so, with the infinite patience and exquisite touch of a man used to dealing in millimeters.

Once more, when she lay naked beside him, he marveled that she was here at all, this beautiful, vital woman who feared so little in the life he found full of reasons to retreat into his work. He let his gaze travel slowly over her, from the pure platinum of her hair to the unexpected fullness of breasts tipped with coral, to the sharp indentation of her waist above hips that flared just enough, the triangle of curls that told him the platinum was indeed her own, and then the legs, those endless, silken legs....

He began his exploration as if he'd never touched her before, and indeed that's how it felt to him—still brand-new and amazing. To have this one woman respond to his touch as if he were everything he knew he'd never been was a heady, luscious feeling. He lingered over each breast and nipple in turn, first with his hands, then his mouth. He traced the long, elegant lines of her body in the same way.

And then, somehow, things turned on him. It began when Samantha reached up and ran her fingers across his belly, causing every muscle there to contract sharply. And then she was touching him as he had touched her, with gentle wonder. Her hands slipped up his sides and over his rib cage. And then inward, until her fingers brushed his nipples and he shivered at the sensation. She didn't miss his reaction, because she returned and gently dragged her nails over the puckered flesh, making him suck in a breath and shiver again.

His body, freshly reminded of this long-neglected activity, began to clamor. But he made himself stay still, loving the feel of her hands on him, loving the very thought of her wanting to touch him like this. Because she left him no doubt that she did want this. When she spoke his name her voice was thick with the same sort of awe and wonder he was feeling.

He loved the feel of her hands, and the sight of her caressing him, so much that he forced himself to lie back and let her continue. And when she moved to straddle him, he groaned aloud, unable to help himself. He could feel her heat and had to set his jaw against the fierce need to move, to lift himself upward those last few critical inches that separated them. Waiting was agony, but he considered it a low enough price to pay when she reached for his swollen flesh and slowly, achingly lowered herself onto him.

She rode him gently at first, then more urgently, until the steady, rocking motion of her body drove him nearly out of his mind.

"Samantha!"

Her name burst from him as she quickened the pace, sliding up and down, pressing herself harder and harder against him each time. Her breasts swayed with every move, tantalizingly, until he simply had to reach up and cup them in his hands. His thumbs slid up to caress her already taut nipples, and to his shock he felt an immediate clench of her body around him. This instant proof of her response to his touch nearly sent him over the edge.

In the moment when he didn't think he could hang on another instant, Samantha arched, her head lolling back on her shoulders. It was the most beautiful sight he'd ever seen, the long curving lines of her body, the feel of her breasts as she pushed them more fully into his hands. He caught the taut crests between his fingers and gently rolled them. They went pebble hard in the same moment her body clenched around him again, this time in a wave of rhythmic contractions, as his name burst from her on a shocked, wondering gasp.

He had little time to wonder at it; the inner stroking of her slick, hot flesh sent him tumbling after her, and he surged upward violently, grabbing her hips to grind her hard against him as he erupted inside her.

Trembling, she sank down atop him, breathing deep and fast. Little aftershocks of pleasure rippled through him, and he wondered how he was supposed to go on; how, now that he knew this was possible, he was ever supposed to live without it.

## Chapter 17

"That's it?" Sam said incredulously.

Rand leaned back in the chair in her Spartan living room and nodded. "They can't come up with any evidence those three have any connection to JetCal or anyone from JetCal. Draven's sure, and so's St. John."

And St. John, Sam knew, never made mistakes. If he said the three men they'd captured weren't connected to JetCal, they weren't.

"Well, great," Sam muttered. "So, who are they?"

"Petty street hoods," Rand said with a shrug. "Long rap sheets, but mostly misdemeanor stuff."

"Then what were they doing—" Samantha cut herself off as Ian walked in from the kitchen. Rand, thankfully, had made the coffee when he'd arrived, and Ian was on his second cup now, as was she.

"What was who doing?" Ian asked.

Rand explained what he'd been telling her, adding regretfully, "Ian, I'm afraid Josh wants you under wraps until we get this all figured out."

"Fine."

He said it so easily, so casually, so unlike his usual protests, that Sam blushed. And she wasn't even sure why. Not, she chided herself, that she hadn't had the thought last night that she wouldn't mind if this went on indefinitely. But sooner or later it would end, and then what? Rare was the man, even in this day and age, who could easily accept her chosen career if he himself had a more...normal life.

Then again, Ian's life—or at least his work—wasn't exactly normal by most standards. But that didn't mean he would be able to, or even want to continue what they'd found here. And she knew enough about bonding under stress to realize that when the threat was over, there might well be little left of the attraction they'd felt.

She looked at Rand thoughtfully. He'd been there, once. With a woman who'd worked for Redstone Aviation, someone he'd rescued along with her young son. It had happened before Sam had joined the security team, but one night on a long, lonely stakeout he'd told her about it. By way of warning, she'd thought, like the big brother she'd come to consider him.

Rand's romance had fallen apart once the situation was resolved. The woman had married someone else within a few months. Even Rand had admitted he wasn't sure how much of it had been genuine feeling, and how much of it had been that he'd fallen hard for the little boy.

"I don't envy whoever it is when Josh finds out who sent those clowns," Rand said.

"What will he do?" Ian asked.

"Add them to the list of people who sadly regret underestimating him," Rand predicted cheerfully. "Ticking off Josh Redstone is a sure road to misery."

"You make him sound vengeful," Ian said.

"No. And that's the beauty of it. He doesn't go after

vengeance, only justice. He gives them a choice, but makes it very hard for people to do anything but the right thing.''

''He's his own kind of irresistible force,'' Sam added with a smile that felt a bit rueful to her. Ian looked at her as if he knew what she was thinking, that not being able to say no to Josh was what had both brought them together and put a wall between them that she wasn't sure they could get past.

A rather musical beep sounded, and Rand shifted to look at the pager on his belt. Sam saw him go still as he looked at the number.

''Mike,'' he said. ''When did you last do a sweep?''

Sam hesitated. ''Yesterday,'' she admitted, hoping she wasn't blushing. She usually did a sweep every night, but last night she'd been quite pleasantly otherwise occupied. She didn't dare look at Ian; the memories of his quiet but intense passion were already threatening to swamp her, and Rand knew her too well. ''I'll do another right now.''

Hastily she got up and retrieved the bug detector from the cabinet she'd put it in. Rand hovered over the phone until they knew the phones and the room were clean. The instant she nodded, he dialed.

''Singleton,'' he said into the receiver. Just by watching his expression Sam knew that Mike was giving Rand his usual dose of tech-talk. Rand stood it for nearly a minute before he cut in. ''Bottom line, Mike.''

Rand listened, then frowned.

''You're sure?'' he asked. Then, after a pause while he listened, he sighed. ''All right. Call Draven and let him know. He'll tell Josh.''

When he hung up, he looked at Sam and grimaced. ''It's JetCal.''

Ian frowned. ''Are you saying the message the Trojan horse sent to me was from JetCal, but those guys who broke in weren't?''

''Exactly.''

"Which means what, that there's more than one party involved in this?" Ian voice rang with obvious disbelief.

"It's hard to believe there's one company out there stupid enough to try and pull this on Redstone, let alone two," Sam muttered.

"Isn't it, though," Rand said grimly. "But unless Draven or Mike made a mistake, and we all know how unlikely that is, it seems we have a whole new ball game."

"It's no mistake."

Josh sounded weary, but certain, Ian thought. He also looked as if he'd had a very long day. Rand and Samantha had driven Ian in late this afternoon, when Josh had notified them he had some information for them. Ian had tried not to think about it, since he didn't want to believe there was still a threat, but it was clear they were acting as bodyguards.

"JetCal's got the phony disks, but didn't send those guys after Ian?" Rand asked.

Josh shook his head. "Yes. I had a little heart-to-heart talk with Joe Santerelli."

Santerelli, Ian knew, was the CEO of JetCal. Samantha had told him there'd been a civil sort of enmity between them since the days Redstone had nearly put JetCal out of business, but that Santerelli would go this far surprised her. But then, she had admitted, anybody going against a man like Josh surprised her. Few ever won, and besides, he was the kind of businessman you rarely saw these days, and Ian tended to agree with her when she said she couldn't imagine anybody not appreciating him for the wonder he was.

"And?" Rand asked their boss.

"He insists they had nothing to do with the attempts on Ian. And that they never initiated any of this."

"You believe him?" Sam asked.

"I do. Because of what he did admit to."

Something flickered in Josh's eyes, something cool and determined. And Ian wondered exactly what he had done, what hammer he had wielded to get the truth out of Santerelli. Redstone by its size and wealth alone could exert a lot of power, but Josh himself could bring to bear even more, by the sheer force of his determination—and the fact that there were people all over the business world who owed him a great deal.

Rand and Sam both stayed silent, waiting, and Ian followed their lead, sensing this was something Josh needed to get to in his own time.

"We've got a snake to hunt," Josh said at last.

Rand and Sam glanced at each other. And Josh's words, *They never initiated any of this,* echoed in Ian's mind, suddenly making sense. As they apparently had to Rand, as well, who said, "A snake? You mean…in-house?"

A traitor in their midst? Ian thought. A leak was one thing, could even be innocent in a way, incautious words in front of the wrong person, but a traitor? With intent? He felt a rush of emotions, shock, anger, an odd kind of hurt. He could only imagine how Josh felt. The man worked so hard at being the kind of boss people wished for that this must seem the worst kind of betrayal.

"Someone contacted Santerelli," Josh said, his expression grim. "Promised they could deliver Ian's research data, for a price. Sent a sample to prove it."

Ian sucked in a breath; when he'd identified the data Josh had shown him, he hadn't realized where it had come from. Both Samantha and Rand turned to look at him, and he managed to say, "It's for real, as far as I can tell. The initial stages of the real thing, anyway."

Samantha seemed to study him for a moment before asking quietly, "We have to ask, Ian. You know her. Do you think it could be Rebecca?"

He shifted uncomfortably, grimacing. He didn't want to think it could be the earnest young lady, but even he had to admit she had, on occasion, acted rather suspiciously. Still, he hesitated. "I can't really say that," he finally said.

Josh sat up straighter. "If you suspect her..." he began.

"Nothing that definite. I wouldn't want to accuse anybody," he said, emphasizing the last word slightly.

"You're not," Rand said soothingly. "You're just telling us a possible place to look."

Still Ian hesitated. This wasn't his bailiwick, and he knew it all too well after watching Samantha at work.

"When it's somebody from Redstone," Josh said quietly, "you know we'll work as hard at proving their innocence as proving their guilt."

Ian sighed. He knew that was true, that Josh would only accept that someone from Redstone had gone bad when the evidence was insurmountable.

"We caught her loitering around your house one night," Samantha said, making him blink.

"You what?"

After her quick explanation, Ian felt a sinking sensation in his gut. "Maybe," he murmured. Then he reluctantly told them about her suspicious actions, her habit of hanging over his shoulder, wanting to get her hands on his work even before he was ready to enter it into the databank, always staying late, often after everyone else had gone, even the occasion when he'd come in and found her sitting at his computer, with that lame explanation of leaving him a note about her dentist's appointment.

"We checked that when we first started looking at her as a possible," Rand said. "She really did have the appointment, but she'd had it for weeks. Could have told you anytime, so why wait until you were gone and write a note, conveniently while sitting at your computer station?"

"Or she could have told Stan," Samantha added. "Isn't that who she would normally tell if she was going to be gone?"

"She tells me most of that stuff," Ian said. "And more,

things that don't have anything to do with work, personal stuff,'' he added, remembering all the times she'd told him things that had made him vaguely uncomfortable. ''I don't know why. Maybe she's afraid of Stan.''

Samantha looked suddenly thoughtful, but said nothing more.

Josh sat twirling a pen between his fingers, quietly considering, for a long moment. Then he spoke decisively. ''I'll talk to her myself.''

Ian shook his head instinctively, barely aware of doing it. Josh lifted a brow at him. ''You don't like the idea?''

''Not you. If it is her, it's me she's been stealing from. I should confront her.''

Josh shook his head in turn. ''We don't know who she's involved with, if she is, how desperate she may be or what she might do if she feels cornered.''

''If she sees you, she's likely to just clam up,'' Ian pointed out.

''I'll go with him,'' Samantha said. ''We can go after hours, if that's when she's there alone, to minimize my exposure.''

''Might work,'' Rand mused. ''She'd likely not see Sam as a threat, and she might open up to Ian more easily than you.''

Josh dropped the pen. ''All right. But only if you're sure she's alone. We're not positive it's her, and if it's not, then we don't want to tip off whoever it really is.''

Ian drew back slightly; he hadn't even thought of that. But he didn't have time to dwell on it as Sam turned to him and suggested, ''Tonight?''

''Sure. Yes,'' he said, feeling oddly flustered.

''Tonight, then,'' Josh agreed.

Ian could think of other things he'd rather be doing tonight, but Samantha was all business now, and as unapproachable as he would have found her before he'd ever met her. He looked at her, even now finding it hard to believe he'd held that slender, wire-drawn body in his arms, naked and eager. For him. Of all people, of all the men she could have had with a snap of her fingers, him.

That he might have been better off if she'd stayed unapproachable was a thought he didn't want to dwell on.

Sam watched Ian as he crisscrossed the floor of Josh's small, private conference room. She knew he paced when he was working hard on a problem, but she wasn't sure what was making him so restless now.

"Maybe it's not her," she said, thinking he might be upset at the thought of his young intern being the traitor. Or at the confrontation that would take place at any moment.

"What?" Ian looked blank. "Oh. That. Yes, maybe it's not. I'd hate to think it is. She's very bright, it would be a shame."

So that hadn't been it, she thought.

The pacing resumed. She waited a while, then asked, "Wishing you could be back at work in your lab?"

"What?" he said again, stopping to glance over his shoulder at her. "Oh. Yes, I am anxious. I always am, when we're this close to a solution. But I wasn't thinking about it at the moment."

Not that, either? Sam wondered. Then what had him walking the floor like an expectant father, if not the brainchild he hoped to hatch soon? If it wasn't the leak in Redstone, and it wasn't his work, what did that leave?

She had an uneasy feeling she knew. Just as she knew the unfinished personal business between them had to wait until the current situation was dealt with. They had a lot to sort out, including how much of what they felt for each other was based in reality rather than the adrenaline rush of danger, but it was going to take time to do it. And time was something she didn't have at the moment; the last thing she wanted was to bring up the subject only to be interrupted when they got word it was time to move.

Still, she thought with a glance at the intercom on the conference table that would crackle with sound at any moment, she didn't know if she would ever get a better opening than the one he'd just handed her. So, tentatively she asked, "What were you thinking of, then? You were in pretty deep."

He turned to face her then. "You," he said baldly, startling her and making her wish she'd stuck to her instincts.

She sighed. "Still pondering how much you hate me for lying to you, I suppose."

"No. Pondering how much it matters. Under the circumstances."

A jolt of hope stabbed through her. This was the first indication she'd had that he perhaps eventually wouldn't despise her for the deception she'd perpetrated on him. On the heels of that jolt came an uneasiness it took her a moment to recognize.

She leaned back in her chair, her eyes unfocused as she tried to work through the revelation that had just struck her. She'd been so troubled about the idea of him hating her forever that she'd never actually thought about how she'd feel—or what would happen next—if he didn't.

*Like it matters,* she thought sourly as old memories rose up to haunt her. Memories of men she'd been attracted to in the past, men she'd let get close enough to actually think there might be a future for them, men who seemed able to accept that her work was not of the garden variety. But those men turned tail and ran the moment they realized Billy was a permanent part of the picture. The two who had lasted beyond that had eventually had the nerve to discuss marriage, with the condition that she put Billy away and kept his presence in their lives to a minimum. When they realized Sam's devotion to her brother would never change, they too had taken to the hills as fast as they could run.

Would Ian run?

Maybe not, she thought. He had enough grace not to do that. And meeting Billy hadn't seemed to bother him at all. But meeting him was one thing...

She'd often wished she could feel something other than sisterly affection for Rand, whom Billy adored and who had a great deal of patience for the boy's ramblings. But it wasn't there. She'd begun to think that spark, that chemistry would never be there, with anyone.

And then Ian Gamble had been dropped into her life. Or she had been forced into his. And she had learned more about that kind of chemistry than she'd ever thought possible. As unlikely as it seemed, quiet, studious, brilliant Ian was the one who struck that spark in her. He had—

"Speaking of being in pretty deep, what are you thinking about?"

Ian's voice snapped her back to the present. She felt her cheeks start to heat as she thought of how he would react if he really knew what she'd been thinking. At the same time she knew she couldn't deny she'd been thinking of him, not when he'd been so bluntly honest about the same subject.

"I—"

"Now." The word crackled from the intercom, saving her. "The lab is empty except for your target."

St. John's words sounded ominous even to Sam. At least, ominous when you considered that a twenty-year-old woman was the target in question.

"Let's go," she said, admitting only to herself how relieved she was to avoid answering Ian's question. Ian gave her a steady look that made her wonder if he knew exactly what she was thinking. But he rose and headed for the door just as she did.

They took Josh's private elevator down to the lab floor.

The main elevator opened just opposite the main double doors and was clearly visible from inside the lab if you happened to be looking that way. From Josh's elevator they were able to reach a side door that was out of the way and get into the lab without being seen.

It was quiet enough to make Sam wonder if St. John had somehow mistaken the woman's presence. *Impossible,* she told herself. St. John simply didn't make mistakes.

They went past the chemical storage vault and the linen room that held lab coats, towels and the like. They passed various different labs set up for various different kinds of work. Sam was curious—avidly curious in fact—about this world that was so strange to her but so familiar to Ian, but now was not the time to ask the myriad questions that popped into her mind.

At the first lab, Ian reached in and flipped off the lights. When Sam gave him a curious look, he said in a low tone, "Might make someone make noise trying to get out, if they're hiding."

Sam grinned at him then. "You want to join my team?"

"No, thanks," he said, so vehemently it stung a little, and her grin faded. Ian didn't seem to notice, just proceeded past empty lab after empty lab, turning out lights as they went.

Sam made herself focus, remembering the layout of the entire department as they approached the junction of two hallways. Ian's office should be to the right, she thought, and quickly confirmed that with him in a whisper.

She stopped him where the halls met, and edged her head around just far enough to see the light that spilled out Ian's office window into the hallway. She held up a hand to indicate he should stay behind her, then began to inch her way around the corner.

Too aware of Ian close behind her, she reached the edge of the window and stopped. He came up against her, and she gritted her teeth against the sensation it sent through her. Ordering herself not to even glance at him, she leaned forward and peeked through the miniblinds that were angled almost too steeply for her to see through. Because of that, it took her a moment to be sure.

Rebecca Hollings was there. Sitting at Ian's desk. Sam watched for a moment as the young woman lounged back almost languorously in the high-backed office chair, then reached out and touched the computer mouse, stroking it almost as if it bore the soft fur of its living namesake. A sad sort of certainty welled up in Sam, and she knew if she was right, it was going to complicate things.

She backed away from the window.

"She's there?" Ian asked, his voice barely audible even to Sam from bare inches away.

Sam nodded. She saw Ian take a deep breath, nod, and draw himself up straight as if setting himself for battle. As, in a way, she supposed he was.

He walked silently to the doorway of his office. Sam hung back, watching the woman inside, wanting to see her reaction.

"I think it's time you told me what you're up to, Rebecca," Ian said, in a tone so gentle it made Sam marvel.

The woman gasped and spun around on the chair she sat in. Ian's chair, Sam thought. Ian's computer mouse.

"Ian! I mean Mr. Gamble," Rebecca corrected, blushing furiously. "What are you doing here?"

"I should be asking you that. It is my office," Ian pointed out.

"Oh. Yes. Well. I…uh…"

Ian let out a barely audible breath. "I really didn't want to believe it was you. Naive of me, I'm sure, but I really didn't want to think a bright, quick mind like yours could be lured by whatever they offered you to betray Redstone."

The young woman drew back, staring. "What?"

"Did you really feel that ignored? Or was it that you

thought it should be easy, that you shouldn't have to earn the attention you wanted?''

"I don't know what you're talking about." For once, Sam thought, the traditional denial sounded almost genuine.

"I'm talking about selling out Redstone. And me."

"Ian, no!" Rebecca exclaimed, apparently unaware she'd again betrayed herself with her use of his first name. "I would never, ever do that! You've got to believe me."

"It's no use," Ian said, his voice weary. "They know."

"Who knows what?" Rebecca asked, bewilderment in her voice now. "What's there to know?"

Ian ran through the list of the suspicions they'd accumulated, ending with, "And they saw you, outside my house that night."

Rebecca flushed. "But that wasn't…anything like that, I swear it wasn't. I was only…I was just…"

The young woman's voice trailed away, and an expression of utter misery distorted her face.

"I didn't. I didn't do any of it. I swear."

Ian seemed to have run out of steam. Sam stepped forward, through the door. Ian turned to look at her. Rebecca Hollings also looked at her and frowned. Her gaze flicked to Ian, then back to Sam. The frown deepened. Sam put a hand on Ian's shoulder. And then she saw, finally, a look of realization dawn in the younger woman's eyes.

"So that's why," Rebecca said, her eyes suddenly brimming with moisture.

Ian looked puzzled. "Why what?"

"Her. She's why you never…"

Rebecca shook her head and turned away. Sam took another step into the room, and when she spoke, it was with a gentleness that made Ian look at her rather oddly.

"Is that what it all was, Rebecca? It wasn't betrayal of Redstone, you were only…following your feelings?"

The young woman looked at Sam, her expression different now, not pained but hopeful. "Yes. I would never do such a thing. Mr. Redstone has been so good to me. I just...I thought..." She sighed loudly. "If I'd known he had someone like you I never would have...."

Her voice trailed away again. Sam glanced at Ian, who by now was looking utterly bewildered. Men, she thought. How oblivious could they be? Then she reached down to the cell phone clipped to her belt. She pressed two buttons in succession. Moments later Rand was there.

"Ms. Hollings has an innocent—relatively—explanation," she told him. She turned to Rebecca. "I suggest you go with him and present it all to his satisfaction."

"Do I have to?" Rebecca asked, a touch of a whine making her voice sound suddenly young.

"Only if you want to keep your job," Rand said, and the young woman dejectedly followed him out of Ian's office and out of the lab section.

When they were gone, Sam turned to Ian. He was staring after the two who had just left. After a moment he turned back to her.

"Would you mind telling me what on earth just happened here? What innocent explanation? She never said a word."

"She didn't have to. I already knew."

Ian expelled a compressed breath. "Knew what?"

"Why she was doing what she was doing around you."

Clearly exasperated, Ian said, "Would you like to enlighten me, if it's not top secret or something? Why was she always in my office and stalking my house at midnight? What was so obvious to you?"

Sam shrugged. "She's in love with you."

## Chapter 18

"That's ridiculous," Ian said as he paced the conference room they'd returned to, to await Rand's report after he finished talking with Rebecca Hollings.

"I thought you'd be glad it wasn't her."

He turned to look at Samantha. "I am. I meant the idea that she's in love with me is ridiculous."

"Why?"

"Because…" He stopped, uncertain how to put into words what seemed so obvious to him. "I'm too old for her," he finally said, knowing it sounded lame even as he said it.

"Hmm," Samantha said. "Now, in this double-standard world of ours, if she was thirteen years older than you, that might matter."

He couldn't think of a way to say what he really thought without sounding as if he was fishing for compliments from her, so he tried another tack. "Whatever gave you this idea in the first place?"

Samantha shrugged. "It was obvious. The way she talked about you, the way she looked at you."

He shook his head, still not quite able to believe this theory. He kept walking, unable to meet her eyes as she explained her incredible idea. He came to a halt in front of a framed photograph on the wall, of Joshua Redstone standing on the wing of the classic *Hawk I*, the first plane of his design ever built. He stared at the photo of the man with the reckless grin. This was the kind of man young women fell for. Not him, not a geeky lab rat with floppy hair and glasses.

"Besides," Samantha said, interrupting his thoughts, "she's young, very intelligent and passionate about this work. Put her in with a sexy, charming guy who's even smarter than she is, it was inevitable."

He wanted to spin around and gape at her. At the same time he didn't dare. *Sexy? Charming? Him?*

"Yes, you."

Samantha's voice as she answered the questions he hadn't even voiced, came from close behind, making him start. With an effort he steadied himself.

"'Smart' I'll give you," he said, fighting to keep his tone even. "But 'charming'? Hardly." He wasn't even going to touch "sexy," he thought.

"I beg to differ. You charmed me, and that's not easy."

He turned then. He had to. Had to see her face, look into her eyes. He had to know if she meant it, or if she was just trying to convince him, for whatever reason.

She was looking at him steadily, those eyes of hers making him feel as if she could see every one of his doubts.

"Or is it the 'sexy' you don't believe?" she asked softly.

He felt heat tinge his cheeks.

"Because if it is," Samantha said, moving even closer, until he could feel the heat of her, until his pulse began to hammer and tightness began to gather low and deep, "I can personally attest that it applies."

"Samantha," he began, but his throat was so tight he couldn't get out another word.

"To me," she said, lifting a hand to place it on his chest, directly over his pounding heart, "you're the best kind of sexy. The subtle kind, the kind that grows on you, the kind that swamps you before you realize what's happening."

"Lord," he muttered, closing his eyes against the intensity of it. Against the stunning shock of a woman like Samantha standing there, saying things like this to him and meaning it. Because he couldn't doubt that she meant every word; it was clear on her face and in her eyes. And he wondered how he had ever missed the tiny edge of unease that he now realized had been there all the time when she'd been acting out her deception.

He opened his eyes again. It wasn't there now. Her eyes were clear and open...and hot. Need surged through him. It was a familiar sensation by now, but for the first time it wasn't accompanied by the thought that he should grab what he could get, because his time with Samantha would end soon. For the first time, emboldened by the way she looked at him in this moment, he dared to wonder if maybe, just maybe—

The door behind them opened. Instinctively, they jumped apart just as Rand strode in. If he realized what he'd interrupted, he had the class not to show it.

"I believe Rebecca," was all he said.

"So do I," Sam agreed.

Rand looked at Ian. "She said she's had a crush on you for months. And that she didn't think there was anyone in your life, so she kept trying to get you to notice she was alive."

Still dumbfounded, Ian shook his head slowly. How could he have missed this? Was he that blind? Or was he so unused to being thought of in that way that he didn't recognize it when he did see it?

Lately, of course, he hadn't been able to really see any woman but Samantha. But that didn't explain the months before, when he'd looked upon Rebecca as merely an energetic nuisance he often wished would simply go away. He felt a pang of guilt. He might not be the most perceptive about people, but he tried to avoid hurting feelings.

His father, he thought, would have known how to rebuff the girl so gently she'd walk away charmed and happy; he himself had just been oblivious and had ended up making the girl miserable.

*And don't forget suspecting her of industrial espionage and worse,* he reminded himself.

"So we're back to square one," Rand said, rattling him out of his bewildered reverie.

"Square one?" he said, pulling his mind back to the situation.

"In other words," Samantha said, "if the leak isn't Hollings, then who is it?"

God, he felt like such a slug. That ramification of Rebecca's innocence hadn't even hit him yet. But it was true; if it wasn't her, then it had to be somebody else.

"Any other ideas, Ian?" Rand asked.

"No," he said.

"Think about it," Samantha said. "I know it's not what you usually put your mind to, but it's a puzzle, like any other project you work on. How do you usually go about it?"

He hadn't thought of it like that. "I usually start by testing each facet of an idea, I guess."

"But how do you decide what facets fit?" she asked.

He thought a moment. "First I eliminate the impossible," he said. "The things I know from past work or trusted research that don't work."

"All right. So we eliminate the impossible suspects. Starting with you."

Ian looked at her. "You're that sure of me? Isn't your job to be suspicious of everyone?"

"From what Sam's said, you're both brilliant and clever, Ian," Rand said drolly. "But I don't think you're devious enough to set yourself up as a target and let yourself end up in the hospital with a concussion."

"Oh."

He couldn't argue with that; that kind of subterfuge would never have occurred to him. Only belatedly did it occur to him that Samantha's praise of his intellect, while warming, had nowhere near the effect that her calling him charming and sexy did. And that thought made him start overheating again, as he did so often around her, much to his embarrassment; he simply wasn't used to reacting like this.

"So," Rand said, "it's not you. It's not Rebecca Hollings. That leaves the rest of the lab staff."

"But none of them works with me as closely as Rebecca did," Ian said. "No one else on the staff really had the access or the awareness of the progress of Safe Transit."

"Are any of them capable of understanding what you're doing?"

Ian looked at Samantha, wondering if she realized how arrogant that made him sound. But what he saw in her face was simple acknowledgment of fact, and somehow that warmed him more than any other praise of his capabilities ever had. No matter about what, he realized, her compliments meant more than anyone else's.

"The entire process? Not really," he finally said.

"Would someone have to understand the whole process to give it away?" Rand asked.

Ian considered that for a moment. "Maybe not. If they just knew what data to steal, how to isolate it on the computer and then copy it, they could probably do enough right to get someone else with the necessary knowledge started.''

''And who could do that?'' Samantha asked.

Ian shrugged and said rather grimly. ''Just about anybody, I suppose. I never thought I'd have to protect my research from the people I work with.''

''Not at Redstone,'' Rand said, looking as grim as Ian sounded. ''And Josh won't stand for it—that you can take to the bank.''

Ian looked at Rand curiously. ''How do you do it? How do you do a job that makes you suspect even friends?''

''You do what you have to,'' Rand said with a half shrug.

''So,'' Ian said thoughtfully, ''that's what makes it worse when it is somebody inside Redstone, then. Because it's like a family member has turned on you.''

''Exactly,'' Rand agreed. ''It's—''

The sound of his beeper cut off whatever his next observation would have been. He glanced down at his belt, then pushed a button on the small black pager.

''No rest for the wicked,'' he said cheerfully, then nodded to Ian. ''I'll leave you to it.''

When he'd gone, Ian looked at Samantha. ''I really don't like sitting here and trying to figure out which person I work with every day is a traitor.''

''Sometimes we all have to do things we don't like doing.''

Even he, unperceptive as he felt just now, couldn't miss the subtext on that one. But she didn't harp on it, just went on.

''Let's go through the R and D roster. We'll start with your division, and begin by eliminating the impossible, as you said. Name by name.''

Ian winced, embarrassed. ''I'm not sure I know all their names.''

Samantha didn't roll her eyes or even shake her head,

she simply picked up the phone and ordered a copy of the employee data from personnel.

"No snappy comment on my social ineptitude?" he asked as she hung up.

She turned and looked at him. For a moment she said nothing, and then, in a seeming irrelevancy, said, "Did you know Einstein didn't know his own phone number?"

He blinked. "What?"

"He was asked why, and answered something like, 'Why should I clutter my brain with things I can look up?'"

It made a beautiful sort of sense to him, but he wasn't sure it should apply to people. And he was certain his parents would insist it shouldn't.

"Unless you work directly with them, there's no real reason you have to know them all," Samantha added. "You've got enough going on in that head of yours."

"My mother," he said wryly, "would say I've too much going on, if I can't remember people."

"Could your mother have created that deicer of yours? Or the computer cable?"

"No, but—"

"We each focus on what's important to us. What's important to you is different, that's all. Not worse, just different."

The tap on the door saved him from having to respond to that. Samantha answered, and moments later was back with a sheet of paper in her hand.

"All right," she said, settling down in a chair opposite him. "Let me see which ones are assigned to your particular lab. Hmm. Mendes, no, he's in the avionics lab, Charles, yes, Marcus, no…."

He watched her as she ticked off the list, fascinated by the intensity of her concentration. He was staring at the sweep of golden lashes and the curve of her cheek when he suddenly realized he should be thinking about the men she was listing.

When she finished, she looked up at him. "Any names seem likely?"

He shook his head. "I just can't imagine it of anyone I know," he said wearily. "But then, I can't imagine it even of the ones I don't really know."

"Well, let's eliminate the impossible first. How about Tran?"

"No. Josh sponsored him to come to America. He would never betray him."

"Okay. Connell?"

"That's one I don't know."

Samantha made a check mark on the list before going on. "Lee?"

Ian shook his head. "He's got three kids he adores. He'd never risk it."

"Rodriguez? Doesn't he have a juvenile record?"

Ian shrugged. "Yes. But he's been straight ever since Josh gave him a chance. I don't think he'd blow it now, after six years."

"Cheng?"

"Another one I don't know."

She made another check mark. "Martin?"

He frowned. "Roger?"

She looked down at the list again before nodding. "Something there?"

Ian hesitated, then shook his head. "I don't think so."

"But something hit you. What?"

"He did grouse a month or so back about some serious money problems. Then suddenly they all seemed solved. But he said a loan came through."

"Timing is right, so it's worth checking," she said.

"I'm not sure. He doesn't really have access."

"Officially, you mean?"

"You mean you think he broke into the system? Or my files?"

"I only mean it's worth checking."

Ian sighed. He *hated* this. He might not have his parents' love of all people, but he hated this suspicion. Even directed at relative strangers, he hated it.

"How can you live like this, suspecting everyone?" He knew he'd asked it of Rand already, but he was still having trouble wrapping his mind around the concept.

"I try to look at it as protecting the innocent more than hunting for the guilty. And the innocent have the biggest stake in the guilty being found."

He sighed. "I still don't think I could get used to it."

"That's why there are people like me," Samantha said with a shrug. "So you don't have to."

She assumed the responsibility so easily, as if it were that clear-cut. And maybe it was, maybe in her mind it was that tidy—there were people who did what he did and people who did what she did. And he knew she would say both were important, just in different ways. Although he had his doubts about himself just now.

"What about Van Owen?" she asked next.

Ian shook his head. "He hung around a lot, but he never really understood what I was doing. Kept talking about how it all was over his head, or Greek to him."

"Could that have been a cover? Playing dumb so you wouldn't suspect?"

Ian frowned. "I suppose, but he wasn't really around that much. And from what I hear, he legitimately is computer-impaired."

The rest of the list went in much the same way. For each person Ian knew, there was a valid reason not to suspect them. As for the others, Samantha agreed that with the hours Ian put in, he would likely know of anyone hanging around enough to know much about his work. It could be someone from another section, but it seemed unlikely to both of them.

But it seemed unlikely to be anyone he did know, either. At least to him.

Finally Samantha sighed. "So you're saying there's no one person who has the computer smarts, the knowledge of what you're doing, access, motive and can remain inconspicuous?"

"I can think of lots who have one or two of those things, but nobody who has all of them."

"How about somebody who is four for five?"

"Nobody I can think of." Ian leaned back in his chair and yawned. "Look, I've about had it. Going over and over this isn't doing any good."

Samantha tossed down her pen. "I can't argue with that. So let's do something else for a while. Put it on the back burner."

It had worked with the adhesion problem, Ian thought, so maybe it would work with this.

"I want to go back to my office. Maybe something will break loose there."

She nodded and followed him out the door of Josh's conference room. He wondered where the boss was, wondered if he, too, was chewing on this problem. From what he knew of Josh, he would be even more determined to find this leak than Samantha, which was saying something.

They went in the front doors of the lab this time, the need for a stealth approach gone now. They headed past the front office, where light spilled out into the corridor— odd, he hadn't noticed that light on earlier—and turned left to go down the hall and around the corner to Ian's smaller, cluttered domain.

They had almost reached the corner when he stopped dead.

*Computer smarts, the knowledge of what you're doing, access, motive and can remain inconspicuous....*

Samantha's words echoed in his head.

*Somebody who is four for five....*

"Ian?"

"Everything but motive," he whispered.

"What?" Samantha keyed off him and kept her voice low, as well.

He turned to face her. "There is one person who has four out of five. Everything but motive."

"Motive's usually the most hidden. Who?"

Ian raised a hand and shook his head to indicate he was thinking, processing. After a moment he leaned forward, peeking around the corner. Then he dodged back.

"My light's back on." His whisper was tight this time.

He felt Samantha tense. Soundlessly she edged around until she was in front of him. She peeked and pulled back, just as he had done.

A sound from around the corner galvanized them. Whatever was happening, Ian was afraid they'd miss it if they didn't move now. Samantha apparently agreed, because she moved quickly, around the corner and down the hall toward his office. Quickly and silently. She seemed to do it effortlessly, while he had to focus on every step to avoid making a betraying noise.

Barely ten seconds later they were at the hallway window into his office. Samantha edged over and peered through the quarter-inch gap between the windowsill and the edge of the miniblinds he always kept closed against the distraction of traffic in the halls.

When she backed away and turned to look at him, her expression was one of surprise. He looked in turn, carefully. Saw the man hunched over his computer keyboard. Saw his research data software program glowing on the screen. Saw file after file disappearing as the man's fingers moved over the keys.

He backed up, his mouth tightening.

He'd been right.

## Chapter 19

It made perfect sense, Sam thought as she stared at Stan Chilton. He knew all about the project, had more access than anyone, she'd heard he was a computer whiz and no one would question his presence anywhere in the lab. The only thing missing was, as Ian had said, motive.

The head of the Redstone R&D Safety Division. This was going to hit Josh hard, she thought. But first they had to wrap him up and deliver him to the boss he'd betrayed.

But Chilton was also part of Redstone, and therefore got the benefit of the doubt. So when Ian took a step toward the office door, she didn't stop him, just moved up to stand just outside the door.

"Ian!"

Sam analyzed the exclamation, trying to determine just how much guilt was in that startled voice.

"What are you doing?" Ian sounded remarkably calm, striking the perfect note of casual puzzlement.

"I was just looking for something," Chilton said. "For my weekly report."

"But you were deleting files."

"Just some old ones," Chilton said.

"Off my computer?" Again, Ian sounded simply puzzled. Sam remembered Ian telling her he'd started keeping his research on his own hard drive rather than the R&D network server.

"Mine's down, so I used yours to access the network."

Plausible, she supposed. But there was an undertone in Chilton's voice that betrayed that he was more stressed than he should be if what he was admitting to was all he'd been up to.

"Those files you deleted weren't on the server."

"You're mistaken," Chilton insisted.

"No," Ian said softly. "No, I'm not. Why, Stan? What was worth betraying us all?"

"What are you talking about?"

"You know what I'm talking about. I'd like to understand why you did it."

"Whatever you're thinking—"

"I'm thinking you're slime, to do this to the man who gave you every chance in the world. I'm thinking you betrayed all of us here, who worked so hard." Sam hung back as Ian hammered his boss, amazed at his cool tenacity. "I'm thinking whatever they promised you, you're still a traitor. Did you know they tried to kill me? Was that with your approval?"

"No! I may hate you, but I would never—"

Chilton's words stopped abruptly.

"Hate me?" Ian asked, his puzzlement genuine this time. "What did I ever do to you?"

"You exist," Chilton snapped, all pretence at denial gone. "All anybody talks about around here is how brilliant, how clever you are. I've built this section up from nothing, but it's you they talk about, you who gets the attention, the credit."

"So you sold out Redstone?" Ian's voice rang with incredulity. "Because you have some idea you're not getting your due?"

"What the hell do you know about it? You've been Josh's fair-haired boy since you got here. I've worked here twice as long, for all the good it does me."

"You're the head of the department," Ian pointed out.

"You just don't get it," Chilton said, and it sounded like he was talking through gritted teeth.

"No, I don't," Ian said. "I never cared about that kind of recognition. The work is the means and the end."

"You always were holier than thou."

"And what are you, Stan?" Ian said softly.

"Rich," the man said bluntly.

"Only if you get away with it."

"Oh, I will."

Sam heard an odd swish of movement, and a sudden intake of breath that had to have come from Ian.

"I never pictured you as a gun-carrying kind of guy, Stan."

Sam's own breath caught at Ian's unmistakable warning. Her heart began to hammer uncharacteristically. This was Ian in trouble. She had to make shooting impossible for Chilton, and fast. She bent swiftly and removed her two-inch revolver from its ankle holster, hit the intercom key on her cell-phone communicator and whispered their location. Then she stepped into the doorway.

Chilton looked over, but the small nickel .380 automatic didn't move; it was still clearly aimed at Ian's chest.

"Don't be any stupider than you have been, Mr. Chilton."

"Who the hell are you?"

"My name's Beckett. Redstone Security." Chilton paled, and Sam pressed her case. "It's over. The rest of the team is on the way."

Chilton's eyes darted to Ian, then back to her face. "I'm

glad you're here," he said. "I've found our leak. It was Gamble all along."

It was, she thought, a good try. If she truly had just happened onto the scene, as Chilton seemed to think, his accusation might have given her pause. As it was, knowing Ian as she now did, she had to stifle a laugh at the idea of him being the leak.

Still, she chose her words carefully. This would all be easier if she could get him to admit his involvement.

"I don't recall seeing your request to carry that weapon on the premises," she said conversationally, nodding at the small automatic.

The slightest pause before he answered told Sam he was thinking fast. "There hasn't been time yet. When I decided to hunt down our leak myself, I knew I'd need to protect myself."

"In that case, now that I'm here, you won't mind handing it over to me. You can have it back later, of course."

His eyes narrowed. "I don't think so."

"Of course we'll give it back. It's your property." She deliberately pretended to misunderstand him as she reached out for the weapon. Carefully. With her left hand. "But for now—"

The man's gun hand jerked dangerously. "Stay back, or I'll shoot!"

*Well, that tears it,* Sam thought. The words were threatening, but his eyes were scared. Sam stopped. Chilton was edging toward panic, and she didn't want to set him off.

"Just remember that once you fire that first shot, you're fair game," she told him. And only then did she move her right hand so that the weapon she held was visible. Chilton went even paler, his eyes wider with fear.

Then he moved, shifting his focus—and the weapon— to Sam.

"Maybe I'll just have to shoot you first, then."

"You plan on killing everyone who's coming through

that door in the next two minutes?'' she asked, noticing as she spoke that Ian was edging by millimeters back toward the wall behind Chilton.

"If I have to."

Bravado, she thought. "You can try," Sam agreed easily, "But I'd be willing to bet I've had a lot more practice at hitting a moving target than you have."

The man swallowed visibly. Ian inched a bit closer, and Sam wondered what he was up to; he was getting dangerously close to Chilton.

"You know," she said quickly, hoping to keep Chilton's attention where it was, on herself, "if you were feeling that way, all you had to do was go to Josh."

"You don't get it, either," Chilton snapped. "He should have seen that I was better. Ian never had to go to Josh. Josh came to him!"

"Did you feel threatened by that, or just by Ian's brilliance?"

Chilton swore, low and ugly.

"Well, you've got Josh's attention now," she said, "after stealing Ian's work and selling it to JetCal. But you're going to regret it."

She gave silent thanks for excellent peripheral vision as Ian moved even closer to the back wall. She still didn't know what he was up to. But he was going to be directly behind Chilton soon, and she hoped urgently he didn't have some silly idea about tackling the armed man.

"I won't. I'll be running things at JetCal, because you can't prove a thing," Chilton said. "I deleted all the evidence that I ever touched his computer. Any good lawyer would get me off."

"What makes you think," Sam said, "that this would ever go to court?"

Chilton blinked. Ian moved ever closer.

"You tried to kill one of Redstone's own. You're beyond the pale to Josh."

"I didn't touch Gamble!"

"But you sent the men who did."

"And they bungled it. He's alive and well."

For a moment Sam's breath caught, fearing Chilton would glance around for the man he was talking about and see that Ian was maneuvering to get behind him. But instead the man smiled, a vicious expression that made Sam's stomach knot.

"But it doesn't matter. I've ruined years of his work. He'll never untangle it now. And there's not a thing he or even Josh can do about it."

Sam really doubted that. She was calmly certain that Ian had a copy of his work safely stashed away, just as before. She didn't even have to look at him to be sure. Which was a good thing, because he was moving again.

"Do you really think Josh would need to have you *arrested* to put an end to your career, anywhere?" she said quickly, keeping him focused on her. "Do you have any idea how far his reach extends?"

A tremor went through the man, and Sam realized he hadn't thought this through at all. He'd no doubt acted in a fit of offended self-righteousness, goaded by a sense of undeserved entitlement, and only now was realizing all the fallout from his ill-advised decision. Still, he tried to recover.

"You can't even prove anything to Josh," he insisted. "And he'll never do anything without proof."

Sam sighed. "Stan, Stan," she said, as if to a recalcitrant child. "Don't mistake Josh's loyalty to his people as stupidity. You're done." She touched the cell phone at her waist. "Draven's been listening this whole time."

It was the final straw. Sam saw Chilton's hand tighten on the pistol's grip. Saw the trigger finger quiver. Regretfully began to raise her own weapon; shooting was the last thing she wanted.

In one instant Sam saw Ian reach out toward the wall

behind the computer on his desk. In the next, a blaring Klaxon blasted through the air.

Chilton jumped. Jerked toward the sound. Sam leaped. Hit him midbody, taking him down with her full weight. His little gun went sliding across the floor under Ian's desk as he hit. Sam's knee came down over his kidneys, and he grunted in pain. She didn't increase the pressure, but neither did she let up; the sight of Ian at gunpoint was emblazoned into her memory forever.

Moments later the thud of footsteps in the outer hall told her the cavalry had arrived. Rand's run slowed to a walk, then a stop as he saw everything was under control. He stared down at Chilton.

"Boy, this is going to tick Josh off in a big way."

"That," Sam said levelly, as she yanked the man to his feet, "is Mr. Chilton's problem."

Another figure appeared in the doorway, tall, lean, black-clad and lethal looking. Draven. For a long moment he simply stood there, looking at the former boss of Redstone Safety R&D. Chilton looked back at Draven, into his eyes. He began to shake, then slowly sank down to his knees on the floor. Draven nodded to Sam, Rand and Ian, then turned and walked away without ever saying a word.

For a few minutes Sam was occupied as they collected Chilton's weapon and Rand called in help to start searching the man's office for anything related to the now solved case of industrial espionage.

Finally she and Ian had a minute alone, and Sam turned to him. "Nice move, Professor. What was that alarm?"

He gave her a lopsided grin that told her he hadn't taken offense at the appellation he normally hated. "My backup alarm. It goes off whenever power to my computer system is interrupted."

She frowned. "Don't most people just have a battery backup that discreetly beeps?"

He colored slightly then. "Yeah. But sometimes I don't

hear it. Or I do, but I get involved again and forget. This one gets my attention.''

"I can see that," she said, returning his grin at last. "I gotta say, though, you gave me some rough moments. I wasn't sure what you were doing. I was afraid you were going to try and jump him.''

He looked surprised. "You were the one with the gun. And the one who's trained for this. Not me. I was just trying to distract him so you could...do your thing.''

Sam tried not to gape, but she wasn't certain how successful she was. She was aware of a tightness deep in her chest, a sort of ache that threatened to spread throughout her body. She'd never, outside of the team, come across such simple acceptance of what she did. Especially from a man.

That it was this man seemed somehow monumentally important. And there was only one reason she could think of for that, only one explanation for that squeezing tightness that made it hard to breathe.

She loved him.

The realization hit her with the force of a blow. She was stunned, apprehensive and nervous. What she was not was surprised. She knew she must have been aware of her feelings on some level, somewhere hidden and protected where she kept hopes she was afraid to acknowledge.

Oh, God. She loved him. Now what?

*Now, nothing,* she told herself. *Just because you've lost your mind doesn't mean he has.*

"Samantha?''

Not knowing—or wanting to know—how long she'd been standing there staring at him, she tried to gather herself.

"What?''

"What will they do with him?''

"That's up to Josh.''

"Can he really ruin him, like you said?''

"I'm sure he could. He carries a lot of weight in a lot of industries. If he puts the word out on Chilton, he'll be lucky to find a job sweeping floors."

Ian shook his head. "I don't get it. Why would he risk it? He had the perfect setup here."

"Some people need their egos stroked more than others, I guess. It takes a dedicated person," she added, "to think the work itself is glory enough."

"A workaholic, you mean," Ian said, the bitter tinge to his voice telling Sam he'd been accused of that before.

"Only if work is the only thing you make room for in your life."

"What if you haven't had much luck with anything else?"

"Then you treat it like one of your projects. Find the pattern, figure out why it goes wrong. Then you can fix it."

A startled look crossed his face. "I never thought of that."

She shrugged. "It's what you're best at. It's natural to you. No reason you can't apply the same principles outside the lab." She gave him the best smile she could manage. "As long as you don't start treating people like lab rats, of course."

Ian became very thoughtful after that. And quiet. But, she thought as she finished up her report to Josh, it wasn't a bad, tense sort of quiet. It was the kind of silence she'd come to know, when Ian's prodigious mind was working on a problem. She found to her surprise that she rather enjoyed watching it, knowing what was going on behind that faintly absent expression.

*Oh, God,* she thought, *I've got it bad.*

She forced herself to concentrate on her own work at hand, using the small details of what had happened to occupy a mind that kept wanting to stray into dangerous territory. Impossible territory. She could just hear it now, jokes about the absentminded professor and his body-guard....

Of course, Ian was probably doing just as she said, working out why he'd had problems with his life outside of his work before. And she doubted very much whether a woman with a job like hers and a brother like Billy would be the answer he came up with. Yes, they'd found an unexpectedly fiery passion together, but you couldn't build a life on that alone, and she knew Ian was smart enough to know that. He and Colleen had had that and it hadn't worked.

His presence was making it hard for her to concentrate, so she was glad when her cell buzzed and the cleanup team requested he come to his office to help them determine what Chilton had removed from his computer. After he'd gone, she set about finishing her lengthy report.

Much later, finished and calmer, she headed for Ian's office. He was alone, the cleanup apparently finished. He was resting his elbows on his desk, and his forehead in his hands. He looked weary, and Sam's chest tightened at the sight.

"Ian?" she said softly

He lifted his head. The weariness in his posture was echoed in his eyes.

"Bad?" she asked as she stepped quietly into the office.

"Bad enough. He wasn't kidding when he said he'd ruined the work here."

"But you have a backup, right?"

He gave her a smile that warmed her. "Yes. But it's going to take a lot of re-inputting. And I'm not sure Rebecca's going to want to do the drudge work, after what I suspected her of."

"She'll get over it. And if she doesn't, then Josh will get somebody else to do it. Come on, it's nearly ten, let's get out of here. We can toast the end of this mess."

She didn't say what else she was thinking, that the end

of this mess also meant the end of their forced relationship. She didn't want to think about what would be left afterward, if anything.

Much later, after a glass of the wine they were sharing over a rich, Italian dinner, Sam gave him an unusually intent look over the rim of her glass.

"So, whatever happened to that friend of yours and his father after their house...er, blew up? Did they get away clean?"

The abrupt non sequitur startled him. "Why?" he asked, warily.

"Don't worry," she said with a smile. "Your secret is still safe. It seems to me you did the best thing anybody could do to help."

"What makes you think it was me?"

"Because," she said softly, "you would."

"Blow up a house?" He'd thought it incredibly wild at the time, hardly something expected of quiet, geeky Ian Gamble.

"No. Use your best strength, your brain, to help a friend."

He grimaced. "Just how many people know besides you?"

"It doesn't matter. None of us would give you up, even if it mattered after all this time. Draven would skin whoever did."

"Draven." Ian shook his head. "That's one scary guy. Those eyes..."

"He is intimidating."

"That's an understatement," he said wryly, lifting his wineglass, "about a guy who makes bad guys break down just at the sight of him."

"Someday," Sam said, "he'll meet the woman who can take that look out of his eyes."

Ian lowered his glass slowly to the table. All the panic

he'd been fighting off came back in a rush. He took a deep breath to steady himself, hesitated a moment longer, then plunged in.

"Are you saying that woman…isn't you?"

"I told you, Ian. I don't love him. And he deserves a woman who will love him madly, passionately, with all her heart." She set down her own glass, ran a finger around the rim in a way he found suddenly maddening. Then she raised her gaze to his. He saw the hesitation, the trepidation in her eyes before she added in a voice so low and husky it sent shivers through him, "Sort of the way I love you."

Ian's breath stopped. It was just as well, since his throat was too tight to let even a whisper of air through. He swallowed with an effort, and managed to suck in enough air to keep himself going.

She'd saved him. Again. He'd been afraid to risk it, afraid to do what she had just done, afraid of making a fool out of himself telling her how he felt. He hadn't even been able to tell her that he'd given up trying to stay mad at her for how they had begun, under false pretenses.

And now, with those simple, wrenching words, she'd turned his sometimes drab world into a brilliantly colored place. And for the first time, he knew how his parents must feel, living with all this joy every day. And what had once bothered him, that intuitive side that clashed with his methodically scientific mind, was now simply one fascinating facet of a woman who could hold him spellbound for the rest of his life.

"You've got more guts than anybody I've ever known," he said softly.

To his amazement she blushed. "You know, I was hoping for something more along the lines of 'Gosh, Samantha, I love you, too.'"

"Gosh, Samantha, I love you, too," he said instantly.

The smile she gave him then did things to his insides

that seemed physically impossible. "Can you accept that I'm not the traditional kind of woman, who does a traditional kind of work?"

"And I'm not a traditional kind of man, with a traditional job. I'm a hermit when I'm in the middle of a project, which is most of the time, while you're out bouncing around the world."

"When I'm home, I like to stay at home," she said. "But when I'm gone, it's any and everywhere. Can you deal with that?"

"I'm my mother's son. What do you think?"

That got him a grin. "There is that," Samantha said.

"Maybe I should be asking you if you can stand her as a mother-in-law."

Her eyes widened. "Was that...a proposal?"

"Yeah," he admitted. "In that, I'm traditional. I'm not like my parents, but I want what they have."

"So do I," Samantha answered, so fervently his gut contracted pleasurably.

"Was that a yes?"

She smiled at the parroting of her words, and used his own back. "Yeah," she said. "It seems in some things I'm traditional, too."

But after a moment her smile wobbled slightly.

"What is it?"

She lowered her gaze to the table. "There's one thing we haven't dealt with, Ian."

"There's probably more than one, but we'll work it all out."

"But this is a big one."

"Who drives?" he quipped. "You got it. You're better than I am at it, anyway."

She laughed, but he could tell there was still reservation behind it. He tried to be serious, not wanting her to think he was belittling whatever her concern was.

"You traveling for your job? I'll save up new ideas to

start when you leave, so I won't hate you being gone so much, or worry so much that you're doing something dangerous.''

''You've really thought about this,'' she said.

''I've thought of little else since the day I realized how we met didn't mean a damn thing,'' he said dryly.

She picked up her fork, then set it down again. She reached for her glass of wine instead, and took a large enough swallow that he knew she was still wound up about something.

''What, Samantha? Are you thinking about where we'll live? We can keep my house or move. I don't care, as long as I have an office. It would be nice to have room for my parents. Or then again, maybe not,'' he said, grinning, hoping to get a smile out of her.

''I like your parents,'' she said softly.

''I know. So I'll live with it. And of course, we'll need a room for Billy. He does come visit you now and then, doesn't he?''

The tiny gasp that broke from her told him he'd managed to hit a nerve. Maybe even the very nerve that had her on edge. He should have guessed sooner, he thought.

''Is that what you're worried about? Billy?''

Slowly, reluctantly, she nodded.

''Then we'd better go see him. I'd like to ask his permission to marry his sister.''

Samantha's joyous expression and her fierce hug told him that for once in his life, he'd done it exactly right.

\* \* \* \* \*

**Coming in March 2003 from**

 *Silhouette®*

# I N T I M A T E   M O M E N T S™

## KAREN TEMPLETON
### Saving Dr. Ryan
(IM #1207)

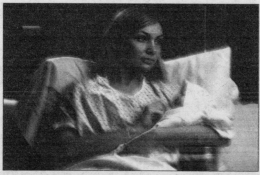

Maddie Kincaid needed a doctor, stat, for a very
special delivery! And the only M.D. in this part of
Mayes County, Ryan Logan, was happy to do the job.
But could she heal *his* broken heart?

**THE MEN OF MAYES COUNTY:**
**Three brothers whose adventures led them far afield—**
**and whose hearts brought them home.**

And look for Hank and Cal's stories, coming in fall 2003,
only from Silhouette Intimate Moments.

*Available at your favorite retail outlet.*

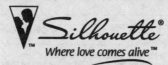

*Where love comes alive*™

Visit Silhouette at www.eHarlequin.com

SIMSDR

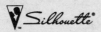

# Silhouette Books

**is delighted to present
two powerful men, each of whom is
used to having everything**

## On His Terms

Robert Duncan in
# LOVING EVANGELINE
by *New York Times* bestselling author
**Linda Howard**

and

Dr. Luke Trahern in
# ONE MORE CHANCE
an original story by
**Allison Leigh**

*Available this February wherever Silhouette books are sold.*

*Where love comes alive™*

# COMING NEXT MONTH